Element Girls
The Lost Goddess

Giulietta M. Spudich

Handersen Publishing, LLC
Lincoln, Nebraska

Handersen Publishing, LLC
Lincoln, Nebraska

Element Girls
The Lost Goddess

Manufactured in the United States of America.

Summary: When Amelia is kidnapped by her sorcerer father, her friends find themselves with new elemental powers. They travel to Hawaii to rescue her, and save a trapped goddess.

Library of Congress Control Number: 2018963515
Handersen Publishing, LLC, Lincoln, Nebraska

Paperback ISBN: 978-1-947854-49-9
Hardback ISBN: 978-1-947854-50-5
eBook ISBN: 978-1-947854-51-2

Publisher Website: www.handersenpublishing.com
Publisher Email: editors@handersenpublishing.com

For Hannah A.,
a fire and water friend.

Tess' Dream

Tess was in the ocean, deep under water. Her red, wavy hair floated like sea sponge around her face. She could see it out of the corners of her eyes.

The water was warm, and a feeling of comfort and peace enveloped her. She knew she was dreaming, but it didn't matter. She felt so safe. Happiness and awe filled her when she saw three mermaids swimming.

The mermaids turned to her, and she recognized the faces of her three best friends. She was delighted and surprised. They looked human from the waist up, but they all had beautiful, iridescent tails.

Amelia's was the blue of deep water.

Susie's was pearl-white like clouds.

Elizabeth's was an earthy, chocolate brown.

If her three best friends were mermaids, Tess must be one too. She wondered what color her own tail was?

But before she could look down, something caught her eye.

The something darkened Tess' mood.

Off in the distance, a black shape snaked toward them. Tess caught the attention of her friends, and they watched the shape approach. All of them were suddenly alarmed.

Fearing a shark, they tried to swim away. Her friends' powerful mermaid tails beat strongly as they shot ahead.

In a few seconds, Tess' friends were far ahead of her, and she was struggling in the currents of their wake.

Why couldn't she keep up?

When Tess looked down, her heart sank. She didn't have a mermaid tail—just human legs.

Amelia, Susie and Elizabeth hurried back to her and urged Tess to swim faster. She tried, but she just flailed in the water.

The dark shape was close now. It was a shark.

A wave of fear ran through Tess when she saw it clearly. Its teeth poked out of its closed mouth in a frightening way. They looked sharp.

Tess kicked and tried to swim, but it was pointless. She couldn't move anywhere. She shivered, feeling small and helpless.

Her three best friends formed a ring around her. Susie was always the one to act first in real life, and it was no different in the dream.

Susie's black hair was wild around her face, and she looked angry. As the shark came close, Susie punched the shark on the nose and shouted at it.

The monstrous fish changed direction, but quickly returned, grinning with large teeth. It opened its jaws wide and clamped down on one of the girl's shoulders.

Tess woke up sobbing.

In the dream, it was always beautiful, mellow Amelia that the shark chose first.

Tess spent a few minutes in bed, breathing deeply and trying to calm down. Sweat covered her whole body.

She had dreamt about mermaids ever since she met her friends, years ago. Usually, Tess and her friends weren't the mermaids, though. They all had legs as in real life, not tails. And the mermaids would swim around them. The dream was always pleasant and comforting.

In the last few weeks, though, the dream had become disturbing. The shark had appeared four times now, in four different dreams. It always went straight for Amelia.

And Tess was always powerless to stop it.

Tess took deep breaths to calm her pounding heart. It was only six in the morning, but she was afraid to sleep again, in case the dream returned, so she got out of bed.

As she got ready for school, she pondered the mermaids and the shark. She wondered why her three best friends were mermaids in this dream, and she wasn't. Why was she the only one in the dream without a mermaid tail?

Though Friday morning was bright and birds sang as she walked along the sidewalks to school, a sense of fear stayed with her. Even the sunny day didn't lift her spirits.

Tess gazed at the sky as she walked, trying to calm her nerves in the beauty of the blue, and forget about the dream.

Though the sky was mostly clear, one dark rain cloud moved across the sky like a shark.

Chapter One

Late winter leaves fell over the little park in Berkeley, California. Nestled among the redwood and oak trees was a wooden table. Tess Gilead sat, playing with the fire amulet around her neck. Her knees bounced up and down with anticipation.

Tess met her friends here every Sunday afternoon, which was normally relaxed and fun. Today, Tess felt nervous. She had the feeling that one of her best friends, Amelia Hilton, was avoiding her.

Tess spied Amelia's long blond hair and fluid walk as she came up the dirt path. Amelia joined her at the table, then put her bag down with a clunk.

"Math books?" Tess asked, noting the heavy bag.

Amelia nodded, but looked away.

"We've been practicing a lot for the math battle next Sunday," Amelia said. She was the star of the Brightcubes, their school's math team. They had a competition with another school coming up, and the math team was practicing hard.

"So, I guess you won't make it to our park meeting next Sunday," Tess said. "How about coming to my house for pizza Friday night? You'll need pizza after all the math practice. We can catch up then."

Tess was dying to hear Amelia's news. She hadn't had a real conversation with Amelia all week. Usually they talked all the time, at school or on the phone.

To Tess' surprise, Amelia's peach-colored cheeks turned red and she looked away.

"I need to practice," Amelia said, not meeting Tess' eye.

"Well, yeah, but even Friday night?" Tess asked.

"We have a chance at making it into the finals this year," Amelia said. "We need all the practice we can get."

Tess didn't know what to say. She looked down and studied her hands.

Amelia was always up for a pizza night.

Was she avoiding her?

Tess would just ask Amelia if there was something wrong. She hoped that she hadn't done anything to make her friend angry or upset about something.

As she opened her mouth, she spied Susie Lang and Elizabeth Brown making their way up the path.

Susie and Elizabeth were often together, both in and out of school. They were practically inseparable, even though Tess couldn't think of two more different people. Susie was thin, athletic and super confident. She was obsessed with volleyball and practiced almost every day.

Elizabeth hated sports or any form of sweating. While Susie normally had her eyes on the sky, especially on incoming volleyballs, Elizabeth had her eyes downward, her nose in a book.

Susie and Elizabeth greeted them and sat down at the round, wooden table.

"We're all here," Susie announced. "Time for the friendship pledge!" They always did the friendship pledge as soon as they all arrived.

Tess loved the friendship pledge. Without needing to speak, all four of them took out an amulet necklace from under their shirts. They held their amulets with their left hands and recited the pledge, which they had been doing since they got the necklaces a few years ago.

"For you, I would walk through fire," Tess said in a soft voice. She touched her necklace, which had the Chinese symbol for fire on it.

Susie's mother, Elaine Lang, who was the coolest mom around, brought the necklaces back from China three years ago, when the girls were all eleven. Susie's mom chose a different element for each of them.

Susie had the element of air.

Amelia had the element of water.

Elizabeth had the element of earth.

The only one that didn't fit was fire. Tess felt about as far from fire as you could possibly get—except for the color of her hair, which was red.

Tess didn't know why she had gotten the fire element. She was calm, didn't get angry much, and wasn't particularly powerful. She still loved the necklace, though, because it linked all four of them together.

"For you, I would walk on air!" Susie punched the air as she said it, and grinned.

Today, Susie's black hair was pulled back in a long ponytail, and she was wearing her usual sweatshirt and sweatpants. That way she could always go to volleyball practice or a pick-up game. Volleyball was her favorite thing. It was really fitting that she had the necklace with the symbol for air.

"For you, I would walk on water," Amelia mumbled. She hid her face in her long blond hair.

"For you, I would walk the Earth," Elizabeth said, looking from one to the other with round, brown eyes.

Tess smiled, her heart warmer. The tension with Amelia still made her stomach feel tight, but now that all four of them were together, things felt more relaxed.

"OK, that's done. Now it's doughnut time!" Susie said, then she grabbed a package of powdered doughnuts. She stuffed a whole doughnut into her mouth.

"Gosh, I'm so hungry," Susie said between bites, white powder dusting the corners of her mouth. "We had practice every night this week. And a three-hour practice this morning."

Susie was a volleyball star on the woman's varsity team, the Hawks, and they were getting ready for semi-finals.

"Don't you normally practice every night?" Elizabeth pointed out. Her fingers drummed the table. "Isn't that like a normal Susie schedule?"

"Yeah, but lots of my practices are with just the girls," Susie said. "This week our coach was there at every single practice. She makes us work twice as hard!" She polished off her doughnut.

"Aren't you supposed to be having healthy smoothies?" Elizabeth pulled out a Tupperware of carrots. "Vegetable, anyone?" She waved the Tupperware around, trying to make it look enticing.

"I already had a smoothie, and a super healthy lunch my mom made," Susie said. "We still have dumplings left over from Valentine's Day."

"It's so cool that you and your mom always celebrate V-Day together," Elizabeth said, resting her chin in her hand. "I was by my lonesome. But I had Mr. Darcy to curl up with."

"You're reading that again?" Susie said with a laugh.

"Of course," Elizabeth replied. "Pride and Prejudice is my Valentine's Day tradition."

"Well, it was fun to make dumplings with Mom," Susie said. "But I've been eating them all week!" She reached for a second doughnut. "These are much more satisfying."

"Are you on another diet, Liz?" Susie asked. She was the only one on the earth who could call Elizabeth 'Liz'. She took a carrot stick from Elizabeth's Tupperware, and crunched it.

"My parents made me take these," Elizabeth said and shrugged. "But they can't make me eat them!" She reached for a doughnut, and bit into it with a contented sigh. "You're right, Susie. Totally satisfying."

Elizabeth smoothed down her loose, cotton dress. Unlike the rest of them, Elizabeth liked to wear dresses. She especially loved anything resembling the styles of England in the 1800's, which was when her favorite author, Jane Austen, lived and wrote. Elizabeth often said she was born in the wrong century, and belonged two hundred years in the past.

Amelia, who in contrast wore jeans and a peach-colored sweatshirt with 'Math Rules' written on it, had finished her doughnut and was now quiet. She looked down, staring at the table and avoiding eye contact.

Tess began to worry. Amelia wasn't being her usual self, not even around Elizabeth and Susie. Maybe something was wrong, and it had nothing to do with Tess.

"Amelia? Hey, Water," Tess asked gently, using the nickname they each adopted from their necklaces.

Amelia barely looked at her. "What is it, Fire?"

Tess pulled at her red curls when she suddenly noticed how her friend's tear-shaped, blue eyes were rimmed with red.

"Are you OK?" Tess said. "You've been quiet. And your eyes are kind of red."

Susie and Elizabeth turned to look at Amelia, who blushed and seemed more uncomfortable. She shifted on her wooden seat.

Tess could tell that whatever it was, Amelia didn't want to talk about it.

The shark dream crept back into Tess' thoughts. If the dream was some kind of warning, then Amelia might be in some serious trouble.

Tess realized she would have to tell them the shark dream. She'd risk being teased for taking a dream seriously. Amelia needed to know about it.

Chapter Two

Before Tess could tell them about her dream, Susie turned to Amelia and squeezed her arm.

"Your eyes do look red," Susie said. "And OMG, your arm is so thin." Susie passed her a second doughnut.

"Are you freaked about the math semi-final?" Susie asked. "Because you shouldn't be. You're going to rock it!" She punched the air.

"I'm not freaked about that," Amelia said as she sat up straighter. "No, we'll be fine. We have a good team this year, and we've been practicing hard."

"Is it your mom?" Tess asked. "Did you not see her this week?"

Amelia's mom worked full-time as a hairstylist, and sometimes got home so late Amelia didn't see her for days. Since her dad had left, back when she was just two years old ("And good riddance," said her mom), the house got lonely.

"No, Mom's been working mornings." Amelia smiled, a real smile, her dimples showing. "We had dinner together almost every night this week. She's on evening shifts again next week, but I'll be practicing with the Brightcubes anyway."

It wasn't the math battle.

It wasn't her mom.

Tess ran out of guesses as to why Amelia was upset.

Did she say something wrong?

Did she do something to make Amelia angry?

Elizabeth watched Amelia closely, and drummed her fingers on the table. Elizabeth did that when she was thinking.

"So what is wrong?" Tess asked. "Is it me?" Amelia didn't answer. She looked away from Tess and bit her lip.

"Tess, I'm sure it isn't your fault," Elizabeth said.

"If I did something wrong," Tess said to Amelia, "I'm really, really sorry."

"Of course you didn't do anything wrong," Amelia said to Tess.

"I know what it is," Elizabeth said, then rolled her eyes. "It's the Valentine. Amelia, you're going to have to get used to it. You with your blond hair, fair skin, blue eyes—you're a regular babe. As for me, I will look forward to dreaming of dashing Mr. Darcy for the rest of my life, without getting a Valentine's Day card from him."

"Look, I didn't ask for a Valentine. I didn't want it!" Amelia said. She turned away, her eyes tearing up.

"Valentine?" Tess said, her voice edgy. "Why didn't you tell me you got a Valentine?" They were supposed to tell each other everything.

"Maybe we're going to have to revoke the 'no boyfriends' rule," Elizabeth said glumly, her chin in her hand. "Now that we're all fourteen, this kind of thing is going to happen. To some of us," she looked intentionally at Amelia.

"We don't have to revoke the rule," Amelia said firmly. "I'm not planning on having a boyfriend."

"You got a Valentine?" Susie asked with excitement. "From a guy? It was from a guy, right? Was it Billy Evans?"

Amelia shrugged and said, "No. It was no one."

"Well, it's just that I've seen Billy staring at you at lunch," Susie said and widened her dark eyes, pretending to gape at Amelia.

"Stop," Amelia said. But she laughed.

"Why didn't you tell me?" Tess asked again.

"I just didn't want to talk about it," Amelia said, looking at the table. "I just want to forget about it."

"Did he give you that pin?" Susie asked. Amelia wore a small, golden heart on her Math Rules T-shirt.

"That was her birthday present from her Aunt Ada. See, you told me about that," Tess said to Amelia. "I don't understand why you didn't tell me about the Valentine."

Amelia seemed to shrink into the bench.

Tess felt guilty. She didn't mean to make her friend feel even more uncomfortable, so she decided to drop it for now.

"Who was it, Liz?" Susie turned toward Elizabeth. "You seem to know about the Valentine. Do you know who gave it to her?"

Elizabeth suddenly looked flustered.

"You do know, don't you?" Susie said. "Must have been someone really bad, if she won't tell us."

"That's for Amelia to say, not me," Elizabeth said, then gave her friend a look. "Amelia, maybe you should just tell them."

Amelia just shook her head, and bit her lip again.

"Don't worry, Amelia," Tess said, trying to be supportive. "Just put it behind you. Valentine's Day only comes once a year, after all."

"Thanks." Amelia tried to smile at Tess, but it looked more like a grimace.

"Why don't you come over tomorrow night?" Tess said. "You can have dinner with us, since your mom will be out working."

"Tomorrow night's not good," Amelia said. Her cheeks flushed red.

"Tuesday?" Tess asked.

Amelia shook her head no.

"Why not?" Tess asked. Amelia was a frequent guest at the Gilead's, and usually jumped at the chance to have dinner there if her mom was working.

"Math battle," Amelia said softly. "Practice."

"But—" Tess started to say that Amelia could practice before or after dinner, but Elizabeth interrupted her.

"Who brought chocolate?" Elizabeth said. "I'm sensing a deprivation in our Sunday ritual."

"I did," Susie said and pulled out four Crunch bars. Amelia took one, and turned away from Tess.

Tess felt her cheeks flame. She felt ashamed and angry and rejected. Not the things Amelia usually made her feel, like loved, comfortable, accepted, and happy. She took a few deep breaths and felt her cheeks cool, then tuned back into the conversation.

"If we do revise the no boyfriend rule," Elizabeth was saying, "then I put in a clause that all love interests must measure up to our standards. He must be a John Knightly, you know, not a Henry Crawford."

Elizabeth started quoting Jane Austen until Susie threw a carrot at her.

"OK, OK, I'll stop," Elizabeth said.

"I had this dream," Tess started to say in a small voice, then stopped. Was it important to tell them about the dream? Her dream didn't seem to have anything to do with a Valentine.

Unless someone was pretending to like Amelia who was as mean as a shark?

Tess chewed on a carrot and thought for awhile. Maybe Amelia didn't want to hear about the dream? It might upset her more.

Tess was halfway through the Tupperware of carrots when Elizabeth's voice broke into her thoughts.

"Hey, Tess, I heard Mrs. Riley asked you to be a summer camp counselor this year," Elizabeth said.

Tess immediately tensed up. She had only told Amelia about that. No one else knew, not even her parents or her older brother Mikey.

"How…how did you know that?" Tess said.

Elizabeth winked, and Susie looked at her with surprise.

"How do you know everything, Liz?" Susie said. "I mean, every time I see you, you've got your nose in a book. Is that a cover? Are you actually spying on the real world?" Susie elbowed Elizabeth.

Elizabeth elbowed her back and grinned.

"Some of us can multitask," Elizabeth said and shrugged. "I just keep my nose in a book and my ears out in the world."

Elizabeth and Susie quit elbowing each other and turned to Tess.

"So?" Elizabeth asked. "Are you going to do it?"

"You totally should," Susie said. "You'd rock as a camp counselor."

Tess felt a nervous fluttering in her stomach.

"How do you know about that?" Tess asked Elizabeth.

"Mrs. Riley talked to me," Elizabeth said. "She asked me if I thought you'd do it – she said I should encourage you. I think she really wants you on the team. Are you going to sign up?"

"I don't think so. I mean, I don't know anything about being a counselor," Tess said. "I don't think I'd be good at it."

"Mrs. Riley said you helped her with the art projects on the Open Day," Elizabeth said. "She said the kids loved you."

"Yeah, and Dana from the Hawks was a counselor last year," Susie said. "She said it was awesome."

"One afternoon of volunteering for Open Day doesn't equal a whole two weeks," Tess said. "Amelia will tell you that. It's simple math."

Amelia looked at Tess with her tear-shaped blue eyes. Tess had already told Amelia about her fears about being a camp counselor on the phone a week ago. It seemed like such a long time ago to Tess. That was such a good conversation. Now Amelia seemed so distant.

"Tess, you should do it," Amelia said. "You'll be great."

But Tess didn't think she was ready to be a counselor. Maybe when she was older and wiser.

"I don't know, Amelia," Tess said. "You won't even tell me what's going on with you. I don't think I could handle upset kids very well. They wouldn't trust me."

Amelia let out a long, deep sigh.

"Come on, Tess," Amelia said. "That's not true at all."

"You'd just help the kids have fun," Susie said. "It would be great."

"Maybe next year, when we're in high school," Tess said. "Though I can't believe we will actually be starting high school this fall. I mean, I'm not ready."

"I'm totally ready for high school volleyball!" Susie said and made a spiking motion in the air.

"I guess it will be OK," Elizabeth said. "We'll know most of our classmates already."

"I don't know," Tess said. "It seems scary to me." She shivered. Not so much because of the cold, it was more to do with the idea of starting high school.

"I wish the sun would come out," Susie said and rubbed Tess' arm. "I'm getting cold!" She pulled up the hood of her sweatshirt.

The fog seemed to roll in even thicker. Though it often burned off in the afternoon, it looked like they might not see any sun today.

When the doughnuts were all eaten, it was time to part ways. Tess decided to try one more time and tell Amelia about the shark dream. Just in case Amelia should be on her guard.

But when Tess came up to Amelia, her friend made a quick excuse and walked away. A knot formed in Tess' stomach.

Why was her best friend avoiding her?

Tess watched Amelia leave, her long blond hair shimmering down her back. It reminded Tess of sunlight on water. As if Amelia was a mermaid and sharks lurked in the shadows of the redwoods, swimming through the fog that covered the park.

Tess hoped she wouldn't have the dream again.

Chapter Three

On Friday afternoon, Amelia walked across the schoolyard to go to math practice. She loved math practice. And no matter how much other girls mocked the students that formed the rest of team Brightcubes, she loved her math friends. Things were simple on the team. It was about numbers and puzzles. They had fun and ate pizza. That was it.

Being on the team was easy. Not like getting a romantic Valentine that could mess up friendships. That wasn't easy. An unwanted Valentine. It was unfair, and she never asked to be liked in that way. She liked the guy as a friend, nothing more.

The Valentine did have a crossword puzzle that she had liked. And if it had been a birthday card, it would have been fine. But it wasn't a birthday card. There was a heart on it. The same kind of heart she wore on her T-shirt from Aunt Ada. Though she never met her Aunt, Amelia always got a sweet birthday gift from her each year. Her mom said Aunt Ada traveled a lot, and was rarely in the country.

So it was OK for an aunt she'd never met to give her a heart pin, but not OK for a boy to give her a card with a heart on it. Amelia had to admit the logic was shaky.

Technically, she should be fine with receiving a card from anyone, heart or no heart. But it had made her stomach churn with nervousness.

Amelia put it out of her mind for now, so she could concentrate on math.

She shivered, which was odd, because it was a sunny afternoon. When she looked down around her feet, she noticed a strange hazy swirl all around her.

She didn't feel scared, not yet.

She was curious about it, wondering if she was seeing only black swirls or if there were also green and purple, when she passed out.

The next thing Amelia knew, she was in a dark, rumbling place. She blinked until she realized she was in the back seat of a car.

Two men sat in the front seats, though she couldn't see their faces. Her heart pounded, and she shrank into the seat. Her hand flew to her heart pin. Then she held onto her necklace with the Water amulet. The thought of her friends comforted her.

She thought back, struggling to remember how she had gotten there. She remembered being halfway to Em's, the building they used for practice. Then there was that colorful, swirling fog.

Had she fainted?

Her body felt stiff, like she had been sitting a long time. She moved her arms and legs to wake them up. She was a little groggy, but otherwise unhurt. A seatbelt restrained her, but nothing else. She wasn't tied or handcuffed.

Where was she going?

Were they taking her to a hospital?

The car seemed like a normal car. There were no sirens at all, and no medical equipment. She was sure it wasn't an ambulance. Her heart skipped several beats, and she breathed quickly in panic.

She recited the prime numbers in her mind. That always calmed her down. Signs for Millbrae and the San Francisco airport rushed past.

Amelia felt the door handle. She could just open it and jump out, but they were going so fast. Maybe she'd wait until the car slowed down, once they turned off the exit.

"Good morning," said the man in the passenger seat. He switched on the overhead light, then turned around and met her eye.

Amelia recoiled into the back seat.

He had the same, tear-shaped blue eyes as her. She had seen those very eyes, clones of hers, in a faded photo her mom showed her. But the photo was of a handsome man with a smooth face and thick, black hair. This man's face was older, and covered with pockmarks. And though his hair was black, it was thin and stringy.

"Are you my…" Amelia's voice was shaky when she tried again. "Are you my father?"

"So, you recognize me. Your mom showed you my picture, huh?" The man had a rough smoker's voice. "Or do you remember me? You were still in diapers the last time I saw you."

"I saw a photo," Amelia said. "I don't remember you."

"Well, we've both changed, darling," he said. "Unless you're still wearing diapers?" He laughed loudly at his own joke, and Amelia could see the driver smirking in the rear view mirror.

"Where are you taking me?" Amelia asked. She felt the words leave her mouth before she planned to say them. "I have a math battle. I have to be there on Sunday."

"Math battle!" Her father roared with laughter, and punched the driver's arm. The driver laughed, too. He was a muscular man - at least his shoulders and arms were, which is all Amelia could see. The driver had a tattoo that circled around his wrist.

She caught the driver's eyes in the rear view mirror. His were dark, and sparkled with amusement.

"Did you drug me?" Amelia asked.

"Something like drugs, but not drugs," her dad said. "You should congratulate me. It wasn't easy to get you. I have had...problems." Her dad's blue eyes narrowed and his face hardened.

"Problems? Like a restraining order?" Amelia said, then clamped her mouth shut. She was shocked at her own words. She didn't normally say sarcastic things like that.

"Girl's got a mouth!" said the driver, and chuckled. "She's just like you, but lots prettier, Jack."

"I used to be pretty, don't you remember?" her dad answered. "I've known you twenty years. Twenty long, painful years."

"You were not so good-looking back then, you just thought you were." The driver grinned at him.

"I was just as handsome as she is pretty, and you know it," her dad said. "Well, not anymore." He sighed.

"I need this off. It's distracting me," the driver said as he turned the overhead light off.

Amelia felt a wave of relief when the light went off. She didn't like seeing her dad's face. He looked so old, and mean. He was much older than her mom. And he looked sick, or something.

"Anyway, smart mouth or not, she's my daughter," her dad said, in the now dark car. When he turned around to face her, he said, "And I don't plan to let her go again. She's mine now."

"You're not my dad," Amelia said. "At least, not in my world. You left when I was two."

"If I'm not your dad," he said, "then why are you wearing the heart pin I got you for your birthday?"

"My Aunt Ada gave it to me!" Amelia said loudly, angrily.

"You sure about that?" he asked. "I bet you never even met Aunt Ada."

Amelia was stunned into silence. How did her dad know that she'd never met her aunt?

It didn't matter. All that mattered was getting out of the car.

Amelia's hand was still on the door handle when the driver put the blinker on. Amelia breathed deeply to calm herself. As soon as velocity was low, she would jump out of the car.

They coasted down the exit. And just before they reached the traffic light, Amelia pulled the handle.

The door didn't open.

Disappointment made her feel heavy all over.

"I'm not stupid," her dad said in a mocking tone of voice. "I put the child lock on. Because that's what you are—a child."

Amelia felt the hairs on her neck bristle at the insult. She decided she didn't like her dad at all. Her mouth opened and she almost yelled, "You are mean and ugly!"

She stopped herself in time. She wouldn't say things like that in normal life. She didn't want her dad or whatever drugs he gave her to affect what she said.

She would have to calm down and not get tangled up in her emotions if she wanted to escape. It was like a math battle.

Don't let the nerves get to you.

Go into the logical space.

She silently mouthed, two, three, five, seven, eleven, thirteen…reciting primes until she felt calmer.

"You probably realize that I need to text mom something, right?" Amelia said in a gentle voice. "I'm supposed to be home." She felt for her cell phone, but her coat pockets were empty.

"Don't worry, I texted her already," her dad said. "I told her you're having pizza with your math team, those nerds. Why do you hang out with those guys?" Her dad turned around, but she couldn't really see his face now that the car was dark.

"How do you know about them?" Amelia said. "Have you been following me? Watching what I do?"

Amelia felt panic at the thought of him watching her. For how long?

Her dad nodded his head and said, "Of course. Like I said, I'm not stupid. This took planning."

Amelia forced her mind back into the logical place. She had to think fast to come up with a way to message her friends.

"So you know about my best friends?" she said.

"Those three you hang around with?" her dad said. "Yeah, I've seen you all on…Sunday, is it? When you all have your little meeting in the park."

Amelia nodded, her heart growing cold. So, this kidnapping (she shuddered as she thought the word) might have been planned for a long time. The idea of she and her friends being watched made her feel sick.

She forced herself to breathe normal.

"I need to text my friends. I text them every day," Amelia explained, though it wasn't true. Her friends probably wouldn't miss her until Sunday, unless one of them texted her. She always responded to their texts, though she didn't often text them first. But she wasn't going to tell her dad all that.

"OK, tell me what to say and I'll type it in," her dad said. "You know, just in case you pull something fast with the phone." Her dad pulled out her cell.

"By the way, you shouldn't use your birth year as a password," he told her. "So obvious. Apparently your mother didn't teach you anything."

"Go to What's App," Amelia said in a clear, calm voice. Her head was clearer, and she felt more in control of herself. She didn't want to share any more thoughts with her dad than were necessary. She didn't want him to know any more about her, so she would only say what was essential.

"I'm there," her dad said.

"Choose 'The Girls'."

Her dad sniggered and said, "So inventive."

"Type this: Capital H, Hello. Full stop," Amelia said and prayed he would do what she said.

"Full stop? What, like Western Union?" her dad said. He and the driver laughed together.

"You said dictate!" Amelia heard the annoyance in her voice.

"I did, I did. OK, I typed 'Hello'. Full stop!" her dad said.

"Capital E, Everything is groovy. Full stop," Amelia said.

"Is that it? I'm getting bored," her dad said, then tapped his fingers on the dashboard. Amelia was reminded of Elizabeth, who had the same habit, and her heart twinged for her friend.

"Capital L, Love. Full stop. Let me see it," Amelia demanded.

He showed it to her.

"OK, could you just type peace at the end, as well?" Amelia said. "Capital P, just like the others."

Her dad rolled his eyes. "All right, peace. Send. It's gone," her dad said. "Though where we're going, phones don't work. So you're not going to get a reply."

Amelia sat back and closed her eyes. She hoped they would understand the message. It was code, after all, which was more her thing than any of theirs. She felt her necklace again, and held the heavy stone in her hand. The weight was comforting.

She took the pin off her T-shirt. She didn't want it, especially if it was a gift from this mean man.

But what if her dad was lying, and it actually was from Aunt Ada? Her mom said Aunt Ada was a really cool person, the only one from Dad's side of the family that her mom was in contact with. If it was from her only aunt, she didn't want to lose it.

Amelia was confused about what to do. She put it into her jeans pocket, until she could figure out who it was from.

My friends will find me, she told herself. They wouldn't let her down. And her mom was smart. Someone would find her.

Tess will find me, she thought as they drove toward the airport. Tess always knew when Amelia was in trouble. Even the other day at the park, Tess could tell Amelia was hiding something.

'Though where we're going...' Amelia replayed her dad's words in her mind. '...phones don't work.'

She had a bad feeling that they were flying somewhere remote, and she hoped it was not so far that no one, not even Tess, could find her.

Chapter Four

It was Saturday morning, and a light fog covered Berkeley. Elizabeth stood just outside Susie's kitchen window, where she watched her friend make a Power Smoothie.

Susie turned on the Nutribullet, blending bananas, peanut butter, coconut water and spinach together. Even with the house wall between them, it sounded to Elizabeth like an airplane taking off.

She rapped on the door and Susie waved her in. Elizabeth made a face as she smelled spinach, bananas and coconut. It smelled like a health food shop, and she hated healthy food. She'd take tea and scones over smoothies any day.

"It's like you're allergic to anything nutritious," Susie said, noticing Elizabeth's face.

"Maybe that smoothie is OK," Elizabeth said, noticing the peanut butter on the counter. "If it has peanut butter, how bad can it be?"

Susie offered her the thick, brown smoothie. Elizabeth took a careful sip. The smoothie was slimy and tasted like mud. Elizabeth made a face and tried not to gag. She spat the smoothie out into the sink.

"Ugh! I was wrong." Elizabeth grabbed a glass and filled it with water. "Even with peanut butter, it's bad."

Susie just laughed.

"More delicious smoothie for me," Susie said.

They went outside to sit on the steps that overlooked the garden. The fog was starting to burn off, and the morning grew brighter. Mint grew in pots along the patio, and a lemon tree looked healthy and full. Susie's mom had a green thumb.

Elizabeth eyed the rainbow chard—a small, lush forest of green, red and yellow.

"That almost looks good," Elizabeth said.

"It is good," Susie said. "Really yummy, I love rainbow chard."

"It's still just a bunch of leaves," Elizabeth said and waved her hand in a dismissive way. "I'm not a rabbit. You know, they didn't eat rainbow chard in Jane Austen's time."

Susie giggled.

"Is that because rainbow chard didn't grow in England then?" Susie asked. "Or they didn't eat a lot of greens?"

"Both," Elizabeth said. "More evidence that I would have been happier in Jane's time."

Susie bumped Elizabeth's shoulder with her own.

"What's so bad about this time?" Susie asked.

Elizabeth wrinkled her nose at the smoothie in her friend's hand.

"That smoothie, for one," Elizabeth said. "Also, it's kind of boring here, isn't it? Nothing really happens. Except in my books."

Susie stared out at the garden for a minute, thinking.

"I'd miss you if you went back in time," Susie said. "But maybe I know what you mean. If I didn't have volleyball, I'd be bored."

Now it was Elizabeth's turn to sit, chin in hand, and stare at the lemon tree. Susie had volleyball, but what did Elizabeth have? She wasn't pretty, or thin, so she felt that dating was out. School was easy enough, but not inspiring.

She had her books. And her dreams, which were usually about a beautiful Pre-Victorian house in the countryside with lots of visitors, tea times, luncheons and plenty of gossip.

"Is this a social visit, or is something up?" Susie stretched her limbs out in the sun, which had won its battle against the fog, and brightened the garden.

"Well, maybe both. Mostly to say hi." Elizabeth smiled and waved. "Hi!" she said, making Susie giggle.

The real reason for her visit swam into Elizabeth's mind. Her body tensed with worry.

"That text Amelia sent last night is on my mind," Elizabeth told her. A chill crept over her body despite the sun. She always got chills when something seemed off. It happened in horror movies, crime novels, or when people tried to spy on her during a school exam. And now it was that same feeling with Amelia's text.

"Didn't it just say hello or something?" Susie said. "I read it kind of quickly."

"Well, she used the word groovy," Elizabeth said and frowned again. "Didn't that strike you as weird? She doesn't use that word."

"Maybe she was in a weird mood," Susie said. "Too much math, you know? Maybe those guys on the team say 'groovy'." She drained her smoothie.

"Well, could be," Elizabeth said and nodded. "If anyone were to resurrect the word 'groovy' it would be the Brightcubes." She reached into her pocket for her phone, but her pocket was empty.

"Oh crap," Elizabeth said. "I forgot my phone. Do you have the text? I want to read it again."

"OK," Susie said. "Hey, do you want to go with me to get some new shorts? My best pair shrank in the dryer."

"Yeah, OK," Elizabeth said. "Maybe I will get an exercise dress."

"Seriously?" Susie said. "What's an exercise dress?"

"My mom wants me to do yoga with her. You know me, I don't wear pants," Elizabeth said. "Don't they have exercise dresses?"

"You totally should do yoga!" Susie said. "We'll find you a Victorian pair of sweats."

"My era is Pre-Victorian. And I don't think Pre-Victorian sweats exist," Elizabeth said. "That's another reason I belong in that century, not this one. I just don't get pants. They are so revealing and constricting all at the same time. Why would anyone wear them?"

"Well, I've never heard of an exercise dress," Susie said.

Elizabeth pictured herself trying to get Lycra yoga pants over her legs, then cringed at the thought.

"Wearing sweats sounds almost as bad as doing exercise," Elizabeth said. "You know, Jane Austen never had to do exercise. I think there is something wrong with our modern-day approach."

"We know more," Susie said. "We know it's good for us. In the 1800s they didn't know anything."

"They knew plenty!" Elizabeth said. "Well, except they were wrong about corsets. But still, the dresses were awesome."

Elizabeth was pretty sure they were wise in the nineteenth century. After all, they spoke better, they wore simple yet elegant dresses, and they had a lot of tea and cookies.

Susie popped up and went into the house.

Elizabeth sighed as she looked out at the garden. At least gardens were something that nineteenth century England would have understood.

She smoothed out her blue dress. The good thing about dresses was that you didn't need a flat stomach or tone legs to wear them.

Thinking about what Susie said, she wondered if she could go back in time…would she do it?

She would certainly miss her friends.

And of course there were no cell phones in the 1800s, Elizabeth considered. That would be hard. She loved texting.

Amelia's text came to mind again.

Elizabeth's chills came back. She knew the things Amelia normally texted. That last text definitely sounded off.

Maybe it was the Valentine thing? It had obviously upset Amelia a lot.

She gazed out at the garden and rested her chin in her hand. She wished it was a doughnut garden, if there were such a thing.

The vegetable patch was doing well. Cucumbers were full at the vines.

Elizabeth was surprised they grew so early in the year. Her parents' garden didn't have cucumbers until July.

Maybe Susie's garden was sunnier than her parents'. Then there was the green thumb thing. Elizabeth and her parents had trouble growing mint, while everything Susie's mom planted seemed to double in size overnight.

Susie came back out with her purse and a jean jacket.

"Let's go," Susie said. She hooked her arm in Elizabeth's.

"Um, Susie, your phone?" Elizabeth said and rolled her

eyes. "The text? Attention span of a…flying volleyball," she teased.

"Oh, right." Susie pulled out her phone and read quickly. "Hello, everything is groovy, love, peace. That's it."

"It still sounds weird to me," Elizabeth said. "Like she's trying to make us think she's OK, but she's not."

"Maybe she wrote it really fast." Susie shrugged. "I know I do that. Come on, let's go."

Elizabeth decided not to worry about the text. Amelia had a lot on her mind, with the math battle coming up tomorrow. She was planning to call Amelia after the battle so she could ask about it then.

They walked through the garden and into the little path to the street.

They didn't see Tess running full-blast to Susie's front door.

Chapter Five

Amelia was so sleepy. All her limbs felt heavy. She couldn't ever remember being so sleepy and comfortable. She curled into a warm ball on her side.

She was dreaming about mermaids again. Her three best friends were mermaids, and they swam in warm, sunny waters. It was a recurring dream, and one of her favorite ones. She never told anyone about the dream. Not even Tess. It was her warm, fuzzy secret.

This time, though, a beautiful mermaid with green skin and green hair swam with them. The green mermaid could swim really quickly—much faster than Amelia and her friends. She wore beautiful, white shell bracelets and anklets. The green mermaid was trying to say something to Amelia, but she couldn't hear.

Amelia felt she was being pulled out of sleep. She sensed noises, light, and a strange, unfamiliar smell. She curled on her side and tried to return to the mermaid dream, but someone was shaking her. She opened her eyes as far as they would go, and blinked in the light.

The sight of those blue, tear-shaped eyes just like hers in a weather-beaten face unlike hers made her sit up, much more alert. She looked around.

She wasn't in her bed.

She was in a small room with a window and one door. Besides the single mattress on the floor that she had slept on, there was a wood-burning stove and a desk. The room was warm, though the stove wasn't lit.

"Good morning," her dad said. "Did you enjoy my sleep charm?"

Amelia looked at him, not understanding what he meant. Did he say sleep charm?

Maybe she was still dreaming. She rubbed her eyes, trying to wake up.

Out the window, dark gray storm clouds were low in the sky.

"Can't sleep all day, beauty. There's work for you to do," her dad said, then clapped his hands.

"Work?" Amelia said. "Where am I?"

"Doesn't matter," her dad answered. "The important thing is, we can finally start."

"Start what?" Amelia's heart began to race. Whatever her dad had in mind, she didn't think it would be good.

"So many questions," her dad said and sighed deeply. "I'm glad I waited until you were of use. Otherwise forget it, no point wading through the boring questions."

Amelia stared at her dad. "Of use?"

What did he mean?

The outside door swung open and let in a gust of warm wind.

Amelia caught a glimpse of large, dark green plants outside. It didn't look like Berkeley, or any part of California she knew.

Through the door came a strong-looking man in his twenties. He wore shorts, sandals, and a yellow T-shirt.

"I've got poi!" the man said. "And water."

He handed Amelia a bowl of purple stuff, a fork, and a glass of water. When she took the items from him, she noticed he had a tattoo around his wrist. It had the same pattern as the driver who was with her dad when they took her to the airport.

She could tell this man giving her food wasn't the same man as the driver. This man was definitely younger.

Amelia studied the purple paste in the bowl.

"What is it?" Amelia said.

"My grandmother's poi," the man said.

Amelia thought he sounded proud. She tried to remember if she knew what poi was, but it didn't sound familiar.

"It's your lunch. Eat!" her dad snapped at her. When he crouched nearby, she could smell his salty, slightly pickly smell.

"Ugh," Amelia said. Her stomach turned over. "I can't eat with you sitting so close."

Her dad rolled his eyes and said, "Prima donna, just like her mom. You better eat, you need your strength. Come to think of it, you better go to the bathroom too." He pointed at a curtain in the corner of the shack.

To Amelia's relief, he grabbed the tattooed man by the arm and they left the room.

"Eat quickly," her dad yelled from outside. "We need to get started."

She should eat, she realized. It was important to keep her energy up. Especially if she was going to escape.

She had no idea what day it was, or when was the last time she ate. She was wearing the same clothes she put on Friday morning when she went to school, jeans and a T-shirt. Her favorite peach-colored T-shirt didn't seem too dirty, even after sleeping in it. She felt greasy, but otherwise OK. Amelia examined her arms. No bruises or anything.

Amelia went over to the desk. She could walk just fine, and her body felt normal. So whatever drug her dad gave her must be out of her system.

She took a tentative bit of the poi, which tasted starchy and really good. Before she knew it, she had eaten the whole bowl, and drunk the whole glass of water. Her stomach gurgled with unsatisfied hunger. She wondered if she could ask for more food.

The curtain in the corner hid a toilet and a small sink.

After she finished, Amelia washed her hands, then drank another glass of water from the faucet. She was dehydrated, so felt better after the water. Her stomach growled, but hunger had to be ignored. Thinking about escape was more important than thinking about food.

"The window!" she muttered under her breath, and went over to the main window in the shack. It was locked. At first glance she couldn't see how to open it.

"You done?" Her dad's voice came sailing through the room from outside.

"Just a minute, I'm in the bathroom!" Amelia lied to buy herself some more time.

Low, male voices came from outside the door as her dad and the other man talked. She crept closer and put the glass up to the door, in hopes that the sound would be amplified. It was a trick she learned from I Love Lucy, an old TV series she often watched with her mom.

Whether the glass helped or not, she could hear them talking, her dad and the other man.

"Do you think it will work?" the strong man asked.

"It better," her dad said, his voice rough.

"If it doesn't, what's Plan B?" the man asked.

"We don't need one," her dad responded.

"But–"

"Hey, Alex!" her dad yelled.

Amelia nearly dropped the glass.

"I'm the brains, so I do all the thinking," her dad said. "You're the muscle. Got it?"

"Yes, sir," Alex mumbled.

"You ready now, girl?" Her dad's voice came loudly through the glass and into her ear.

Amelia quickly returned the glass to the desk, and opened the door. A sea-scented, warm breeze blew into the room. The fresh air cleared her head, and she felt more alert.

"Yes, I'm ready," she told him. "What's this work you're talking about?" She tried to sound confident. She didn't want her dad to think she was afraid.

Her dad's lips curled into a grin that didn't look friendly or happy. It looked…mean.

"Follow me," he said, then headed outside. "Alex, make sure she comes."

Amelia chose to follow her dad, rather than be pushed into it. She figured the more she appeared to behave, the less they would watch her. Maybe she could escape while they were looking the other way?

The trio walked down a dirt path, bordered by dark green plants. Alex, the strong man, made no move to force her, though. He just walked along beside her.

Amelia took quick glances around. She spied coconut trees, a sloping mountain with a flat top that must be a volcano, and the ocean. Plenty of places to hide, to get lost. It looked tropical—a theory that was supported by the warm, humid feeling in the air.

Storm clouds gathered low in the sky.

Alex surprised her by leaning over and asking if the poi was good.

Amelia nodded. "I wish I had more," she whispered.

"My grandma's cooking is like that," Alex said in a quiet voice. "You always want more."

Alex seemed OK. Not mean like her dad. So maybe he would answer some questions.

"Where are we, anyway?" she whispered to Alex.

"Kahi Kanaka Mai I Hele," Alex responded. "This island is named The Place Where People Do Not Go."

"Why is it called that?" she asked, a nervous feeling stealing up her spine.

"An old legend," Alex said, but her dad cut him short.

"No talking," her dad said, "unless it's me." He laughed at his own joke.

The wind picked up, a lot. Although it was warm, Amelia felt a chill prickle her neck.

It was bad enough missing her mom, friends, and the math battle. And bad enough being with her mean dad. But being on an island called The Place Where People Do Not Go sounded like an extra heap of bad news.

Chapter Six

When Susie and Elizabeth entered the house with shopping bags, they were laughing.

"I can't believe you bought a dress instead of yoga pants!" Susie pinched Elizabeth. "Though I guess you were looking for an exercise dress."

"I can do yoga in it," Elizabeth said.

Susie laughed loudly.

"Seriously? It's from the vintage shop!" Susie said. "Do you really want to sweat in that?"

"Yeah, you're right," Elizabeth said. "Fanny Price wouldn't have wanted to ruin a dress like this." Elizabeth referred to one of her favorite characters by Jane Austen.

"Who's Fanny Price?" Susie asked. "Someone at school?"

"Susie, we watched Mansfield Park over Christmas break, remember?" Elizabeth said. "Fanny Price, the one who wore that gorgeous wine-colored dress—just like the one I bought. Frances O'Connor played her."

"Oh, sorry," Susie said.

Elizabeth rolled her eyes.

"I guess I might have been going over volleyball plays in my head," Susie said. "Anyway, my point is, yoga is much easier in pants."

"I leave the pants to you, Air Master," Elizabeth said, laughing.

They stopped laughing at once when they saw Tess standing in the doorway to the kitchen. Tess knew she looked terrible. Her eyes were puffy and red, nearly the same color as her hair. Her face was blotchy, and a tear slid down her freckled face.

"Tess, what happened?"

"What's wrong?"

Both girls dropped their bags and went to hug their friend, wondering what had her so upset.

"It's Amelia," Tess managed to choke out. "She's in trouble."

Tess pulled out her phone and showed the text to the girls.

Hello. Everything is groovy. Love. Peace.

"Look. Read the capital letters in the text. H–E–L–P," Tess said. "You know how Amelia likes codes."

"Oh my gosh!" Elizabeth exclaimed. She moved to the kitchen table and sat down, putting her head in her hands. "I knew it! I just knew there was something funny about that text."

"I'm so sorry, I didn't see that at all," Susie said and whipped out her own phone. "I'm calling Amelia right now."

The mood in the room turned to panic and worry.

"I've been trying her phone since last night, and this morning," Tess said with a sob. "There's no answer."

"Her mom?" Elizabeth asked. "Does her mom know where she is?"

Tess shook her head, and her voice came out choked. "No, her mom said Amelia didn't come home last night."

Susie slid down to sit on the floor, with a lost expression on her face.

Elizabeth had the opposite reaction. Her brown eyes narrowed with focus. She looked like she was thinking hard.

"Let's call the Brightcubes," Elizabeth said. "They might know something."

"I did," Tess said and started to cry. "I called Pete, from the Brightcubes, and he told me that Amelia didn't turn up to practice on Friday."

"She missed math practice?" Susie said with surprise.

"I don't think that was her choice," Tess said. "Something awful must have happened."

Tess and Susie held hands for a moment.

"Let's think, girls. She was in history class on Friday at four o'clock," Elizabeth said. "I know because I was in the same class. So she would have gone straight from there to math practice."

"Okay, so we know when she disappeared," Susie said, brightening. "And it was probably from campus, so–"

"Better than that, girls," said a new voice.

Susie's mom, Elaine Lang, came into the kitchen.

"We know where she is," said Ms. Lang.

Ms. Lang was an older version of Susie. Her build was thin, like Susie, but she didn't have the muscle of her athletic daughter. She had the same dark, energetic eyes, though her black hair had lots of gray streaks in it.

Tess felt relief as soon as she saw Susie's mom. Ms. Lang was so confident, and so kind. She had raised Susie on her own. Despite the fact her husband left when Susie was a kid, she managed to get an engineering degree, and be a great mom. There was probably nothing Susie's mom couldn't do.

So if Susie's mom knew where Amelia was, Tess felt sure everything would be OK.

Susie jumped up off the floor, and all three girls crowded around her mom.

"Did you say you know where Amelia is?" Elizabeth asked, her face hopeful.

Susie's mom nodded. She held up a glass ball, which on closer look was a globe of the Earth. All the continents were blue, except for one small island in the middle of the Pacific. That island was black.

"What's that?" Susie asked.

"Looks like a globe," Elizabeth said. Her face and eyebrows were knotted in concentration. "Did Amelia leave that as a clue?"

"In a way, yes," said Ms. Lang.

"What do you mean?" Elizabeth asked.

"It's a clue, though Amelia didn't leave it," Ms. Lang told

them. "That island in the Hawaiian archipelago is where she is right now."

"How do you know?" Elizabeth asked.

"Why is she there?" Susie asked at the same time.

Susie's mom turned to Susie and answered her question.

"That, I don't know," Ms. Lang said. "But I already booked a flight for Maggie, Amelia's Mom. We leave this afternoon."

Tess felt hope soothe her heart. She just knew if Susie's mom was on the case, Amelia would come home safe.

"What about us?" Susie said. "We want to come too!"

"It's safer if you stay here," her mom said and put a comforting hand on her shoulder. "Safer for all of you." She looked at each girl with her kind, dark eyes.

Tess wished she could be the one to save Amelia. But what could she do? At fourteen, she was basically powerless.

"Yeah," Tess said. "What can we do, anyway?" Tess' shoulder's sagged.

Why hadn't she told Amelia about the shark dream? Maybe if she had warned Amelia, her best friend wouldn't be missing right now.

Susie's mom frowned.

"You are her friends. You can do a lot," said Ms. Lang. "Tess, that text was a valuable clue, and you noticed it right away."

She hugged Tess. Tess felt mildly better, but still worried.

"And what if Amelia does come back home? You three will make sure she's fine and safe if that happens," Ms. Lang said. "Someone trustworthy needs to be here in that case."

Ms. Lang squeezed Tess' shoulder.

Tess' spirits lifted at the idea that Amelia might just walk back home like she normally did. Maybe something terrible hadn't happened. Maybe Amelia just got lost, or hit her head, and she would come back soon. Tess hoped she could be there to help her if Amelia came home to an empty house.

"Maybe we could stay at Amelia's just in case," Tess said. "I mean, if the house will be empty, she might come back and not have a key."

Ms. Lang seemed like she was about to disagree. But her face changed and she nodded.

"Yes, do. Maybe there are clues in the house," Ms. Lang said, "but don't go there alone. Take Mikey—it's better if your brother is also there."

Tess shivered with an unpleasant fear. Ms. Lang was clearly worried Amelia's house wasn't safe.

Ms. Lang looked at her watch. "Oh! I have to go pack." She raced out of the kitchen. Her footsteps pounded up the stairs.

Elizabeth had the globe in her hands and studied it carefully.

"I'll stay with you, Tess," Elizabeth said. Then she went back to studying the globe.

Susie chimed in, "Me too. We can look through Amelia's room, just in case there are clues."

The three girls were silent for awhile, each lost in her own thoughts. Elizabeth examined the globe, turning it over in her hands. Tess studied the text, reading it again and again. Susie sat on the floor and looked off into the distance, braiding and unbraiding her hair.

"Do you think she has her necklace on?" Susie asked, touching her Air amulet.

Both Elizabeth and Tess touched their own amulets, Earth and Fire.

"I hope so," Tess said. "I'm sure of it. She never takes it off."

Amelia would be fine, Tess told herself. But her heart beat fast with worry.

Chapter Seven

Amelia felt sweat run down her back as they walked in the hot, humid air. Her dad led her and Alex along a winding dirt path. Most of the path was level, but after about half an hour, they started to climb. Her dad wheezed as soon as they started ascending, so Amelia figured they couldn't be going too far. He didn't sound like he could hike much farther.

Amelia held her Water amulet in her hand as they walked. It helped to think she was still connected to her friends, even if it was just through the necklace. She hoped they understood her text for help.

The air was so thick that Amelia felt she was walking through a hot cloud. She slapped at a mosquito that stung her neck. She wished she wasn't wearing jeans—they felt heavy in the heat.

Amelia caught glimpses of the sea as they made their way up a hill. The volcano towered over them in the distance. Amelia was glad they weren't climbing that.

Her dad wheezed heavily, and she was out of breath herself when they got to a level place covered with tall, swaying coconut palms. She kicked a fallen coconut and watched it roll down the path.

Considering all places to be kidnapped and taken away to, at least she was in the tropics. It was good to have the ocean so nearby, and the wind so warm against her face. Although it would be nice to have the sun rather than those dark clouds in the sky.

She breathed in deeply, feeling her back and shoulders relax. They stiffened again when her dad called her name, shaking her from her peace.

"Amelia!" His rough voice seemed at odds with the quiet surroundings. She thought even Alex winced.

"No time to chill out," her dad said. He made an exaggerated peace sign. "Time to work. In there." He pointed to a cave.

Amelia tensed further as she studied the cave. The mouth of the cave was shaped like a hunched figure—a ghoul. And it looked dark in there.

She thought of the name of the island—The Place Where People Do Not Go—and hoped the island wasn't named for the cave.

"Inside!" her dad said sternly, as if he noticed her hesitation. "Now."

He snapped his fingers and a ball of light appeared in his hand.

"What is that?" Amelia stared at the light. Her dad had definitely made the light appear from nowhere.

"That's impossible," Amelia said.

It must have been a trick.

Not magic, just a trick.

"Well, I figure all will be revealed in a moment," her dad said. "No need to keep hiding it from you."

Alex picked up a palm leaf and twisted it nervously.

"Hide what? That you're a magician?" Amelia said and studied her dad carefully.

"No, a sorcerer," he said and laughed. The sound felt evil, and it gave Amelia chills down her spine.

Oh great, he's crazy, Amelia thought.

"Alex. Amelia. In the cave, now," her dad said.

Alex snapped the palm leaf and scowled at her dad.

"What's wrong with you?" her dad asked Alex.

"You know I don't go in there," Alex said, pointing to the cave.

"Well, today I need your help. So you will if I say you will," her dad said. "Come on, bring the girl if she won't come."

Amelia took a step toward the cave. She definitely didn't want some stranger forcing her to move, even if he seemed nice. Alex looked big and strong. Her dad was thin and stringy. She wondered why her dad thought he could order Alex around.

Alex stayed at the edge of the clearing, making no move to get closer to the cave.

Amelia's mind raced as she walked toward the cave, she needed time to think. Her dad was clearly insane. Alex seemed frightened of the cave, or something else waiting in there. So whatever was in the cave, it must be bad.

"I'm not going in there," Amelia said.

Her dad went to the mouth of the cave and motioned for her to follow.

"Why would I follow you in there?" she asked.

Her dad gave her a tired, annoyed look. "I'll make you follow if you don't behave," he said.

She felt a stubborn strength tighten her jaw, and she planted her feet into the ground and crossed her arms.

Her dad suddenly softened.

"Look, kid. I'm not going to hurt you, and nothing will hurt you in the cave," he said, his voice almost kind. "Please just trust me a little? I'm your dad."

He was her dad. And he hadn't hurt her so far. Except he had hurt her feelings a few times.

What if she refused to go in the cave? He and Alex were stronger than she was, and could force her to go into the cave.

"One last chance, Amelia. Follow me, or I'll make you follow," her dad said and took a step inside the dark mouth of the cave. "Just come in here, I don't want to push you. I want us to be friends."

She decided to follow him. At least no one would push her. She hated being pushed.

When she entered the cave, her eyes were plunged into blackness. She could just make out the ball of light her dad held. She hurried toward it.

A rock wall stood to her right, but the light didn't extend very far, so she couldn't see how big the cave was. Even though he smelled pickly, she stuck close to her dad, but breathed with her mouth.

It was cool and musty inside the cave.

They came out of the tunnel, and Amelia couldn't see the stone wall anymore. Their steps were louder, and echoed. They were inside a larger room within the cave.

Her dad led her to a rocky corner. He grabbed her wrist, which she really didn't like, and placed her hand on the stone.

The rock felt like ice.

"This rock is freezing!" Amelia said and gasped.

"Yes, Dark is cold." Her dad's voice was low now, almost humble. "And look at this."

He held the ball of light up higher, next to her hand on the rock. Instead of the spherical glow, the light shone in a half moon. It was blocked by the rock.

"Why does the rock stop the light?" Amelia asked. She took her hand off the freezing stone and rubbed warmth back into it.

"It's Dark. The rock is a great source of it. No light can touch it," her dad said. "Dark cannot coexist with the light. You see?" Her dad sounded passionate, and not his usual snide, joking self.

"It can't coexist—that means this Dark stuff and the light can't be in the same place at the same time," Amelia said.

"But I've never heard of Dark."

"You wouldn't have heard of Dark," her dad said. "It's not known to most of the world."

"But if it blocks light…" Amelia looked at her dad. "I mean, if light cannot touch it, then the Dark would be studied, right? We study things like that on my math team. Things scientists and astronomers know about, like black holes."

"Ha!" Her dad laughed so loud that Amelia took a step back away from the cold rock, and the sphere of light her dad was holding.

"Science doesn't know about Dark," her dad explained. "Only the legends come close to explaining it. But what we know about it doesn't matter. Only that it's very special. Now come closer to the rock."

Amelia was getting a bad feeling about all this. The cave was so dark, anything could be in here. She tried to think of a subject to distract her dad, or get him talking to avoid whatever weird thing he had planned. Maybe she could distract him and step farther away from him, then run.

"Why doesn't Alex like coming in here?" she asked.

"No concern of yours!" her dad yelled. "He just doesn't like it in here."

Maybe if she asked more about Dark, she could keep him talking?

But she didn't get the chance.

Her dad grabbed her arm and pulled her toward the cold rock.

"Back to business," her dad said.

She suddenly remembered stories of daughters being sacrificed for ancient gods. It was sometimes done in caves, on stones.

Amelia's heart raced.

"You're not going to sacrifice me, are you?" Amelia swallowed. She touched the pin in her pocket. Hopefully he had some fatherly feelings toward her, and wouldn't consider sacrifice.

"No, I need you alive, kid," her dad said. "You and me, we'll be a team. You're going to do what I do. I'm going to show you how it's done. Then you'll do it. You'll be fine."

Amelia watched in silence. First, her dad put the sphere of light on a ledge. The Dark rock cut into the sphere of light, making it look like a not-quite full moon.

Her dad placed his right hand on the rock.

"See, you have to really feel it. You can't just touch it, you have to let the Dark enter your hand," he said.

"Enter your hand?" Amelia realized her dad really did think the rock—the Dark—was entering his hand. Her dad seemed completely loony. Though it was interesting what the rock did to the light. That was definitely strange, and it was really happening because she could see it.

She wondered if she could run while he was absorbed in his task. But he stood so close to her, she didn't dare try.

A strange, eerie sound filled the cave.

It took Amelia a few moments to realize her dad was singing. The song didn't have a happy melody, as each note seemed to clash with the one before. Amelia covered her ears and winced.

"Oh, no, no," her dad said and stopped the unpleasant sound. "You're going to have to do it. You need to listen."

"I can actually hear you with my fingers in my ears," Amelia said. "Unfortunately," she added.

She was surprised at herself. She wasn't normally sarcastic. Maybe her dad was rubbing off on her.

He continued singing the awful notes.

Then Amelia noticed something she didn't understand. She could see her dad's right hand and arm, bathed in the light. A shadow came up over his fingers. Soon she couldn't see his hand. It was like his hand was eaten by shadow.

She screamed.

"Ah, you see? You see?" Her dad sounded happy, and kept singing.

Black veins ran up his right arm.

"What's happening?" she asked him.

"Look at my left hand," her dad said. "Just look! It's working, just like it's supposed to."

Black veins ran down his left arm. The tube he held in his left hand began to fill up with shadow.

"The Dark enters my body from the stone, and runs through me. The power is amazing! You'll feel it, once you try," her dad said. "The Dark runs out into this tube, and we sell it. Get rich. Easy."

Her dad stopped when the tube was a quarter full. He stopped singing, and took his hand off the stone. He put both hands on his knees and gasped for breath, sagging.

"Are you…OK?" Amelia asked. She wasn't sure she liked worrying about him. He was so mean to her, and clearly weird. But after all, he was her dad. And he did seem sick all of a sudden.

"Mining the Dark…it takes…a lot out of me," her dad said between gasps of air. He sounded terrible.

His breathing slowed to normal. This might be the chance to run for it, while he was still hunched over. She took a step away from him.

But her dad reached out and grabbed her arm.

"That's why I need you," he said and stood upright. "You're young and strong. You try."

Amelia's entire body stiffened at the idea of touching that awful rock. Watching those black veins run up and down her dad's arms made her pull away from the rock. She knew without doubt that she had to get out of the cave somehow.

Her dad stared at her, waiting for her answer.

There was no escape. She would have to mine the Dark, or her dad would make her do it. There was no telling what he was capable of, or how mean he could get. She was sure he would do anything for his precious Dark.

Chapter Eight

Tess sat at the kitchen table in Susie's house. She was thinking about the mermaid and shark dream, and if it held any clues to what happened to Amelia, when a honk outside startled her.

Elizabeth, who was investigating the globe, jumped as well. Susie got up from the floor, and her mom hurried into the kitchen with a bag.

"It's the taxi to the airport," said Ms. Lang. "OK, girls, you know where Amelia's house key is, right?"

"Yeah, spare key drawer," Susie answered.

"Don't worry," said Ms. Lang, then she hugged each girl in turn. "We'll get Amelia back. In the meantime, if you look for clues at her house, let me know if you find anything. And above all, be careful."

"We'll be fine," Susie said and hugged her again. "You be careful, too."

Susie's mom flashed a smile and went out the door.

The girls were left in silence.

"Huh," Elizabeth said. "That's weird."

She showed Tess and Susie the ball that she held. It wasn't a globe anymore. It looked like a normal, clear glass ball.

"Where did the countries all go?" Elizabeth said.

Susie shrugged.

"Maybe it's like Etch A Sketch, where you shake it to clear it." Susie said. "Did you shake it?"

Elizabeth shook her head. "No, I kept it pretty still," she said.

"That is weird," Tess said, agreeing with Elizabeth. "But I guess we have more important things to worry about. Let's get the spare key and go to Amelia's."

"Yeah, let's go. I hate just sitting around," Susie said.

Tess placed the ball on a side table.

"Actually, I'll take it," Elizabeth said and as they left the house, she put the glass ball into her shopping bag along with the vintage dress.

Susie looked at her curiously.

"Just in case," Elizabeth shrugged. "Maybe the countries will come back or something."

It was normally a twenty-minute walk from Susie's to Amelia's, but they walked so fast they got there in fifteen. Elizabeth panted as Susie opened the door.

"You have got to get more exercise," Susie said to Elizabeth.

"Isn't that what we just did?" Elizabeth said between wheezes. "See, starting today, power walking."

Susie smiled, but her face grew serious when she opened the door.

"Let's spread out," Susie said.

"I'll take Amelia's room," Tess offered.

Susie went into the living room, Elizabeth the kitchen, and Tess headed up the stairs.

After half an hour they met in the kitchen. Susie poured glasses of water for the three of them, and they sat with the only item of interest they had found on the table in front of them.

Amelia's diary was a small, thick book with a pink cover. Bits of paper stuck out of the pages.

"She would kill us if we read that," Susie said. "She never even told us she kept a diary."

"Amelia's not going to kill anybody," Elizabeth said and she took the diary in one hand and weighed it. "She wouldn't be happy if we read it for no reason, but I'd say being kidnapped is a very good reason. Maybe we'd finally see what she's like when she's angry."

"I know what Amelia's like when she's angry," Tess said, wincing at the memory. "When she was nine, I accidentally lost her math homework."

"What did she do?" Susie asked.

"Well..." Tess put her chin in her hands and tried to remember. "She wouldn't speak to me for a couple days. And she wouldn't even look at me."

Tess suddenly realized it was much the same behavior as Amelia showed Tess at the park last Sunday. Amelia had trouble meeting Tess' eye then, too.

"It's so cool you've known her since you were kids," Susie said.

Tess realized that she never didn't know where Amelia was. She always knew what she was doing. Amelia had never disappeared like this before.

"I hope she's OK," Tess said in a small voice.

"My mom will find her," Susie said and grabbed Tess' hand.

"Let's focus," Elizabeth said. "Do we read her diary or not?"

"What if my mom finds her right away and we don't need to read it?" Susie said. "Then I'd feel bad."

"Tess?" Elizabeth drummed her fingers on the table and cocked a brown eyebrow at her friend.

Tess tried to think, but her thoughts swam as if in an ocean. She felt a deep tiredness fill her body. She tried not to yawn, but ended up yawning anyway.

"You look like you need some rest," Susie said.

Tess' eyes were closing against her will.

"I didn't sleep at all last night," Tess explained. "I was so worried about Amelia."

"Get some sleep," Elizabeth said. "We'll wake you up if anything happens."

Tess shuffled out of the kitchen and into the living room, where she sank down on the couch. She could still hear the conversation in the kitchen, and was grateful to be lying down.

"Still waters run deep," Tess heard Elizabeth say. "I wouldn't be surprised if Amelia had some secrets. And if she wrote about them in her diary, it might help us find her."

"I don't know, Liz," Susie said. "She might be angry with us if we read it. It's private, you know?"

Tess tried to stay awake and listen, but she relaxed more and more into the comfortable cushions.

"Maybe just one of us should read it," Tess heard Elizabeth saying. "That way, only one of us gets in trouble…"

Elizabeth's words faded out as Tess dropped off into sleep.

Tess dreamed that she was swimming underwater in a warm ocean. She felt her heart lift when Amelia swam into view, looking happy and graceful with a shining blue mermaid tail.

She scanned for anything threatening, but could only see clear, blue water.

"I'm OK," Amelia mouthed to her. "I'm fine."

A large shadow passed over them, and Tess looked up, expecting a shark. But it wasn't a shark. The shadow belonged to a big boat on the surface.

Tess and Amelia swam in its shadow. A large net descended from the boat, heading straight for Amelia. Tess grabbed her friend and tried to pull her out of the way, but a second later, Amelia was caught in the net. Amelia struggled and called out to Tess.

"It's him!" The words came bubbling down to Tess.

Amelia twisted and wiggled in the net, but she couldn't break free. The net was almost out of view when the next word came down to Tess.

"Daddy!" Tess heard.

The voice was a young child's.

"What–? Where–?"

Tess woke up speaking aloud. The dream was gone. She was in Amelia's living room, on the couch. Not in the ocean.

The kitchen was full of people–she could hear them chattering. She rubbed her eyes and shuffled in.

Elizabeth and Susie were chatting, and three guys from the Brightcubes were on their iPads. Tess knew them from school: Damian, Pete and George.

"One in fourteen," Damian said, not looking up from his tablet. He had on a T-shirt that said Math Rocks.

"I got one in three," Pete said. He did look up, with a look of confusion. He wore a Math Rolls T-shirt.

"That's optimistic," George said and tapped his screen. "Especially considering flights from Honolulu." George's T-shirt had no words on it, just plain black.

"There are other airports, you know," Pete said and rolled his eyes. "Private jets, too."

"Private jets!" George and Damian both said. They went back to their iPads with renewed energy.

"What are they talking about?" Tess asked Susie and Elizabeth, who were both watching the Brightcubes.

"No idea," Susie said with a shrug.

"I think they're calculating the probability that Amelia will make the math battle tomorrow," Elizabeth said.

George met her eye, then nodded.

"One chance in fourteen?" Tess felt her breath come short. "That's terrible!"

"Totally agree," Pete mumbled. "Gross overestimate of the odds."

"Hmm." Elizabeth had her chin in her hand and was staring at the guys. "Not sure this is the best use of time, boys," she said loudly.

Pete gave her an intense look.

"Amelia's better at imaginary numbers than any of us," Pete said. "She will be sorely missed if she isn't back by tomorrow afternoon, ready to battle. We're trying all the possible ways to help. OK?" He stared Elizabeth down.

"OK! Fine," Elizabeth said.

"Well," Susie said to Elizabeth. "At least they are here, trying to help. Maybe they can help us find her."

Tess, feeling more awake now, met eyes with her older brother Mikey. He leaned against the kitchen counter, apart from the others. His short, red hair stuck out at funny angles, as if he'd been pulling it. That was his habit when he was stressed.

"Tess?" Mikey walked over and gave her a rare hug. "I came as soon as Elizabeth called me."

She sank gratefully into Mikey's warm shoulder and felt a sob coming on. She pulled away and noticed his eyes were rimmed with red.

"He brought the pizza," Elizabeth said and held up the slice she was eating. "You know, for a guy he's not bad. A definite Edmund," she said, comparing him to the male hero from Jane Austen's Mansfield Park.

"He's my brother!" Tess said, shocked. "Not an 'Edmund.'" Tess knew Edmund was a love interest. Elizabeth couldn't get them to read Mansfield Park, but all four of them watched the movie one Friday night.

"I'm not saying I like him like that," Elizabeth said. "I'm just saying, if someone did like him one day, she would be lucky." She seemed on the verge of saying something else, but closed her mouth.

One of the Brightcubes looked up.

"The weather report says a storm is hitting all the islands in a few hours," Damian said. "I amend my previous estimation. One in thirty."

The other two Brightcubes groaned.

"We better call our alternates for tomorrow's battle," Pete said, sounding tired.

"One in thirty," Tess repeated. Her heart sank.

"Those are just the odds for her coming back by tomorrow morning," Pete quickly said. "I mean, the odds are much better for her coming back at all. Those are..." He quickly did some more research.

"We don't need to hear it," Elizabeth said, cutting him off. "Unless it's a one hundred percent chance."

The Brightcubes all looked down.

No one spoke for a long time.

Pete took his phone into the living room to call the alternates for the math battle.

Tess woke hungry, as if it was dinnertime.

"How long did I sleep?" Tess asked.

"Well, it's eight o'clock, so...about five hours," Elizabeth said. "Have some." She opened the pizza box and shook it at Tess.

Tess took a slice of cold pizza and ate it tentatively. Though she was hungry, her stomach was tight with worry.

Susie's phone lay next to her on the table.

"Any messages at all?" Tess asked hopefully.

Susie and Elizabeth shook their heads.

"My mom and Amelia's mom should be in Hawaii soon," Susie said. "Maybe we'll hear some news."

After the horrible image in her dream of Amelia caught in a net, Tess felt more worried than ever. Surely Susie's mom and Amelia's mom would find her and bring her home.

But what if they didn't?

Elizabeth drummed her fingers on something in her lap. Tess peeked down and saw Amelia's diary lying in

Elizabeth's lap, hidden from the others.

"Did you read it?" Tess whispered to Elizabeth, not wanting the Brightcubes to hear.

Elizabeth shook her head.

Maybe it would be worth looking through, Tess thought. Even if it meant Amelia would be angry later.

Just in case Amelia's mom and Susie's mom needed some help finding Amelia, Tess would look through it. Even if it was an angry Amelia, at least they'd have her back, safe.

She held out her hand for the diary, and Elizabeth handed it over.

Chapter Nine

Amelia realized she couldn't run out of the cave without her dad stopping her. He was standing too close for that.

Maybe she could distract him while she tried to come up with an escape plan.

"Come on, girl," her dad said, apparently getting tired of waiting. "Put your hand on the rock."

"Me? But I don't even understand what's going on," Amelia told her dad.

"Well, it's Dark. There were Dark miners in the world before, but never very many," her dad explained, still breathing hard from mining the Dark. "There are Dark spots in other places, not just in Hawaii. But this is my Dark spot. No one else knows about it."

Amelia made a mental note that she was in Hawaii. At least now she knew where she was.

"The Dark miners died out," her dad explained. "But the way to mine Dark was written down, and remembered by a few sorcerers through time. Not everyone can mine it though. In fact, few can."

Amelia thought it was a good thing that few people could extract that weird Dark from rocks.

"I am one of the few who figured out how to do it, through books and what I learned from great sorcerers," her dad said. "And for some reason, I have the rare power of Dark mining."

Amelia wasn't sure what to believe. Her mind began to swirl with confusion.

"Dark mining is hereditary," her dad said. "Though you don't necessarily have the gift. But you look like me—a lot like me. Or at least how I used to look. So I guess you have the gift."

He took her right hand and pressed it against the ice-cold rock. Amelia shuddered.

"I mined Dark for forty years. Made a fortune," her dad said. "But I'm getting too old for it. So now it's your turn." He pressed an empty tube into her left hand.

"What is it used for?" Amelia asked in a small voice.

"Powerful spells. The most powerful ones," her dad said with reverence.

Amelia thought that over. She didn't understand what the rock was made of, or what her dad had in the shadowy tube. But she was quite sure there was no such thing as spells.

"There's no such thing as magic spells," Amelia said confidently.

"Ha!" Her dad laughed. "How do you think I got you off your campus and into the car? Why do you think you slept so well this morning?"

"Um, drugs for the first answer. Exhaustion for the second," Amelia answered, feeling calmer. She liked being rational, it made her feel safe. She went through the prime numbers in the back of her mind. It made her feel clearer and calmer.

She was still listening to her dad, with half a brain.

"Teleportation for the first one. Sleep charm for the second," her dad said. "Though I don't know why I bothered. Seems a good night's sleep was wasted on you."

"You're completely nuts," Amelia said, not caring if she was being rude. "There are no spells, no magic."

"Well, you asked what Dark is used for. Serves you right if you don't believe me."

She didn't believe him, not a word.

"And now…" Her dad tapped a finger on his daughter's right hand, the one that was still pressed against the freezing rock. "Let the Dark in the rock claim your hand."

"What? NO!" Amelia said.

"What do you mean, no? Don't you want to be a Dark miner?" her dad said angrily.

"Um, no. Actually, I want to go home," Amelia said.

"You'll be rich! Look, I'll give you a nice room. Not that shack. And all the beautiful dresses you'd like. How about a boat? A yacht! A sleep charm every night. Just try."

Amelia shook her head. "It's cold, and I don't like it," she said.

Her dad sighed deeply.

"I can't say I'm surprised," he said. "I mean, you're my kid. Stubborn, just like me. But I hoped we could be partners. Instead, I've got to convince you the hard way."

Her dad waved his hand back and forth, as if swatting mosquitoes.

Amelia felt her ankles grow heavy. She tried to take a step, but couldn't.

"What happened?" Amelia asked. Her mind swirled. "What did you do?"

"It's a spell. Like the kind you don't believe in," her dad said, mocking her.

Amelia pulled her hand away from the rock. She could do that, at least.

"Magic doesn't work on the Dark," her dad said, as he studied her free hand. "I did try to bind your hand, just like your ankles. It's a good sign. It means the Dark was probably on your hand. If it likes you, you'll be able to mine it."

"If it likes me? Eew," Amelia said. Fear made her heart pound.

What strange things were happening here?

"My silly daughter. Don't you understand the honor of it? Do you know we might be the only ones left? I don't know of a single other living Dark miner," her dad said and shook his head. "Some sorcerers, even great sorcerers, they would kill to have the ability."

"It just doesn't sound very positive," Amelia said. She wasn't sure what she had against trying it, really. Since she didn't believe in spells, or magic, what harm could it do?

But all her instincts told her not to touch that cold rock again.

"Oh well, I'll leave you here awhile," her dad said. "When I come back, I'm sure you'll be singing a different song." Her dad laughed at his own joke.

He took the ball of light and started to go.

"Hey!" Amelia said, suddenly afraid. "At least leave me the light!" Her feet were still stuck in place, and she was starting to feel cold, wearing only her T-shirt and jeans.

"You want the light? Then go ahead and start mining," her dad said. "The sooner you do that, the sooner you can get out of here. I'll even let you go to the beach, have some free time. You like swimming? There's a nice beach a mile's walk from here…" Her dad's voice sounded eager.

Amelia had to admit the sound of a beach, outside in fresh air, sounded much nicer than her present situation. But she didn't believe him. What would stop him from sticking her in that shack again once he was done with her?

"Food? I can make a nice grill, too. You must be hungry," her dad said. "You've only had a little poi."

Amelia's stomach rumbled so loud that it echoed throughout the cave. Her dad laughed.

"Kid, I want us to be friends. Partners. Really," her dad said.

She was hungry. And he was her Dad. Maybe they could be friends. But the Dark seemed like a terrible thing. Her instincts were to get away from the rock. And her dad did kidnap her, after all. That wasn't the action of a friend.

Amelia was afraid that if she opened her mouth, she would agree to do this weird Dark mining thing, just for the promise of food.

"No!" Amelia finally trusted herself enough to yell.

"Suit yourself," her dad said. "We'll do this the hard way."

Amelia reached into her pocket and held the pin out.

"If you really gave me this, you must care about me," she said. "You can't leave me here in the dark, if you care about me."

Her dad gazed at the pin. A sad look came into his eyes. But then he shook it off, and looked mean again.

"I do care," he said. "And staying here for awhile to think things over isn't going to kill you. Believe it or not, if you mine the Dark, it will be the greatest thing that ever happened to you."

"What do you mean?" Amelia said. "Why is it so great?"

"We were poor," her dad said. "You don't remember, but your mom and I had nothing. When I started mining the Dark, I made money. I bought that house you're living in now. We could afford doctor's bills. You had a ton of ear infections when you were little. Don't you understand?

Darkmining was the best thing that happened to me. To us."

"So why did you leave?" Amelia asked. "Why does Mom hate you?"

"She didn't understand where I got the money. Didn't trust me," her dad said. "Didn't like my friends, either."

Amelia bit her lip. Her mom definitely hated her dad, and told Amelia to stay far away. So her dad must have done something to deserve that.

She held up the pin again.

"Does Mom know this was from you?" she asked.

"She wouldn't have let me give that to you," he said. "So I pretended your birthday gifts were from your Aunt Ada. I knew you'd never meet her. She's always traveling—Egypt, Japan, Nepal. Anywhere but home."

"Wait, all the birthday pins were from you?" Amelia asked, stunned.

A smile lit up her dad's face. Amelia was amazed. Her dad actually looked handsome in that moment, and kind.

Then his smile disappeared.

"I can't be too soft on you," he said. "If you don't mine that Dark, I lose everything."

Her dad quickly walked away, and the cave was plunged into darkness. She heard him talking to Alex outside.

"Girl's going to stay until nightfall," her dad said.

"A storm is coming. We can't leave her all alone in there!" Alex said. "What if the rock dragon comes?"

Rock dragon?

Amelia's heart pounded harder.

"She'll be fine. Mind your own business," her dad said, his voice rising. "The rock dragon never climbs that hill. Well, almost never."

"Hey, you said she'd be into this," Alex said. "I don't like how this is going. She doesn't want to Darkmine. I heard you talking in the cave."

With an especially evil tone, her dad said, "When she mines the Dark, you will see that change. She'll become like me, lose all that stupid, childlike goodness. She'll want to do it, once she knows the power of the Dark."

The voices grew more distant. Amelia guessed they were walking away. She wondered what the rock dragon was all about. Maybe she didn't really want to know. It sounded scary.

Soon it was silent, except for the very faint, low howl of the wind. She felt the smooth surface of the pin with her thumb. Her dad was so complicated. He kidnapped her, then left her in the dark in this cave…but he also gave her a gift every birthday.

Surely he wouldn't leave her in danger.

Her arms prickled in the cold air. She wished she had her jacket and not just a T-shirt on. It was so quiet that she could hear her own breath, fast and panicked.

When she calmed down, she realized something was wrong. She should feel alone, but she didn't. She felt a presence next to her. It came from the direction of the Dark rock.

It seemed like something was waiting. Something cold, with lots of eyes. She shook off the image.

Just my imagination, she thought.

There's no such thing as magic.

Though…why can't I move my feet?

When she reached down to feel around her ankles, she could tell there was nothing around them. But her feet felt so heavy.

"A trick!" Amelia yelled. "A trick from my dad! The kidnapper, not a sorcerer!"

Her words echoed through the cave, unnerving her. To comfort herself, she touched the Water amulet she wore around her neck. She said the names of her friends.

"Tess. Elizabeth. Susie." She recited their names over and over again. It calmed her, filled her with comfort.

When she stopped, it seemed that the rock had lost interest. She couldn't explain how she knew that, it just seemed like she was no longer being watched.

She squatted down, cold and alone.

Amelia held her Water amulet, and thought of her friends and their strong, simple love.

"Come get me," she whispered.

Chapter Ten

Susie, Tess, Elizabeth and Mikey stayed up all night with the Brightcubes. Except for the occasional power nap on the sofa, they all stayed awake until dawn. They kept ordering pizzas as they researched Hawaii, flights, kidnappings and anything else they could think of which might help find Amelia.

At dawn, the Brightcubes left to get ready for their math battle. Their spirits were low. They found an alternate named Dirk, but they said he was 'no Amelia'.

Tess picked at a cold slice of pizza. She had read part of Amelia's diary, starting with January 1st of this year. Mostly it was a logbook of what classes Amelia went to, if she had dinner with her mom or not, and what problem she solved during math practice. There was a lot about imaginary numbers in it, and math theorems.

Tess had thought it would be filled with personal feelings, so hesitated to read it. But there was almost nothing personal in it. Her diary was downright boring. Tess got so bored that she gave up reading it when she got to February.

No interesting news had come up, either. Nothing from Susie's mom, and that had them worrying more and more.

Normally, Susie's mom texted her daughter a lot. Had something happened to Susie's mom?

Hopefully she just got really busy or her phone battery was low so she couldn't text.

Susie rummaged through the fridge looking for 'anything healthy', as she put it.

"I need to stress-eat, and I'm tired of pizza," Susie said from the fridge. "You'd think there would be at least one fruit or vegetable in here."

"Frosted Flakes! It's cereal, so it must be healthy, right? Good enough for me," Elizabeth said and poured herself a bowl.

Tess' brother walked in holding his phone. His hair stuck up all over the place. He had been pulling it all night. He had waited until 7 a.m., then he called Amelia's teachers. He hoped to find out if they had seen anything strange, like her talking to anyone they didn't recognize over the last week.

"Anything, Mikey? Any leads?" Tess asked him.

He shook his head.

When Susie's phone buzzed, all four of them leapt to the table to look at the screen. They read the message on the phone.

"It's your mom, Susie. All it says is Plan B, Didus," Elizabeth said, as she read the message. "What does that mean?"

"Yes, she texted!" Susie said with relief. "She's OK!" She punched the air. "But I don't know what she means by Plan B. And the only Didus I know is a dog." Susie had found a jar of peanut butter and was eating it with a spoon.

"I'll try to call her," Elizabeth said. She picked up Susie's phone and hit the 'Mom' button.

"Voicemail," Elizabeth mouthed, then left a message: "Hi, Ms. Lang. We're not sure what Plan B actually means, so could you tell us more? Thanks. Bye. Oh! Call us back."

"Wait," Elizabeth said, staring out the window. "Is that Didus?"

Tess looked out the window. A huge, furry face was staring back at her. It was a beautiful dog—a collie. Its long, soft fur was white, reddish brown and tan. She found its deep, dark eyes friendly and comforting.

The dog at the window barked once, getting the attention of everyone in the kitchen.

"That's Didus!" Susie gushed. "I know him. He's an awesome dog. But I don't understand how he can be part of the plan." She went to the window, and the collie opened his mouth, seeming to smile.

"Don't let it in," Elizabeth said. "Its teeth look sharp, and it probably smells."

"He doesn't smell!" Susie said. "And he's not an 'it'."

The phone vibrated in Elizabeth's hand.

"This is weird," Elizabeth said and showed Susie the phone.

"Please give him water," Susie read. "That is weird. How does my mom know Didus is here?"

"I don't like dogs," Elizabeth said. "Maybe your mom means something else about the water. Let's just stay away from that one. It looks big."

Tess eyed Didus, who looked back at her with friendly eyes. He pressed his paw on one window, and panted.

"Didus is friendly," Susie said. "I know that dog. He hangs around our house sometimes, and we let him in. He's cool. I've known him since…well, forever."

Elizabeth complained about the dog, but Mikey went to let him in.

The Collie came into the kitchen. Elizabeth cowered on her chair, even though Didus stayed near the entrance to the kitchen. He sat down and cocked his head, as if listening and following the conversation.

"Hello, sweetie," Susie said and pet the dog.

Tess put a bowl of water on the floor, and Didus lapped it up.

Susie tried to call her mom again, but got no answer. She spoke aloud as she texted.

"Are you OK, Mom?" Susie texted. "Is Amelia there?"

For the next few minutes, they all stared at either the phone or the dog. Nobody was sure what to do next.

Finally, another text appeared.

Susie read it aloud.

"Find green envelope under sofa. Instructions. Can't text anymore. Will try to contact you another way. Love."

"Green envelope?" Elizabeth read the text herself. "Instructions under the sofa? What is she talking about? And why can't she text anymore?"

Didus padded out of the kitchen. He came back with a green envelope.

"Oh, he's smart," Tess said. "He understood what you said, Susie. Good boy!" She scratched him behind the ears. Didus placed a paw on her leg, as if in thanks.

Elizabeth took the envelope, but with two careful fingers. It had dog slobber on it.

"Oh, disgusting," Elizabeth said.

Susie rolled her eyes. She grabbed a tea towel and wiped it down. She returned the letter to Elizabeth, who opened it with the tips of her fingers as if it was toxic.

Elizabeth held the letter close to her eyes, reading it over several times. Then she put it down on the table, and placed her head in her hands.

"This is too weird," Elizabeth mumbled.

"What?" Susie said and grabbed the paper. Her eyes grew big as she read. She quickly put it back on the table.

"Some sort of joke," Susie said angrily, and crossed her arms. She paced the kitchen.

"What?" Tess took it and read aloud.

If you read this, it means we've been captured.

"Captured?" Tess' eyes grew wide with surprise, and she exchanged a look with her brother.

Didus whined.

"Keep reading," Mikey said and Tess picked up where she left off.

I need to tell you some things you won't believe. I'm a...

Tess stared at the word before going on.

I'm a sorceress. I use my magic for good. Amelia's dad is a dark sorcerer. He deals with evil magic. That's why I had to try to rescue Amelia. There aren't a lot of sorcerers left these days, neither good nor bad. I don't think there is anyone else who can help.

If you are reading this, I must have failed. I triggered Plan B texts to be sent to you if my phone falls into the wrong hands. Give Didus the green stone in this envelope. He will activate your amulets. They will give you powers that will protect you. If Didus has not yet come, wait for him. My capture will have sent him a signal, and he'll find you.

Tess stopped reading and looked at Didus, who looked sadly back at her. She cleared her throat, blinked a few times, then read on.

'Do not—I repeat, do not—come after us. If I failed, Amelia's dad is too powerful. Use the magic in the amulets to protect yourselves. Susie, I left my credit card, passport and veil of mom in your sock drawer. Only use them as a last resort. Be safe.'

Tess held the paper in stunned silence. Elizabeth sat still with her head in her hands. Susie stomped up and down, pacing the small kitchen. Mikey took the paper from Tess and read it himself.

"A trick. A joke from the kidnapper," Elizabeth said. "Though, it doesn't really make sense. I mean…why?"

"Stupid joke," Susie practically yelled.

Tess picked up the green envelope. There was a stone in there. She held it in her hand, turning it over. It was smooth and small, and seemed totally normal.

Didus watched her with interest.

Elizabeth pulled out the glass sphere she had in her bag. "This is weird, too. I still don't know where the countries went." She turned the clear ball around, inspecting it. "I don't know what it is, but…magic?"

Give Didus the green stone.

Tess recalled the words from the letter.

Didus whined and put a paw on Tess' leg. He opened his mouth wide, as if he was inviting Tess to put the stone there.

Tess placed the stone on the dog's long pink tongue, then snatched her fingers away in case his sharp teeth snapped shut.

Didus closed his mouth gently. He bounded away and scratched at the front door.

"Should I let him out?" Mikey asked from the living room.

"Yes!" Susie shouted.

"No!" Elizabeth yelled. "Get that stone out of its mouth, wash it, then give it to me. I need to find out what's going on here."

"The letter said to give the stone to Didus. I'm going to let him out," Mikey said and opened the door. "Don't worry, I'll follow him."

Didus ran outside, while Mikey jogged to keep up behind him. Tess watched from the front window until they were out of sight, way down the street.

When she came back to the kitchen, both Susie and Elizabeth were holding their necklaces.

"Is my mom OK, do you think?" Susie asked. "I mean, if she's texting, she has to be OK. But she said she was captured."

"Your mom might not have been texting us real-time. The letter said those texts were triggered to be sent if her phone fell into the wrong hands," Elizabeth said, thinking out loud.

At the horrified look on Susie's face, Elizabeth changed her approach.

"Of course, your mom is the coolest, and the strongest," Elizabeth said. "I'm sure she'll be fine."

Susie held on to her amulet.

"Do you think this could really be magic?" Susie was asking. "I mean, real magic? That's impossible."

Elizabeth shrugged, looking tired.

"Well, one thing I can say," Elizabeth said. "This century is getting a lot more interesting. But I still prefer Jane Austen's world."

Tess massaged her temples. She wasn't sure what she thought about all this. Everything seemed to be going in a bad direction. First, Amelia seemed weird with her at the park. Then, Amelia disappeared. Now Susie's mom claimed to be magical. Unless, of course, it was all made up by the kidnapper, whoever that was.

"If these necklaces are magic," Tess said, pulling out her Fire amulet. "I hope they can help us find Amelia."

"For you, I would walk through fire," Tess said, quietly reciting her part of the friendship pledge.

"I don't believe in magic," Susie said. "But for you, I would walk on air. Now let's go find Amelia and my mom."

Susie took Tess' hand in hers. Elizabeth added her hand as well.

"For you, I would walk the Earth," Elizabeth said. "Magic or not, let's find our friends."

Chapter Eleven

The wind had picked up. Amelia could hear it howling outside. Only a light breeze made its way into the cave, though. It was warm and smelled like the sea.

She had no idea how long she had been sitting in the same place. Though it was dark, her eyes had adapted enough that she could make out shapes of rocks here and there. The Dark rock remained an ink-black hole.

Her fear had subsided. It seemed pointless to worry about things like starvation. And the rock dragon. What could she do about it anyway? It felt better to just keep calm and not let fear get to her.

She sang all the songs she knew. Cyndi Lauper, Beyoncé, even the Spice Girls.

She recited prime numbers until she got bored. She stopped at 1,061, which was much higher than she normally recited them to.

She tried to decide what she would do when her dad came, but she hadn't come to a conclusion yet.

Option A was to pretend she felt too sick to stand up.

Option B was to tell him she had to pee, then go outside behind a coconut palm and run as fast as she could.

Option C was to pretend to try to mine the Dark, but actually keep her hand off the stone.

Option D was to actually try to mine it.

It might not work, anyway.

But Option D twisted her stomach nervously, and made chills run up her spine. There was something very wrong with Dark, she could feel it.

Steps echoed through the cave.

"Option B," she said to herself, the pee and run plan. "At least I'll get to breathe some fresh air."

She turned as far as she was able with her ankles held to the ground. She was surprised to see a normal flashlight, rather than the light ball her dad had earlier. She looked closely at the face of the man that held it.

It was Alex.

"Aloha," he said. Amelia knew it was a Hawaiian greeting.

"Aloha, Alex," she said. "I thought you said you don't come into the cave."

"It's funny," Alex said. "It usually feels so creepy in here, I don't want to go in. It doesn't feel as bad just now."

His sweatshirt was marked with rain, and his hair was wet and plastered to his head.

"Your dad can't come. He's too weak to walk through this storm after the mining," he said and handed Amelia an energy bar. She ate it quickly, realizing how hungry she was. Her stomach felt horribly empty.

"Is he OK?" Amelia asked.

"You care?" Alex said, surprised. "I mean, he hasn't been nice to you." He indicated her trapped ankles. "You're trapped in a cave in a storm."

"I noticed," Amelia said. "But he's still my dad." Her fingers touched the heart pin in her jeans pocket.

"Man," Alex said. "I can't imagine having a scary dad like that. I think I would hate him."

Amelia's stomach rumbled.

"I knew you'd be hungry," he said and grunted. "My sister is your age. When I see you trapped in here, I see her. So I want to help you." He handed her something that looked like purple bread in the flashlight.

"Taro bread," Alex said. "Go ahead and take it."

"Are you going to try to make me mine the Dark?" Amelia asked, and took a bite of the bread. It was so delicious she wolfed it down.

"Nope." Alex shook his head. "I said I want to help you. I'm here to give you food and that's it. Though your dad gave me different orders."

"Won't my dad get mad at you?" Amelia asked.

"How's he going to know?" Alex sat next to her. "Your dad wanted me to give you the energy bar only if you tried mining the Dark first. But if you're stubborn like him, that wouldn't have worked. Right?"

Amelia nodded.

"I don't think I would have tried to mine the Dark," she said. "Not even for food."

The sound of the wind picked up. The breeze in the cave stirred her hair.

"Do you want me to mine the Dark?" Amelia asked.

"Me?" Alex looked surprised. "Well. It's how I make my living. I sell the Dark that your dad mines. I've done it for a year now. My sister, the one your age, she's smart and wants to go to college. So this is how we're getting her there."

Amelia understood.

"Also, it's good money. I can take my girlfriend to nice places sometimes," he said and grinned.

"But this Dark…it changes things," Alex said. "I met your dad's buddy, Zoro, before he died. That's how I got the job. Zoro offered it to me. Anyway, he said that once, your dad was handsome, and kind of nice. Can you believe that? But the Dark changed him."

Amelia shuddered at the thought. She recalled the black veins that ran up her dad's arm.

"So, maybe my answer is no," Alex said. "You seem nice. Pretty, too. I don't think you should Darkmine. I don't like working for your dad, anyway. He's too mean. I will get a different job."

"Thanks," she said. "For being honest."

He nodded, looking surprised again.

"I'd be so mad if someone trapped me here. You seem all chilled," he said.

Amelia pulled at her blond hair and reflected.

"I was angry, but a lot of time has passed. Now I'm just tired," Amelia said. "Anger doesn't help anyway."

"Wise," Alex smiled. "Look, I can't free your ankles. I don't know how. I wish I could."

Amelia smiled and said, "You helped. The food helped. Thanks."

Alex gave her a sad look.

"I'll leave the flashlight," he said. "You'll be OK in the cave. That storm looks like it's going to be a bad one."

"Thanks," Amelia said in a small voice. She didn't want to be in the cave all night. But she didn't want Alex to know she was afraid.

"I guess your dad will come in the morning," Alex said. "After he's had a good night's sleep. Mining takes a lot out of him. Anyway, he's not so good walking at night. He has bad night vision."

"Even with his magic?" Amelia asked.

"He could use magic to see better, but he's too weak now," Alex said. "And the rock dragon is more active at night."

"The rock dragon?" Amelia felt alarm clench her heart. "I heard you guys talking about it."

"Oh, don't worry about it," Alex said quickly. "It won't come up here in the storm."

"What does it look like?" Amelia asked. "You know, in case it comes here."

"Believe me, you would know if you saw it," Alex said. "Big, hungry, made of rock."

A shiver passed up Amelia's spine.

"But really…" Alex's voice softened. "It hides out in bad storms like this one. You'll be fine."

Alex handed her the flashlight.

"Yeah, well, thanks for the help," Amelia said. "Bye, Alex. Good night."

Alex stood in place for awhile, hovering.

"My name is Akoni," he said. "Your dad just calls me Alex. It's not my real name."

Amelia was surprised.

Why didn't her dad call him by his real name?

"Akoni, it's nice to meet you," Amelia said.

"Aloha," Akoni said and his voice caught. Then he took off his sweatshirt and gave it to Amelia.

"Sorry it's not so clean," Akoni said. "But you'll be warmer."

Amelia put the sweatshirt on, enjoying the instant warmth. It didn't smell bad. It just smelled like smoke.

"Thanks, it's really helpful," Amelia said. "I'll be much warmer now."

Akoni found another taro bread roll in his bag, and gave it to her. He didn't seem to want to leave her there. But he eventually said goodbye, and she heard his footsteps as he left the cave.

Amelia thought about their conversation. She didn't like the sound of the rock dragon. But she decided to believe Akoni that it wouldn't come up here in the storm.

Akoni's visit had also brought her good news.

She had learned that her dad couldn't make his way in the dark, so she had a good chance of escaping by night. She had also learned Akoni's true name, and thought that maybe, if she wanted to escape, he'd be on her side.

To calm herself, she hummed "True Colors" in between bites of the starchy taro bread. The cave echoed it back to her, and it almost seemed it was singing along.

Chapter Twelve

Mikey and the Collie had not returned. Tess called her brother's cell, and when he answered the phone, he was panting. He was still running after Didus through the fire trails up in the hills.

Tess let him know they were going to Susie's house to search through her mom's study for anything that could help them rescue Amelia.

Tess had a sinking feeling they might have to rescue not only Amelia, but also Amelia's mom and Susie's mom too.

The girls had decided that, whether or not the amulets were magical, they had to go to Hawaii.

While Tess and Susie searched the study, Elizabeth sat downstairs on a laptop. She was trying to book them all a flight, hopefully, for later that day.

Tess examined the bookshelves in the study. Whether or not Susie's mom was a sorceress, or just thought she was a sorceress, she was bound to have some helpful items, like the glass ball that had showed Amelia's location.

"You know…" Susie opened and closed her mom's desk drawers with small slams that made Tess jump. "I always thought of my mom as being really together. I mean, an engineer, a master gardener, and a single mom. And now I find out she's just…crazy!" Susie opened a drawer she had already looked in and slammed it extra loud.

"Well," Tess said. "I don't really understand what's happening. Maybe this is all a trick, you know, planned by the kidnapper. But even if your mom has some sort of secret life, it doesn't mean she's not really together."

"Magic?" Susie said, her dark eyes flashing. "Doesn't that sound crazy to you?"

"Well, either magic or some sort of…" Tess shrugged. "I don't know, a bag of clever tricks, I guess."

"There's nothing useful in these drawers," Susie said loudly. "Just paper."

"How about trying the cabinet?" Tess motioned to a wooden cabinet in the corner, then turned her attention to the bookshelves.

Susie stomped over to the cabinet, rattled the locked door, then searched around underneath it for the key.

"You know," Tess said, as she watched Susie out of the corner of her eye. "I always wondered why your mom gave me the Fire amulet, and not you."

Susie stopped what she was doing. Her anger seemed to calm for a moment.

"Well, I'm clearly Air," she said in a more normal voice. "I mean, I love spiking the ball. Jumping and spiking."

"Yeah, and I guess Amelia is more water than fire, for sure," Tess said. "And Elizabeth's clearly Earth."

"Nineteenth century Earth!" Susie said and laughed.

"But I don't feel like fire either," Tess said. "Except for my red hair, I guess."

Susie stood up and faced Tess. She gave Tess her full attention, which was a rare thing. Tess felt exposed under her strong gaze.

"I think you could be fire," Susie finally said and dropped to her knees again, feeling around for a key.

"Why?" Tess scanned the books. They were all on math, materials, engineering, and gardening. "I don't have a temper."

"But you flicker," Susie said.

"Flicker?" Tess asked, confused.

"Yes. And I get the feeling that you could be really powerful, like fire, but normally you just flicker," Susie said.

"Aha!" Susie held up a silver key. "I found it. Mom always leaves them in the same place."

"Is that bad?" Tess asked. "I mean, that I just flicker?"

"No, of course not!" Susie said, as she unlocked the door. "Flickering is very Tess. But I wouldn't mind seeing a full flare one day."

Tess stood up, stunned. She had never thought of herself as flickering. But she really couldn't see herself flaring with a fiery power. That didn't seem to be her at all.

"That's weird," Susie said and stood there with her arms crossed. "It's empty."

"Empty? Then why was it locked?" Tess came to stand beside Susie. The doors of the wood cabinet were both open, and two light-colored, empty shelves were revealed.

"What if…" Tess thought aloud. "In stories, magicians say passwords sometimes. Oh, I don't know, that sounds so weird. Forget it."

"That's not so weird. There's no such thing as real magic but maybe there's some trick to use," Susie said. "But anyway, what password would we use?"

"Susie!" Tess said. Nothing happened. "Susie Elisa Lang!" Still nothing happened.

"Elaine Lang!" Susie tried her mom's name.

Susie and Tess were shouting random words at the empty cabinet when Elizabeth entered the room.

"Um, what are you two doing?" Elizabeth asked. Her eyebrows raised with amusement.

"We're yelling at the cabinet. Did you book flights?" Susie asked.

"I booked the red-eye for ten p.m. tonight," Elizabeth said, "so we'll arrive tomorrow morning. We have one stop. All the non-stops were full. The flights were expensive! I booked tickets for us three, and Mikey."

"Did you use my mom's credit card?" Susie asked. "I guess she thought she might run into trouble, or she would never have given it to me."

Elizabeth nodded.

"I guess it's good to take the red-eye," Tess said. "It

might be better to get there tomorrow morning rather than tonight, anyway. We can start looking as soon as we arrive."

"Susie, your mom's credit card was in your sock drawer with her passport and this," Elizabeth said and held out a silky fabric that was nearly transparent.

"What's that?" Susie asked.

"Well, I think it might be the 'veil of mom' your mom mentioned in her message to us," Elizabeth said.

Tess had a sudden feeling she knew what the 'veil of mom' would do.

"Put it on," Tess said.

"Exactly what I was thinking," Elizabeth said.

Susie reluctantly put the veil over her head.

Elizabeth gasped and a shockwave ran through Tess, stunning her into an open-mouthed silence.

With the veil on, Susie looked exactly like her mom, down to the styled waves of black hair streaked with grey.

"What?" Susie asked, as the girls stared. They brought her to a mirror and it was Susie's turn to stare open-mouthed.

"I was wondering how we were going to get on the plane without an adult." Elizabeth said. "But this will work, you're going to fly as Elaine Lang."

Susie shook her head no.

"You've got to!" Elizabeth said. "We're fourteen, Mikey's sixteen...we need an adult to fly with us."

Susie sighed deeply and took the veil off.

"Look, I'll do it," she said. "But I don't want to talk about it. This is just a trick, right? No such thing as magic."

Tess didn't think it was only a trick, but there was no point in arguing with Susie. Elizabeth calmly took the veil and Susie knelt before the empty cabinet, searching, pretending she hadn't just turned into her mom.

"So, what's with the cabinet?" Elizabeth indicated the empty shelves.

"Well, it was locked," Tess explained. "But there's nothing in it. So we wondered if there was a password." Her cheeks flamed as she heard her own words. She suddenly felt embarrassed.

"A password?" Elizabeth nodded, and didn't seem to find the idea silly. "Well, her laptop password was Verdant."

"Verdant?" Susie said. All of a sudden, the air in the cabinet shimmered. All three girls watched as objects and papers cluttered the previously bare shelves.

"Magic!" Elizabeth said.

"A trick!" Susie said and crossed her arms.

Tess picked up a map of the world on the top shelf.

"Maybe this map is like, not a normal map," Tess said. "I don't know, it could be a trick map."

"Yeah, could be," Elizabeth said. "Let's look for anything that can be used to find Amelia, and the missing moms." She took a box from the shelf.

"Look at this!" Susie took a very normal-looking wallet from the shelf. "Money!"

"Well, money's kind of like magic," Elizabeth said, joking.

"We'll definitely need some of this. Looks like we've got forty bucks," Susie said and took the bills out.

Two more bills appeared in the wallet as soon as she did. Susie gasped and dropped the wallet.

Tess picked it up, and extracted $40 several times. Soon she had $200 in her hand. All three girls stared at the money in her hand.

"I can't believe she said I had to wait a year for a new pair of sneakers," Susie said, "when she has that wallet!" Tess and Elizabeth stared at her.

Suddenly, Tess and Elizabeth both burst out laughing.

"What?" Susie asked.

"That's your first thought?" Elizabeth said through her laughter. "You find a magic wallet, and all you can think about are those shoes you wanted?"

"It's not magic," Susie said, but she grinned.

Tess felt the tension of the last couple days leave her body as she fell onto the floor, hiccuping and laughing. She couldn't meet Elizabeth's eyes without exploding again.

When she recovered herself and could breathe normally, she felt more hopeful. Whether it was a magic wallet or a clever trick, the money would come in handy in Hawaii. They were a step closer to finding Amelia, Tess could feel it.

Chapter Thirteen

Amelia woke up on the floor of the stone cave. Her arm was numb where she had pressed it against the rock floor while she slept. Her hip hurt as well. Most of all, her ankles were killing her. They felt like they were trapped in steel vices.

At least she hadn't had a visit from the rock dragon.

It was dark, so she couldn't tell if it was day or night. A breeze whistled through the cave, and she could hear sounds of strong winds outside. She figured the storm was still going.

She blinked her eyes sleepily. She was deeply hungry. Her stomach gnawed, so she put a hand on it to calm it.

Voices outside the cave reached her ears, so she guessed it was morning. Her heart sank when she heard her dad's voice.

Would he make her mine the Dark?

She couldn't hear what they were saying, but Alex seemed to be arguing with her dad.

No, his name is Akoni, she corrected herself.

Maybe she could get her dad to take the ankle spell off, so she could rotate them. She was worried she wouldn't be able to walk, considering how stiff they were.

"Amelia," said a soft, female voice. "Water."

Amelia strained her ears to listen. Did she really just hear a woman's voice? Or was it the wind?

Had it come from inside or outside the cave?

But there was only the whistling of the wind, and the men's conversation. Maybe she was just hearing things.

A thin, high whistle began.

The melody was from True Colors.

Unsure of who was whistling, Amelia hummed along. It gave her a strange sense of comfort.

Maybe someone had come to save her.

Could it be Tess, Elizabeth or Susie?

The voice had called her 'Water', their nickname for her. She hoped it was one of her friends.

The Dark rock was nearby, but Amelia wasn't getting that cold, gloomy feeling from it anymore. She had the strong feeling it knew she was there, it just wasn't interested.

She sang the chorus of True Colors and the whistling got louder. Soon the whistle turned into singing. It didn't sound like any of her friends—she knew their voices well. Amelia wondered if she was hallucinating. But it was nice singing with someone else.

Amelia realized that the singing was coming from inside the walls of the cave.

How was that possible?

The singing stopped as soon as her dad walked into the cave. The sense of Dark became stronger, and Amelia shivered. It felt like the cave got colder.

Amelia wondered if she had imagined the singing after all.

Her dad was holding his lightball. He immediately noticed the flashlight and sweatshirt Amelia had on.

"That's it, he's fired," her dad said.

"No, I begged Akoni for these," Amelia said. She didn't want to get him in trouble. "Really, he tried to be mean."

Her dad looked surprised. "You know his name? His real name?" He rolled his eyes. "Amateurs."

"What's wrong with that?" Amelia felt a great annoyance fill her. "It's his name. What, you don't like it?" She didn't like being around her dad. He made her so angry.

"You never give your real name in the magic world," her dad said. "It gives spell-casters way too much information, and too much power over you."

"Is your name really Jack?" Amelia said, thinking back to what Akoni and her mom had called him.

Her dad grinned.

"You're not so slow after all," her dad said. "Now, get up, it's time to mine some Dark." Her dad rubbed his hands together.

"Amelia, Water," the gentle voice spoke softly.

"What's that? Did you say that?" her dad asked.

"No. I thought I was imagining things," Amelia said. "I'm glad you hear her too." The thought that the soothing voice might be real made her happy.

"Well, it's not important. Let's get to it," her dad said. "Before anything else strange happens."

"Please. Please unshackle my ankles," Amelia said. "They really, really hurt."

"Good! My plan is working then. Mine the Dark, and you can go soak them in the waves. I'll give you the whole day off for five minutes of work."

Amelia wanted to cry. She didn't want to stay shackled in this cave. But the Dark seemed more powerful and disgusting now that her dad was here. She didn't want to touch the rock.

As her dad put a tube in her left hand and pressed her right hand against the frigid rock, Amelia thought of the ocean. The waves, and swimming. The warmth of the water. She could imagine kicking her ankles, turning them freely.

The water necklace hung around her neck like it always did. She thought of the gentle voice in the walls saying her name. Her real names—Amelia, and Water.

"Now, sing!" Her dad's voice was impatient.

True Colors came sailing out of Amelia's mouth, in a clear, high song.

Her dad stamped his foot. "Not that song!" he shouted. "The Dark won't like it."

Another voice joined Amelia's, and the cave was filled with a rich, beautiful melody.

"What's going on?" her dad asked. "Did that Lang

woman escape? She was under my sleep spell. Maybe it wasn't strong enough."

"Elaine Lang? Susie's mom is here?" Amelia asked. She felt her spirits lift. "What do you mean did she escape? Do you have her trapped?"

"Never mind," her dad said. "Elaine is not a problem at the moment. All you need to do is change your tune. Sing something sad, the Dark likes it better."

With the extra boost of energy Amelia gained from learning Susie's mom had come to rescue her, she put all her strength into singing True Colors. The woman's voice sang along with her. Amelia wondered if it was Susie's mom, somehow.

The Dark rock under Amelia's hand trembled. Maybe it didn't like the song. Amelia sang louder, and the other woman's voice became stronger.

Akoni ran into the cave.

Amelia was shocked to see his face full of joy when he came into the light.

"It's the goddess! The ocean goddess!" he said and clapped Amelia on the back. "She sings!"

"Are you sure it's not Susie's mom?" Amelia asked. "I thought, maybe, it was Ms. Lang singing."

"It's coming from the walls," Akoni said. "There is a legend that the goddess has been trapped in this cave for hundreds of years. It's got to be her!"

"That goddess has long lived in these walls. The Dark has long been stronger. Now leave!" her dad said and stared Akoni down.

"No, see, the girl has broken the spell! The girl woke the goddess!" Akoni said. "We must help free her from the walls."

Her dad waved his hands like Akoni was a mosquito.

"Incantus Akoni Akoni newt," her dad said.

When her dad clapped, Akoni was gone.

"Where is he? What did you do?" Amelia asked, her voice shaking.

"I did what I do to troublemakers. Do you want to be next?" her dad said.

Amelia felt something scurry up her leg. She wanted to look down, but just in case the old legends about sorcerers turning people to newts was true, she didn't want to give Akoni's whereabouts away.

She felt the sensation of tiny feet scurrying all the way up her leg, then whatever it was plopped into her pocket, where it stayed.

"Amelia," the voice said again. "Water."

"Are you a goddess?" Amelia asked.

"My name, say my name," the voice said.

"What's her name? This is important!" Amelia asked her dad.

Her dad pulled at his hair.

"I have a shipment of Dark to make by sunset," her dad said. His voice had lost its irritation, and was cold. It scared Amelia.

"I've been far too good to you. Akoni, too. Clearly, you need to see the gravity of the situation." Her dad waved his hands in front of him. Amelia's heart beat double-time. Was she about to become a newt?

Amelia quickly took her mind to the ocean.

"I am Water," she said to herself, and felt her amulet warm against her chest. A swirling feeling swam through her.

"Amelia, Amelia dolor dolor," her dad said.

But nothing happened.

Her dad studied his hands. "I must have been weakened by that newt spell," he mumbled to himself.

Amelia thought about her friends, and how they called her 'Water'. She felt full of happiness, remembering them. She felt like an ocean of love.

Amelia felt the Dark repelling her. It gave a mighty push, and she flew across the cave, landing on the hard floor. She had the wind knocked clear out of her, and her magical restraints were broken. Her ankles were free!

Before her dad could collect himself, she pulled herself to her feet and started to limp out of the cave. Her feet were numb, though, and she ended up crawling.

"Amelia, Amelia arret arret!" Her dad's angry voice filled the cave.

111

She got to the mouth of the cave. It wasn't far. Soon she was out in the wind and rain. She heard steps rushing toward her, and she rolled to the edge of the hill. The drop looked steep, but not deathly steep. She bet she could roll down the hill and survive.

Her dad stood at the ghoul-shaped mouth of the cave, leaning against the stone. He spotted Amelia lying near the edge.

"Amelia arret," he said, but his voice was weak.

"That's not my name!" she yelled back. He took a step toward her and she rolled down the hill. Rolled, or flowed, as she skidded and slid in a half controlled, half wild way. Because now, covered with rain and sliding down a muddy slope, she was Water.

Chapter Fourteen

Elizabeth pulled another two twenties from the wallet of unending money, and added it to the stack. She closed the wallet, opened it again, and shook her head.

"I can't believe it," Elizabeth said. "Twenties keep filling the wallet. I can't figure out how it works. Unless, of course, it really is magic."

"There must be a trick," Susie said.

A bark interrupted them.

Mikey and Didus had returned.

"Look at this, Mikey," Elizabeth said as she took money out the wallet and showed him how it reappeared. Maybe Mikey would be able to figure out what was going on.

Mikey was stunned by what he just witnessed.

"Did you just take money out of that wallet, close it, and then more money appeared?" Mikey asked.

"Cool, huh? We haven't decided if it's magic, or just a really useful trick," Elizabeth said. "I think it's magic. Susie thinks it's a trick. Tess?"

"Undecided," Tess said truthfully. "Though if it helps us get Amelia back, I don't really care either way."

"Hey, boy!" Susie bent down and greeted Didus, whose eyes were shining. Didus greeted Tess next. When he went to rub against Elizabeth's leg, she ran across the room.

"Don't worry, Elizabeth, he's friendly!" Susie said.

"Yeah, well, he can be friendly from across the room," Elizabeth said, then waved at the dog.

Didus lifted a paw up, as if waving back, but made no move to approach Elizabeth.

"What happened?" Elizabeth asked Mikey. "Where did you go?"

"I followed Didus into the hills, and we came to this water well," Mikey said. "It's weird, I swear I've been to that area before, but I never saw that well. All made of stone, you know. Anyway, he dropped the green stone into the well. That was it."

"Doesn't sound very magical to me," Susie said.

"It actually does sound kind of magical to me," Elizabeth said. "A well, like in a fairytale."

Susie rolled her eyes.

"Do you girls feel any different?" Mikey asked. He looked from one to the next, just as Didus had.

All three girls touched their amulets.

"Mine might be warm," Tess said, after a minute. "But I can't tell if it's warmer than normal."

"I really feel like playing volleyball," Susie said.

"Well, nothing strange about that!" Elizabeth said. "I don't think I feel anything."

A sense of embarrassment hung in the air.

"I kind of expected to feel something, like some kind

of special power," Elizabeth said. "I guess I believed your mom's note."

"Yeah," Tess said. "I wasn't sure either way."

"Well, I'm glad. I don't think I could take it if magic was real," Susie said. She sat on the floor and pet Didus.

"How do you explain the wallet, though? And the veil?" Elizabeth asked.

"Just tricks," Susie said and shrugged. "Very useful ones."

"Well, there might be more useful things in here," Elizabeth said. The box she had taken out just contained seeds, so she replaced it on the shelf. She looked through the cabinet and took out another glass ball, smaller than the one she had in her bag.

Tess took a long, purple candle out of the cabinet. She turned it over in her hands. It seemed like a normal candle. She opened the map of the world she had taken out of the cabinet, and started talking to it.

"Amelia," Tess said. "Where is Amelia?"

"Are you talking to the map?" Mikey asked, and clapped his sister on the shoulder.

"Mikey, if you're not going to help..." Tess said and playfully fake-punched him.

"I'll get out of the way and go make dinner," Mikey said. "Bye-bye, map!" He waved to the map. Tess stuck her tongue out at him.

"He's making dinner?" Elizabeth said, once he was gone. "I bet Mr. Darcy never made dinner."

"Stop comparing Mikey to your Jane Austen boyfriends!" Tess said.

"I'm just saying," Elizabeth said. "Actually, I don't normally like guys our age. They're boring. But Mikey's something special."

Susie paced the room, stomping and muttering to herself. "So my mom is just deluded. There is no magic. It's all just a bunch of tricks."

"Verdant," Elizabeth said to the ball. Nothing happened.

"Amelia Hilton," Tess said to the map. Then she held her necklace, and said her nickname for Amelia.

"Water."

The map changed immediately.

A small island close to the eight main islands in Hawaii glowed.

"Oh my gosh! Is that where Amelia is?" Tess said.

Elizabeth looked over at the map.

"The globe showed Amelia was on that little island, too," Elizabeth said and drummed her fingers on the carpet.

"Maggie Hilton," Elizabeth said, saying Amelia's mom's name to the map. A bigger island glowed.

"Oahu." Tess read the island's label. "Honolulu! That's where they flew to. Maybe Ms. Lang and Ms. Hilton are still there."

"I have an idea," Elizabeth said. "A way we can test the map."

"Mikey John Gilead," Elizabeth said to the map. Hawaii stopped glowing, and a glow appeared around the San Francisco Bay Area, California.

"I think it works," Elizabeth said. "Mikey is here, after all."

Susie looked at the map, then at the wallet and stack of money by Tess.

"It's all so weird. I feel like I'm going crazy," Susie said. "And I'm totally worried about my mom. Why hasn't she texted again? I need to play some V-ball. Otherwise I'll explode! And there is a practice today."

"Go," Elizabeth said and looked at her watch. "Makes sense to me. Go burn your energy, girl!"

Tess nodded.

"Good idea, Air," Tess said, using Susie's Element name. "Better than pacing."

Didus barked as if in goodbye as Susie flew out of the office to go change.

"I'll go home and pack," Tess said. "Do you think our parents know that Susie's mom and Amelia's mom are missing now?"

"No, I don't think so," Elizabeth said. "I called mine earlier. I said we're staying at Amelia's house again. I told them everything was fine, except we haven't found Amelia yet."

"I hate lying, but I think you're right," Tess said. "My parents would make us come home if they knew more people have gone missing. And they definitely wouldn't let me and Mikey go to Hawaii."

"Guess we'll miss school on Monday," Elizabeth said.

"Yeah, but it will be worth it when we get Amelia back," Tess said.

"I can't believe Amelia's missing the math battle today. She worked so hard," Elizabeth said.

Elizabeth rooted around the cabinet some more. Tess turned the purple candle over in her hands.

"Here, take this," Elizabeth said and handed her a key. "Maybe it opens another cabinet or safe in here." She took out a small, golden key, and looked around the room but didn't see anywhere it might fit.

"Well, we have the wallet, so we have money," Tess said. "And we have the map, so we know where we're going. I think we're doing OK."

"Nice to hear you being confident, Tess," Elizabeth said. "Normally you, um…how can I put it?"

"Flicker?" Tess asked.

"Yes, exactly!" Elizabeth turned and smiled at her. Then her face fell, and she pointed at the candle.

The candle was lit.

"No magic, huh?" Elizabeth said.

"Could be a trick candle," Tess said and blew it out.

Elizabeth found a few more candles in the desk drawer.

She gave them to Tess.

"What am I supposed to do with these?" Tess asked, studying them.

"I don't know. Try saying 'flicker' again," Elizabeth suggested.

"Flicker," Tess said. Three of the four candles lit. Tess nearly dropped them.

"Awesome, Tess, you have fire power!" Elizabeth said. "Finally, something cool happens outside my books."

Elizabeth hugged Tess and gave her a huge grin.

"You try it," Tess said and took the Fire amulet from her neck. She exchanged it with Elizabeth's Earth amulet, and put Elizabeth's necklace on.

A sickly feeling stole through her. She shivered.

"I feel sick," Elizabeth said. "I don't like this amulet."

"I feel sick, too," Tess said. "Nauseous."

"Nauseated," Elizabeth said, holding her stomach. "Let's exchange back."

Tess felt better as soon as she took Elizabeth's necklace off and exchanged it for her own amulet. She patted her Fire necklace when it hung from her own neck once again.

"Well, I guess no one else can use my Fire amulet," Tess said. She wondered if she was the only one who had a magic amulet?

She felt the weight of responsibility sitting heavy on her shoulders.

Would she know what to do with it?

Chapter Fifteen

Amelia half slid, half rolled down the wet, muddy hill. She tried to keep her left side away from the ground. Akoni might be in her left pocket, so she didn't want him to get smashed.

Once she rolled onto flat ground, she pulled herself up. Her ankles were so stiff, but at least she could walk slowly. She made her way through a tangle of lush leaves toward the sound of the roaring ocean.

The wind felt hurricane-force. Her hair blew out of its ponytail and whipped her in the face.

When she emerged onto sand, her eyes took in the huge waves of the ocean in front of her. Though they looked dangerous, Amelia felt some comfort being near the water.

It was her element, after all. She held her pendant and it soothed her.

She shielded her eyes from the wind and sand blowing around. Through her fingers, she could see the beach. It was beautiful, shaped like a perfect crescent moon. Enormous shells lay on the sand. In better weather, Amelia would love to study the shells and walk on the sand for hours. She wondered if this was the beach her dad had mentioned back in the cave.

A chill stole up her spine when she saw the shape of what looked to be a Tyrannosaurus Rex silhouetted at the end of the beach. The illusion of the perfect beach was destroyed by the frightening rock formation.

The beach was under attack by the weather. All the crazy wind blew sand into Amelia's eyes. Rain pelted her face. The waves were way too fierce and choppy to swim in, so escape by water looked impossible.

Amelia moved from the beach into a grove of coconut palms, looking for shelter from the wind and rain.

The wind died down as soon as she was among the trees. She found palm leaves all over the ground, and dragged some of them over by one of the trees. She managed to lean a few in tepee style around the tree, and used her shoelaces to tie them together. Now she had a makeshift tent.

It was surprisingly calm under the palm leaves. A little rain dribbled in, but it didn't bother Amelia too much. She let her ears relax after the sound of the relentless wind. It was much quieter in here, and the rain pattering was peaceful.

She recited the primes to 1,061. Still not calm by then, she kept going until she reached 1,601.

As she rotated her ankles and massaged life into her feet, she focused on her situation, using her logical mind. It made her feel calmer to think through things.

She doubted her dad would find her in this weather. He had looked weak and tired when she saw him at the mouth of the cave. She didn't think he would come after her. Then again, she didn't know the extent of his magic. Maybe he could magic himself to her, or vice-a-versa.

She could hide, and once the weather was better, explore the island and try to find a way off. Her dad and Akoni must have a boat, or a plane, or something.

"Akoni!" Amelia shouted out loud. She had forgotten about him.

Amelia put her hand in her left pocket and removed the smooth, warm, curled-up thing in there. When she brought it out, she saw it was a lizard.

"Well, you're not a newt," she said.

It had dark brown eyes like Akoni's. She peered at it closely. The lizard had the same tattoo as Akoni's around its front, right foot.

"Oh, Akoni," Amelia said. "I'm so sorry."

The lizard bowed its head and licked her palm with a red, forked tongue. She thought it looked sad. It curled up on her palm, and trembled. She stroked its back, and wondered if it might be hungry. She gave it a leaf from nearby, but it curled deeper into itself and ignored the leaf.

"What do we do?" Amelia said and sighed.

She sat there as the rain came down. Amelia's stomach gurgled and moaned. There was nothing to eat, except for the coconuts. She eyed one that was sitting not far away.

She could probably figure out how to break it open, once the rain calmed down. But she felt too tired to try now.

Amelia heard a low growl in the distance. She shivered and curled under the palm leaves, just like the lizard was curled up in her hand. She didn't know what wild creatures lived here. Hopefully the T-Rex she saw was really just her imagination and not a rock monster.

She thought back to the strange things that happened in the cave.

Who was singing along with her?

Akoni had called it an ocean goddess. Her dad said the Dark kept her trapped.

The voice had asked her to say its name. Maybe Akoni knew it. She looked at the lizard, but its eyes were shut. He seemed to be sleeping.

Her logical mind started to drift, and a kind of panic set in. She was just a little girl with a lizard for a friend.

Cold, wet, and hungry.

She had no food, no money, and the wind and rain beat down. And an evil sorcerer was after her, who also happened to be her dad.

She lay down on the ground and stroked the lizard's back more for her comfort than anything. At least she wasn't completely alone.

Chapter Sixteen

Tess, Susie and Elizabeth sat in a row on the plane to Hawaii. It was late, the middle of the night in California. Tess was asleep in the aisle seat. She was dreaming.

The dream wasn't underwater like her other mermaid dreams. In this one, she was on land, in front of a turbulent ocean with great green-gray waves, and swaying palms in a fierce wind.

There was a mermaid resting on the beach, staying out of the strong waves. She held a palm frond above her head. The mermaid had blond hair like Amelia, but Tess couldn't see her face. Tess worried for her, alone in the awful wind and rain.

Tess woke up to a bump. The seatbelt sign was on - there must be turbulence. So maybe that's where the dream came from. But Tess couldn't help feeling the dream was real—that somewhere there was a storm and Amelia was caught in it.

She checked the flight display on the little screen in front of her. They were halfway to Honolulu.

Elizabeth read *Sense and Sensibility* in the seat next to her, and Susie had the window. Stars were visible outside the little airplane window, shining in the deep night sky.

Susie had been strangely quiet since she came back from volleyball practice. She even drank a cup of coffee at the airport before they boarded. And she never drank coffee, usually preferring smoothies or vitamin water. Of course she looked like her mom at that point, since she was wearing the veil. It was uncanny to see what looked like Susie's mom bounce up and down in the airline seat and inhale two chocolate bars. Tess guessed the veil didn't actually change Susie's personality. Except for drinking that cup of coffee.

Tess smiled to herself. She was happy, now that they were all on the red-eye flight, and one step closer to finding Amelia.

Mikey had a seat at the back of the plane. He always preferred the back seat, ever since they were little. Tess caught a rare look of pure delight on her brother's face when she passed him on the way to the bathroom, just before takeoff. He was watching some kids play video games and poking each other. Tess suspected he sat there to spy on other passengers.

A distant bark sounded—either for real, or in her mind, Tess wasn't sure. She was worried about poor Didus, who had refused to leave them. He used every means possible of informing them he was coming along, from climbing into their suitcases as they packed, to curling up in Susie's lap in the taxi and snapping his jaws at anyone who tried to extract him.

In the end, they had to bring Didus. They also had to pay extra money for his travel crate, and for his place in the hold. All of it was paid for with the very useful wallet of replenishing money.

Tess hoped he was OK. It couldn't be fun traveling in the hold, but the airport personnel said he was too big to go under the seat in front.

Since Elizabeth was reading and Susie was quietly staring out the window, Tess decided to read more of Amelia's diary.

Elizabeth had nicknamed it the Chronicle of Math Battles, when Tess told her it was a logbook of math. She thumbed to the beginning of February. Maybe there would be something in it closer to the time Amelia disappeared.

Tess felt a deep pain in her heart as she pictured the poor mermaid from her dream in that awful storm, with only a palm leaf to protect her. Tears stung her eyes as she hoped Amelia was better off than the mermaid, somewhere safe.

As she flipped through February, she scanned the pages for anything that did not involve math. Her stomach fluttered uncomfortably when she realized there might be something in the diary to explain why Amelia had been avoiding her before she disappeared. Maybe Amelia was angry at her.

Tess shook her head to clear it. She had to focus on

getting Amelia back, no matter if Amelia was angry or not. Tess could deal with that later.

The important thing was finding Amelia. And they had an advantage now—magic.

After Tess lit those candles by saying 'flicker', she hadn't lit anything else on fire. She didn't feel particularly powerful, but lighting a candle without a match was pretty cool in itself.

In addition to the veil they had the wallet, purple candle, map, and key from Susie's mom's office—five magic items. That had to be an advantage. That had to be enough to get Amelia back.

Tess opened the diary, and her heart lifted at Amelia's careful, curly script. She missed her friend so much her stomach felt like an empty pit.

Amelia did have the water necklace, Tess considered hopefully. She wore it all the time. Maybe she would have some water magic to help her.

Tess sighed and began to read. Ten minutes into the diary, her face flushed with heat. She felt a wave of anger pass through her. What she read explained something - explained a lot.

Chapter Seventeen

When Amelia woke up, it was quiet except for the sound of a breeze through the palm trees. The rain had stopped. She crawled out of the palm-leaf tent.

The sky was clear enough to show some stars overhead. A half-moon was visible and shed some light. She looked around nervously for Akoni, hoping he wasn't lost...or worse.

"I hope I didn't roll on him!" she said to herself. She spied a lizard near the tent, munching on a leaf. It turned his head to see her, and Amelia swore it looked embarrassed.

"It's OK. I'm hungry too," she said. "Are you Akoni?"

The lizard nodded.

Akoni darted over to her on his little legs. He sat down in the muddy ground and dragged his tail end over it with his front legs. Amelia stared at him.

"I don't think that's what lizards do," she said to him. "Why are you doing that?"

It took her awhile to realize he was forming letters, drawing them in the dirt with his butt.

"Not safe," she read aloud. "Well, that's stating the obvious, isn't it?"

Her stomach rumbled.

"Do you know how to break open a coconut?" she asked the lizard. He looked around, and then darted over to a rocky area. Some sharp stones were sticking up. Maybe she could smash the coconut onto the rocks.

"While I'm doing that..." she said, studying the lizard. "Do you know the goddesses' name? The one in the cave, I mean."

To her delight, the lizard nodded vigorously. He began to drag himself over the mud again, forming letters. Amelia could see it was a lot of effort for him. He stopped and stretched out his back legs a few times.

Finally, the lizard held still, panting. Amelia came over to read what he wrote.

"Alanawaiwai," she said.

The lizard nodded. He limped away and sat in a leaf full of water. Amelia imagined it probably felt cool on his sore bottom.

"Thanks, Akoni. Sorry it was painful," Amelia said. "If I know her name, and end up in the cave again, maybe I can help her. Though I hope I never have to go back to that place."

Akoni gave her a long look, and then turned his gaze to the moon and stars.

Amelia took the nearest coconut and smashed it against the rock. It just bounced off the rock and rolled away, completely undamaged.

She tried a few different coconuts, and was soon sweaty and out of breath from the effort of smashing them against the sharp rocks.

After ten minutes, then twenty, then half-an-hour, she still couldn't get one to open. She had nearly given up, when a coconut finally split.

Unfortunately, the liquid all spilled from one half, but she drank the other half. It was delicious, and she swore it was better than anything she had tasted before. It was sweet and fresh, and she wanted more. She scooped out cool, tasty coconut jelly with a flat stone.

Though she could have easily eaten a few more coconuts, her thirst was, for the moment, quenched. She forgot her hunger, and looked around for Akoni. No lizards were in sight.

A few minutes later, Akoni—the human Akoni—walked out from behind the palms. He wore nothing but a skirt made of palm leaves. He looked angry.

"Akoni!" Amelia threw her arms around him, glad to see him. Then she backed off, embarrassed. He was nearly naked, after all.

"Your father! Of all the awful tricks to play…" Akoni spit a huge wad onto the ground.

"Are you all right?" Amelia asked.

"Well, I have indigestion, probably from the leaves," he said. "And my okole is sore."

Amelia guessed that okole was probably Hawaiian for butt.

"I guess if we had known the spell would wear off, you wouldn't have to write Alanawaiwai's name in the mud," Amelia said. "Sorry."

"We didn't know," Akoni said and shrugged. "Actually, I thought I'd be a liz…liz…Oh, I can't say it. But I thought that was a forever spell."

"I'm glad it wore off," Amelia said.

"Me too," Akoni said. "We can't stay here, I was trying to tell you."

"Where can we go?" Amelia asked. "Is there anywhere on the island that is safe?"

"We can go to the other side. It's better there," Akoni said. "As far from the Dark as possible."

"Can the Dark reach us here? I don't think it likes me," Amelia said and remembered how it had pushed her across the cave. "I'm glad it doesn't like me."

"It's not just the Dark. It's what the Dark calls," Akoni said. "Do you know why this island is called 'The Place Where People Do Not Go?'"

"I thought it was the weather," Amelia said.

"Partly it's the weather, the storms called by the Dark. But it's partly things like the Rock Dragon," Akoni said and nervously looked around.

"That sounds…bad," Amelia said. "It doesn't look like a T-Rex, does it?"

131

Akoni's eyes widened.

"That's exactly what it looks like," he said. "You didn't see it, did you?"

Amelia waved toward the beach and said, "Last night, I thought I saw it on the beach."

"It likes to hang out there and sink ships, if they get too close," Akoni said.

A low growl raised the hairs on the back of Amelia's neck.

Akoni stared at her, alarmed.

"Did you hear that, too?" Amelia asked.

Akoni nodded.

"If it gets bored looking for ships, we might have a big problem," he said.

"OK, let's go to the other side, then," Amelia said. Her heartbeat sped up with fear.

"I know the way," Akoni said and picked a leaf out of his teeth as they started walking. He cursed, which would seem more menacing if he wasn't wearing a skirt.

"Are you cold?" Amelia asked. "Would you like your sweatshirt back?"

"If that's OK with you, girl. It would at least make me feel like I was dressed!" Akoni said.

Amelia took the large, loose sweatshirt off and gave it to Akoni. She felt the night air chill her arms, but she wasn't cold.

He gratefully put it on.

"Ah. I feel more like me," he said. "The me without a tail. I don't have a tail, do I?" Akoni said and suddenly looked nervous.

"No." Amelia stifled a giggle. "At least, not that I can see."

As they walked along the coast, Amelia thought of something.

"So why are you human again?" she asked. "Did my dad's spell wear off?"

"Wore off," said Akoni, "or he might have passed out, or maybe fell down. Maybe too weak, or too sick."

"What do you mean?" Amelia asked.

"Well, according to my grandmother Tutu, when a sorcerer is really sick, their spells stop working," Akoni explained. He moved a big plant out of Amelia's way as they walked inland.

"My dad? Sick?" Amelia said nervously. Maybe he needed help.

"He's a bad man," Akoni reminded her. "He trapped you in that cave. He turned me into a—well, you know. He tried to make you feel a lot of pain with his spell, too. I heard him say 'Amelia dolor'. That's a pain spell."

"But…" Amelia felt conflicted.

A roar shook the trees and the ground, followed by a high screech that caused Amelia's teeth to clench together. She nearly lost her footing.

"The Rock Dragon! Something has rattled it," Akoni said. "Let's get to the other side of the island. And fast."

He grabbed her hand and ran through the lush vegetation. Amelia hurried to keep his pace, picking up her feet and trying not to trip. Her heart pounded harder every time the Rock Dragon roared.

She didn't know what to do if her dad was sick. She could go back and try to find him. But what if he was strong enough to trap her in the cave again?

She thought Akoni was right. Her dad was a bad man. And he had a temper.

If he had changed Akoni to a lizard, it probably wasn't a temporary spell. He probably meant it forever.

So her dad might be in trouble. He could have fallen, or fainted.

Amelia felt sad. She felt sorry for him, and hoped he was OK. And she desperately wanted to try to free the goddess, now that she knew her name.

But what could they really do, but get away from the Rock Dragon? Or even better, get off the chilly, dark island altogether?

Chapter Eighteen

Tess was fuming mad. She had her arms crossed against her chest. Her jaw felt tight from clenching her teeth. She stared at the back of the airplane seat in front of her, as if she could burn a hole in it. Elizabeth looked over at Tess.

"What happened?" Elizabeth asked. She looked up from her book, and her brown eyes flew open in alarm.

"What do you mean?" Tess heard her own voice come out gravelly.

"Well...let's just say you are living up to your name, Fire-o," Elizabeth said.

Susie looked over at them.

"Wow! Seriously, you're all red!" Susie said. "Your face matches your hair."

"Um, Susie, you're not exactly looking normal yourself, mom-hair," Elizabeth said and elbowed her.

"Well, it's just—I can't believe what I found in here. I can't believe...my brother!" Tess' voice came out much louder than she intended, and several people turned to look at her.

"What do you mean? Why is Mikey in there?" Susie asked.

"Uh-oh." Elizabeth's eyes were big with worry. "I think I know what this is about."

"You know?" Tess asked.

"I bumped into Amelia just…just after," Elizabeth said, with a calming hand on Tess' arm. "She was worried about what you would think, and if you would be mad at her. So I promised not to tell you."

"Why would I be mad at Amelia?" Tess said, her face hot. "It was Mikey who was totally out of line, and broke all the rules!"

"What?" Susie looked from Tess to Elizabeth. "Will someone tell me what's going on?"

The food cart came at that moment. Susie ordered an orange juice and a cheese sandwich. Elizabeth ordered an orange juice and a chocolate muffin.

When the flight attendant asked what Tess wanted, she spat, "Nothing!" The airline attendant jumped back.

"Um, my friend will have something with no caffeine," Elizabeth said and ordered for Tess. "Do you have chamomile tea?"

When the cart moved on, Tess leaned over to Elizabeth and Susie, who shrank back.

"My brother gave Amelia the Valentine," Tess said. "The one that made her so upset. That's why Amelia wouldn't come to my house."

"Mikey?" Susie screwed up her mouth. "Eew. But he's old."

"A junior!" Tess nodded fervently. "In high school! We're not even in high school yet."

"Maybe he really loves her," Elizabeth said. "Maybe they'll get married one day. Tess, Amelia could be your sister, really your sister."

Tess crossed her arms and shook her head.

"No wonder Amelia was upset," Tess said. "She definitely doesn't like Mikey that way. Not anyone. She's not really into guys, not like you, Elizabeth."

Elizabeth shrugged.

"Hey, I'm into fictional guys, not real ones," Elizabeth said. "Amelia and Mikey get along. That's all I'll say." Elizabeth took a big bite of the chocolate muffin, and offered Tess a piece. "I don't normally share muffins, but it might make you feel better."

"What does her diary say?" Susie said. "Come on, you got to read it. What did Amelia say? Does she like him back?"

Tess glared at her, then lifted the book to read the entry aloud.

"Mikey gave me a Valentine. I felt sick. Hope Tess is not mad at me. Can't deal. Am going to recite primes to calm down," Tess said.

"Does it sound like she likes him back to you?" Tess' voice raised again.

"OK, OK," Susie said. "I was just asking."

Elizabeth pushed the chamomile tea toward Tess.

"Maybe you should drink this," she said.

"Sorry, it's just—it's just been so much," Tess said, "with Amelia being all weird at the park last Sunday, then going missing…"

Elizabeth offered her shoulder, and Tess rested her head on her friend.

She stared ahead as bright sunshine streamed through the windows. The plane was getting noisy with voices of excitement as they approached Hawaii.

She finally picked up her tea. It was cold. She was about to drink it that way, though she hated cold tea.

"Heat up," she said quietly, with the cup held close to her mouth. She was rewarded with a hot cup of tea that steamed in her hands.

Even though everything was all topsy-turvy, and Mikey was being gross and everything…at least she could make a cold cup of tea warm again.

That wouldn't be enough to save Amelia, but it made Tess feel better all the same.

Chapter Nineteen

Amelia and Akoni ran for what felt like hours. Before dawn, they finally reached the beach on the other side of the island. The rock dragon's cries had continued through the whole night, and they could still hear it even from this new beach.

The monster's screeching was an awful sound, which sent chills up Amelia's spine.

The wind was calmer on this beach. A slight drizzle of rain fell, and lots of clouds blocked out the stars. It seemed warmer, though. Amelia was so hot and sticky from all the running, it was hard to tell. She collapsed on the sand, breathing hard.

"Good running, girl!" Akoni high-fived her. "We made it."

Amelia nodded, still trying to catch her breath. Akoni sat on the sand next to her and looked at the waves rolling in the dark ocean. Whitecaps showed in the dawn light.

"The waves are still high on this side. But the farther from the Dark we are, the better the weather," Akoni said. "The wind isn't very strong here."

He massaged his bare feet. "Man! My feet are still cramped from all that running around, when I was a...Oh,

I can't even say it," he said. "You promised not to tell my girlfriend Malie, right?"

"That you were a lizard?" Amelia said. "It's nothing to be embarrassed about. But, yes, I promised you eight times already that I wouldn't tell her."

"Good. Just the tail alone would freak her out," Akoni said and shivered.

"Don't worry, I won't tell her. Are you warm enough in that?" Amelia asked. She examined his palm leaf skirt and sweatshirt.

Now that they had stopped, and the rain was getting them wet, Amelia cooled down fast. Her arms broke out into goose bumps.

"I'm fine. But you're cold," Akoni said, noticing the goose bumps on her arms. He gave her back his sweatshirt.

She put it on, enjoying the warmth.

"Tell me about my dad," Amelia asked, lifting her face to the drizzle. She was thirsty, but the rain was too fine and misty to drink.

"How did you meet him?" Amelia asked.

"I knew your dad's assistant, Zoro, though I don't think that was his real name. He used to come into the shop where I worked," Akoni said and dug his toe into the sand.

"We got to talking last year, when Zoro was sick. He said he had a great job that paid well," Akoni said. "I heard the 'paid well' part and agreed to meet your dad."

"Oh. That sounds normal enough," Amelia said. "But did you know he was a…you know, a sorcerer? I mean, did you know about magic?"

"Oh sure, I knew about magic, living here in Hawaii," Akoni said. "But I didn't know there were magic men walking around here. I thought that magic belonged only to the spirits and gods."

Akoni looked out over the water. Dawn was breaking, and pink and orange highlights lit the sky. The rain stopped.

"Hungry?" Akoni asked. "I can catch some crabs here. It's shallow and I know where they hang out."

Amelia nodded. She was as hungry as a rock dragon.

"You build a fire," Akoni said, then headed off into the water.

Amelia had never built a fire in her life. She searched for sticks, twigs, and palm leaves along the ground. She wanted to know more about her dad, and more about what Akoni thought about magic. But food definitely took priority.

Amelia piled the damp sticks and leaves up on the sand, hoping they would dry quickly. She sat gazing out at the ocean. Akoni was a black silhouette against an orange-pink sky, knee-deep in the water. She wondered if he had a boat. If so, maybe they could get off this island soon.

This beach had much calmer waves, though in the distance they looked quite big. Once the shallow part ended, there was probably a sand bank where the waves broke.

141

Amelia wished for nothing more than a nice, cool glass of water—or better yet, coconut water. While she waited for Akoni, she twisted a palm leaf in her hands.

Amelia did a double-take when she looked down at the leaf. It had only been damp before, but now it was dripping wet.

She was so thirsty that she licked the leaves. Had she created the water just by thinking about it?

Just to try it, she cupped her hands and thought about water. Soon she had enough for a satisfying gulp collected in her hands. She refilled her cupped hands a few times just by thinking about water.

She remembered feeling like water in the cave. She had really stopped feeling like Amelia, and started feeling so...fluid.

A nervous feeling twisted in her stomach. Could magic really have passed on to her from her father?

Her dad was a bad man. Did magic make him bad? Or was it the Dark that made him bad?

It seemed so innocent, just using magic to get a drink of water. She would give some to Akoni, too. Or would he be afraid of her?

Or should he be afraid of her, she wondered, and shivered.

Chapter Twenty

Tess, Susie, Elizabeth and Mikey left the plane in various moods, once they landed in Honolulu. Susie whipped off the veil as soon as they stepped into the arrivals hall, and told Elizabeth to bury it deep in her backpack and never mention it. Once she looked like herself again, she pulled her gray-free black hair into a ponytail and walked with a bounce in her step.

Tess, on the other hand, was not in a good mood. She was fuming, and Mikey was confused as to why Tess was so mad at him. But Tess didn't want to talk about it just then.

They decided to pick up Didus and find some food before they began the search. They hadn't brought much luggage, as they weren't sure how much traveling they would be doing. Each had a carry-on backpack, and that was it.

Susie ran to Didus as soon as she saw him sitting near a collection point. She gave him a hug and he licked her face. Some nice airline attendant had put a bowl of water by him. His friendly eyes looked from one human friend to the next.

Most of the group greeted him by petting him—except for Elizabeth, who just waved. Didus barked at her as if to say 'hello'.

Mikey attached the leash onto Didus' new collar, and they walked out of the airport. The air outside was warm and humid. Tess breathed in deep and smiled. The fresh air smelled like flowers and sea salt.

"Ouch!" Tess said. She slapped a mosquito on her arm.

"Good thing they like you," Elizabeth said. "They'll stay away from the rest of us."

Tess had to laugh. Mosquitoes always chose her to bite.

Susie's phone beeped. She pulled it out of her pocket.

"It's from my mom!" Susie said, excited.

They gathered around to read the text, but Tess kept her distance from Mikey. She was too annoyed with him to stand close.

I am stuck somewhere but OK. I'm in and out of sleep. I will find a way out of this soon. Love you all.

Susie tried to text her mom back, but teared up, staring at her phone.

"What is it?" Elizabeth asked, putting a comforting arm around her friend.

"My text is undelivered," Susie said, her voice shaking. She sat on the curb.

"I'm sure your mom will be OK," Elizabeth said, sitting next to her.

Tess agreed. "In her text, she sounds strong," she said, trying to comfort her friend.

"She says she's stuck somewhere, in and out of sleep. That doesn't sound too good," Susie said and put her head in her hands.

"It's your mom," Tess said. "She can do anything. And she says she'll find a way out soon."

"Tess is right," Elizabeth said. "Your mom is so smart. If she said she'll find a way out, she will. She has magic, after all."

Susie nodded, sniffling.

"We can deal with all this better on full stomachs," Mikey said. "Then we'll find Susie's mom. And Amelia's mom. And Amelia."

Tess was feeling light-headed. The thought of food was a very good idea, though she wasn't going to tell Mikey that she agreed with him.

Susie brightened at the mention of food. She hopped up to her feet and wiped the tears from her face.

"Yeah, OK," Susie said. "Let's eat something."

They weren't sure what sort of restaurants might be nearby. They were about to ask a taxi driver when Didus barked. He wouldn't stop barking until Mikey let him pull him along down the road. After a few yards, the Collie stopped, and held a paw up, staring at something.

"Is he pointing to that hotel?" Tess asked.

"Dogs don't point," Elizabeth said.

"Well, he's a magic dog," Tess said.

"I think he is pointing to the hotel," Mikey said excitedly. "Maybe Susie's mom and Amelia's mom are there!"

Didus was still staring at the hotel.

"It's worth checking it out," Mikey said.

Tess stood with her arms crossed, and refused to meet Mikey's eye. But at this statement, she reached into her bag and took the map out. She sat on the ground between Elizabeth and Susie, and said 'Maggie Hilton'.

Honolulu glowed.

"It's not showing us the hotel, though. It's the whole city. Zoom in," Tess said. Nothing zoomed, the map stayed the same.

"It's not Google maps," Elizabeth said.

"How about we just ask at the reception desk?" Mikey said.

Tess didn't want to admit it, but that did seem the easiest way to find out if the two missing moms were at the hotel.

"Oh, yeah. Good idea," Elizabeth said.

Susie agreed. Tess didn't say anything, she only glared at her brother.

"Um, Tess?" Mikey asked. "What's wrong?"

"I know!" Tess said and the words came out angrily. "I know about the Valentine!" She glared some more.

"Oh." Mikey turned as red as Tess, but not from anger.

"Hey, Tess?" Elizabeth said. The map in Tess' hands was starting to smoke at the edges.

Tess dropped it.

"Sorry," Tess mumbled.

Susie stared at the smoking map on the ground, and blinked at it a few times.

"Tess, you just lit that on fire with your anger," Susie said.

Elizabeth nodded.

"She's got fire magic!" Elizabeth said. "She lit the candle back in your mom's study. And now the map."

"I warmed up a cup of tea, too," Tess said.

Elizabeth and Susie stared at her.

"Well, that's...handy," Elizabeth said.

"And kind of lame," Susie said.

The three girls laughed. There was so much tension in the air, Tess felt relief when she laughed. She felt a little giddy.

But then she looked at Mikey, and felt her face grow hot with anger again.

"I just can't believe you did what you did," Tess said to Mikey.

"This isn't the time to discuss the Valentine," Elizabeth said. "We have a friend to find. And two very cool moms."

Tess still fumed.

"Sorry." Tess's arms were crossed hard against her chest. "I'm just so mad." A mosquito bit the back of her elbow.

"Another mosquito!" Tess said. "Now I am even madder."

"How about this…" Elizabeth said. "Mikey, you take Didus to the hotel and find out if either Ms. Lang or Ms. Hilton is registered there. We'll go look for a restaurant. And mosquito repellent."

"It would be good to split up," Tess said. "I can't think with my brother here."

"Why? What was so wrong about giving Amelia a Valentine?" Mikey said. "She's so cool."

Tess felt heat rush through her again, and Elizabeth put a hand on her arm to calm her. A stick near them burst into flames. Susie stamped it out quickly.

"Because she's one of my best friends!" Tess said loudly. "And besides, we're a lot younger than you. And because…because…"

Mikey stared at the ground, embarrassed.

"Oh, never mind," Tess said, feeling guilty for yelling. "Look, we'll explain it later. Let's just find everyone, OK?"

Didus strained toward the hotel. Mikey agreed with Elizabeth's plan, and with a sheepish look at Elizabeth and Tess, followed Didus in the direction of the hotel.

"I can't believe he actually asked why it was wrong," Tess said, still mad.

Elizabeth pinched her. "He's gone now. Let's focus on Amelia," she said. "Also, you need to calm down. Who knows what else you'll light on fire."

"I need food," Susie said. "Or I won't be able to go on."

"Food first," Elizabeth agreed.

Tess, Susie and Elizabeth walked along the road, figuring a McDonald's or something would pop up.

"Wow, it's hot!" Susie said and stripped her sweatshirt off to reveal a pink tank top. Tess was glad she was wearing her shorts. The heat baked every inch of her.

"I'm actually OK," Elizabeth said, gazing at the sky in her sunglasses. "This dress is nice and cool, perfect for this weather."

"So, Tess, that fire power is getting stronger for you, is it?" Elizabeth said and waved the singed map.

"I guess," Tess said.

"I'm not sure why our amulets didn't work," Elizabeth said.

"Mine works," Susie said.

"What?" Elizabeth and Tess said.

"What happened?" Tess asked.

"Well, I sort of jumped up for a spike," Susie explained, "and I might have jumped a little higher than expected."

"How high?" Elizabeth asked her.

"Um, the ceiling?" Susie said.

Tess and Elizabeth were stunned. The ceiling in the gym was high, stories high.

"Half the team went crazy excited," Susie told them. "But the other half looked at me funny. And one of the girls called me a witch."

"Oh no," Elizabeth said.

"I played it off, telling them that it only looked like I touched the ceiling," Susie went on, "but that I really didn't jump that high. I told them it was one of those optical illusion things."

"And they believed that?" Elizabeth asked.

"Yeah, I think so," Susie said with a shrug. "I took the necklace off, and it didn't happen again."

"But you did touch the ceiling?" Elizabeth asked. "You're sure?"

"Scraped it," Susie said and showed them her raw knuckles.

"That is so cool," Elizabeth said. "Now you can jump all the way to the moon, knowing you. Isn't that great?"

"Well, I'm a little freaked. You know, at magic being real," Susie said and scuffed her shoe on the sidewalk. "Though since it's real, maybe my mom will really be OK. You know, if she's a sorceress."

"I bet your mom is really powerful," Elizabeth said, sounding excited. "And it's so cool you have air power. Jumping high suits you, Air-o."

Tess laughed.

"Feeling better, Tess?" Elizabeth said.

"Yeah," Tess admitted. "I'm enjoying picturing Susie jumping so high she touched the ceiling!"

"You're right. It's totally cool," Susie said. "I don't know why it bummed me out like that."

Susie was taking two steps and leaping, two steps and leaping. Her leaps were getting higher and higher.

"Careful, Susie," Elizabeth warned. "We don't want to draw too much attention to ourselves."

"It is awesome, though," Susie said. "Now that I think about it, it's so cool to have jumping power. I wonder if I can fly?"

"Well, be careful when you try that one!" Elizabeth said.

"I wonder what your power is, Elizabeth," Tess said.

"With this Earth amulet?" Elizabeth said. "It's probably making dirt. Or mud pies."

All three girls laughed.

Their spirits lightened even more when they spied a cluster of buildings down the road.

"Pizza!" Tess read one of the signs.

"Perfect," Elizabeth said.

As they walked, Elizabeth's phone rang. During the call, she said "oh" a bunch of times, but not much else.

Susie had gone off ahead, racing toward the buildings, racing toward pizza.

"It was Mikey," Elizabeth said, not looking too happy after she hung up. "Amelia's mom is at the hotel."

"That's great!" Tess said. "Isn't it?" She studied Elizabeth's dark expression.

"She doesn't remember anything. And she doesn't know where Susie's mom is," Elizabeth said.

A silence fell on the girls.

"I wonder how powerful Amelia's dad is?" Tess said. She gave voice to the fear that Amelia's dad had kidnapped Susie's mom, too.

She watched Susie way up ahead. She was jumping up and turning in the air, landing like an ice skater. Cars were slowing down to watch.

"Should we tell Susie?" Tess asked.

"I think we better," Elizabeth said. "But maybe after we get some pizza. Hey, Susie!" She waved at her friend to come back, and Susie took long, super-human leaps back to them.

Elizabeth took one of Susie's arms, and Tess took the other. Now all three of them were linked.

"Let's ground you," Elizabeth said. "That will be my Earth power."

"Elizabeth, I hope we find your real power soon," Tess said. "We may need it."

Chapter Twenty-one

Amelia and Akoni rested on the sandy beach. Akoni made a breakfast of crabs, cooking them over a warm fire. Amelia had been ready to learn how to start a fire with sticks or rocks, and had laughed when he pulled out his lighter.

Amelia was soon pleasantly full of baked crab, and a little sleepy from all the food and the warmth of the fire. The fire also seemed to keep away the mosquitoes. Amelia had been bitten numerous times during the night, making her itch all over.

Across the water, she could see a big island. She watched a plane fly close to the island, though the plane was tiny from where they were.

"Does that island have an airport?" Amelia asked.

"Honolulu Airport," Akoni said.

"We're that close to Honolulu?" Amelia asked. "I thought we were in the middle of nowhere."

"Yeah, it's basically nowhere. No one comes here because of the rock dragon, for one thing. The Dark, for another. And the waves," Akoni said and indicated the choppy ocean. "This is pretty calm for this island. I have a boat here, but your dad has to use magic to calm the waves for me to use it. I need him to come and go."

"So there's no way off this island unless my dad helps us out?" Amelia asked. "There must be something, another way."

"There is one way," Akoni said. "But we would need to go back to your dad's house to use it. And I'm not getting anywhere near your dad."

"Is it a magic way?" Amelia said and watched him closely. She hadn't revealed her water power to him, in case it freaked him out.

"A little bit magic, yeah," Akoni said. "Normally I don't deal with magic. Not my thing. But this is pretty harmless."

Amelia thought maybe that meant her magic ability was harmless too. She didn't want Akoni to think she was anything like her dad, so decided not to reveal her water power to him.

She stood up and dusted sand off her jeans.

"OK, let's go back to my dad's and get off the island," she said.

"No way, girl!" Akoni stared at her in shock.

"Look, he might be sick. If he is, we can help him," Amelia said. "In return, he can help us get off this island."

"He turned me into a lizard!" Akoni said.

"I can't just sit here until...forever. That's boring and just...stupid!" Amelia said, words failing her.

"You think I like sitting here doing nothing?" Akoni said angrily. "I'm bored too! I am still hungry. And thirsty."

Amelia looked at her hands. She could take the risk and reveal her water-making ability to Akoni. At least he wouldn't be thirsty anymore.

Before she could say anything, a screech set Amelia's teeth on end.

"Oh, ka!" Akoni said loudly. "It's the rock dragon."

"The rock dragon? I thought he was asleep!" Amelia said.

"Why did you think that?" Akoni said, puzzled. "It doesn't sleep."

Tremors shook the ground. Palm trees swayed violently in the distance.

"Oh, no. I think it's coming," Akoni said.

"I must have been too loud," Amelia said. "I'm sorry for shouting like that, and arguing."

"It's the Dark. It affects people like that," Akoni said. "They argue, get mad."

A great roar shattered the air. It sounded like a lion's roar, only much worse. Amelia put her fingers in her ears to block the awful sound.

"The rock dragon likes anger," Akoni said. "Probably it came to sniff it out."

Amelia couldn't answer Akoni. She just couldn't speak anymore. She could only stare at the giant monster made of rock that was moving toward them.

It was almost as tall as a palm tree!

The rock creature was shaped like a T-Rex, only made entirely of jagged rocks, all stacked together. Its eyes burned with fire. Through the cracks in its body, it glowed orange.

Akoni grabbed Amelia's hand and ran down the beach.

The rock dragon spotted them. It gave out a great roar, then headed straight for them. The ground shook each time it took a giant step, closing the gap quickly.

Amelia looked out at the ocean as they ran. Maybe the ocean would cool the rock dragon's fire.

"Let's go in the water," she said. "Maybe it can't follow."

"It can!" Akoni said and pulled her inland. They raced through lush, green plants.

They reached a dead end.

Amelia gasped for breath. She and Akoni stood against a rock wall, their backs pressed against it.

Her heart beat like a wild drum when the dark figure of the rock dragon burst through the lush green plants they hoped would hide them.

The rock dragon roared.

The sound was so loud, Amelia's eardrums hurt. The monster stared at them with its burning eyes. She could feel the heat coming off its body.

Akoni grabbed her hand.

"It is a good day to die," he said.

"No, it's not!" Amelia yelled as loud as she could. She

yelled, not because she was angry, but because she could find her courage that way.

Amelia squeezed Akoni's hand, her fear like a fist gripping her heart. But she knew she'd have to have courage to do what she wanted to do next.

She took a deep breath, and sang "True Colors" as loud as she could. She let go of Akoni's hand and waved her arms and hands around in swirling motions. She didn't think about how those things might seem strange. They just felt right.

She was dimly aware of Akoni staring at her with an open mouth, shocked. Her attention was on the rock dragon. Its burning eyes blinked. It looked at her, and made a high, squeaking noise.

Was it charmed by her song?

Amelia became aware of a power, a great power, coming from the ocean. She was calling it with her hands, and as she sang, she called it with her heart.

The ocean rolled up, closer and closer. Water came across the sand, through the lush green jungle, and covered her feet and ankles.

Steam raised from the rock dragon's feet, where the water touched it. But it made no move to get free of the water.

Amelia tried to tell the ocean to come, to cover them. She thought maybe if the water got up to the rock dragon's neck, it might cool the fire in its glowing body.

But the ocean wouldn't come further. It got as high as their ankles, then began to recede.

Amelia felt her strength fade. She was so thirsty, her voice cracked and her song got weaker.

The rock dragon shook its head, as if to clear it. It roared, shattering Amelia's song.

It reached an arm out and batted Akoni aside. Akoni fell into the ankle-deep water. Amelia felt heat like a dry oven cover her body as the rock dragon came closer. She screamed, and the rock dragon gave an answering scream.

The rock dragon's jaw opened wide, revealing sharp, pearl-colored teeth, and a tongue like a burning flame.

She glanced at Akoni, who was facedown in the water.

A wild thought ran through her mind.

Was it better to drown?

Or be eaten by the rock dragon?

The rock dragon roared again, and her face felt like hot sand in its breath.

Maybe it was a good day to die.

Chapter Twenty-two

Tess, Susie and Elizabeth entered the pizza place near Honolulu airport. Surfboards and fake palm trees decorated the inside of the small and cheerful restaurant. Ukulele music piped softly through the speaker system.

A friendly man in a T-shirt decorated with palm trees and a woman in a loose-fitting, flowery dress behind the bar said, "Aloha". They both asked Susie if she was a surfer.

"Volleyball," Susie told them. They grinned and gave her a thumbs-up.

The girls sat down. Susie scanned the menu and suggested "Dragon's Bane," a pizza covered in pineapple and spicy peppers. Tess and Elizabeth agreed, and they ordered two large ones.

"Surfer?" the waiter asked Susie.

"Volleyball," Susie answered. The waiter made a "shaka" or "hang loose" sign with his hand, which was a friendly greeting in the surfer community.

"Guess it's the way I'm dressed," Susie said to her friends. Her hair was pulled back in a ponytail, and her tank top revealed her muscled arms and shoulders. She looked ready for volleyball, as usual.

"They have beach volleyball here," Tess said. "I remember when a girl from school went to Hawaii.

Remember how she was talking about it?"

Susie's eyes grew big.

"Oh, yeah," she said. "Beach volleyball would be perfect just now. I'm so wound up, I just want to spike the ball and watch it smash into the sand."

Elizabeth took Susie's hand and said, "I know you're worried. But we will find your mom, and Amelia."

"Hope you're right," Susie said, though she slumped in her chair. When the pizza arrived, her back straightened with new energy.

Susie dug into a piece, cheese dripping off her hands. Tess and Elizabeth were less messy, but once they started eating, everyone had cheese and grease on their faces.

Tess exchanged looks with Elizabeth. They hadn't told Susie that Amelia's mom was at the hotel, but not her mom. They didn't want to worry her more, but she should know. And now that she was at least full of pizza, it would be a good time to tell her.

Susie wiped grease off her face as she polished off her fifth slice.

"Um, Susie," Elizabeth said. "Mikey called awhile ago. Amelia's mom is at the hotel."

"That's great!" Susie said. "But why didn't you tell me before?" She took a big sip of her Coke through a straw.

"Well, because your mom wasn't with her," Elizabeth explained. "Mikey doesn't know where your mom is. Neither does Amelia's mom. She doesn't remember anything."

Susie slowly put down her Coke.

"Are you OK?" Elizabeth asked.

"Liz, I'm worried but..." Susie pulled at her ponytail.

Elizabeth patted her hand.

"No, I'm OK," Susie said. "I bet my mom went to find Amelia," she said. "She's probably with her now, helping her escape."

"Your mom is awesome," Elizabeth said. "I'm sure she's rescuing Amelia right now. Right, Tess?"

Tess agreed. "Even without magical abilities, your mom could do anything," Tess said to Susie. "If she's really a sorceress, I'm sure she's OK."

"Yeah, I mean that's best case scenario," Elizabeth said. "Let's go with that."

"So, let's go find them," Susie said.

"OK. Where to?" Elizabeth said.

Tess pulled out the map. "Water," she said and the tiny island to the west of Oahu turned black.

"We know which island it is," Tess said. "Why don't we just ask one of the locals how to get there?"

"Susie, you ask," Elizabeth said and thrust the map into her hands. "They like you."

Susie went to ask the staff about the island. When she approached the bar, the Hawaiian man and woman greeted her with big smiles. As Susie talked, their smiles faded. Soon, the friendly staff were frowning.

When Susie came back, she looked stunned.

"They said people don't go there," Susie explained. "They got kind of mad."

The girls looked over at the bar. The people behind the bar looked back with unfriendly faces.

"Is it an off-limits island?" Tess asked. "Like for the army or something? Or privately owned?"

Susie shrugged. "I guess. They said I shouldn't even know about it. They said it shouldn't be on our map."

"What do we do?" Tess asked. "We need to get there."

The waiter came over. He had apparently been listening to their conversation. He clicked his tongue and shook his head.

"Don't go looking for that island. Don't look for things you don't understand," the waiter told them, and handed them their bill.

"Go surf, go play in the ocean," said the woman behind the bar. "Don't look for dark places. Enjoy our land and water."

"But stay on Oahu," the waiter said.

"But we think my mom is on that island," Susie said. "Our friend, too."

The waiter shook his head.

"If they are on Kahi Kanaka Mai I Hele, you cannot help them," the waiter said.

"Kahi what?" Susie said.

"Kahi Kanaka Mai I Hele. The Place Where People Do Not Go."

"That's the island's name?" Susie said. "Why?"

"I have said too much," the waiter said and walked away. The woman behind the bar looked down and busied herself straightening bottles and glasses.

Tess, Susie and Elizabeth sipped the last sips of their sodas.

"Well, I have an idea," Elizabeth said. "Let's go to the coast. Here–" She pointed to the west coast of Oahu. "That island looks like it's pretty close. Maybe we can even see it from the coast."

"If we're that close, maybe we can rent a boat, find someone to take us," Tess said, feeling hopeful.

"Let's go," Susie said.

"Yeah," Tess agreed. "Going to the west coast of this island can only get us closer to where Amelia is, right?"

"And my mom," Susie said.

They paid their silent waiter, who gave serious looks to Susie. As the girls walked to the door, they felt eyes on their back. Susie turned around and gave a tentative wave. The woman waved to Susie but didn't smile.

A shiver traveled through Tess. She was glad when they stepped out into the hot Hawaiian sun.

An island named The Place Where People Do Not Go didn't sound like a place they should be heading to. But if Amelia was there, and Susie's mom, that's exactly where they needed to go.

Chapter Twenty-three

Oven-hot heat blew through Amelia's hair as the rock dragon's jaws opened next to her face. Despite the temperature of the creature's breath, an icy fear ran through her. She threw her hands up to guard her face.

"Water," she thought, and tried to connect with the feeling of being fluid. But she could only feel heat and fear. Her knees locked. She couldn't move, couldn't run.

The rock dragon was going to eat her.

"Goodbye, Tess. Goodbye, Air and Earth," she said quietly to herself. "Goodbye, Mom. I'm sorry I wasn't strong enough to survive."

A swirl of dust stung Amelia's eyes.

The dust storm was followed by a clap of thunder, then a flash of lightning.

Someone came into view–a man, though she couldn't see him clearly. Amelia couldn't tear her eyes away from the jaws of the rock dragon.

"Ahiweliweli incantus, incantus newt," the rough voice said. Amelia recognized it as her dad's voice.

She felt relief unlocking her knees. Even though her dad might capture her again to mine the dark, at least she'd be alive.

But her dad's voice sounded weak.

And the rock dragon was certainly not a newt.

The rock dragon turned its horrible face toward her dad, with its massive jaw still open.

Amelia crept sideways along the rock wall, to get away from its heat. She moved slowly, hoping it wouldn't notice.

Maybe she could reach Akoni, and turn him around so his face wasn't planted in the water. Her heart pounded with a new fear—that he would drown.

"That should have worked. I'm too weak," her dad said. "I'll have to settle for the pain spell."

"Ahiweliweli, dolor dolor," her dad said, his voice a bit stronger.

This time, the rock dragon yelped, as if it had been poked. It hissed through sharp teeth, then looked from Amelia to her dad. Amelia hoped it wasn't picking who to eat first, but that was what it seemed to be doing. Her heart raced and she felt dizzy.

Her dad took a pebble out of the pocket of his long coat. Weirdly, her dad opened his mouth wide and roared at the dragon. Her dad's roar wasn't very loud, but the monster turned toward him at once.

The rock dragon studied her dad. It opened its huge jaws and roared so loud that all the hairs on Amelia's body stood up.

Her dad threw the pebble in its open mouth, covered his head with his arms and crouched to the ground.

A puff of smoke came out of the rock dragon's mouth. The monster shook its head and gave a loud, scratchy-sounding cry. It ran away, its tail whisking back and forth, breaking down whole palm trees.

"Dad!" Amelia said. "You saved me!"

Her dad stayed crouched down in the ankle-deep water, taking deep breaths.

Amelia quickly went over to Akoni and rolled him over onto his back. His eyes were closed. She didn't want to think about how long he'd been face down in the water.

"Akoni?" she said to the unmoving man.

He didn't respond. She wasn't sure how to check to see if he was breathing.

"Do you know CPR?" Amelia asked her dad.

Her dad ignored the question. He got shakily to his feet, using the rock wall behind him to help himself up.

"Why is the ocean here?" her dad said. "It never comes this high."

He glared at Amelia.

"It's you," he said. "You have magic."

"I guess I must," Amelia said. "I mean, I only just discovered it. I think it's...water magic."

"Did you undo Akoni's newt spell?" her dad asked. He looked angry, with his eyes narrowed.

"No," she said. "We thought it just wore off."

Her dad backed off. "Yep, had me some blackout time," he said. "A few of my spells stopped working."

He studied her.

"Do you realize you're lucky it wasn't you who undid the newt spell?" her dad said. "That would mean you had training. Only a powerful sorceresses would be able to undo such a complex spell. And if you're a powerful sorceress…I don't know you at all."

"Magic's as new to me as this island," Amelia said truthfully.

Her dad came closer and looked deeply into her eyes. It was unnerving to see eyes so much like her own up close.

"In that case…" her dad said.

Amelia's heart constricted. He looked so serious.

To her surprise, he broke out into a rare smile. It transformed his face. He almost looked…healthy.

"Good work, kid," her dad said. "Calling the ocean is no small thing for a rookie."

Amelia tried to absorb the compliment. She couldn't quite accept that her mean dad had actually said something positive about her. She tried to say thank you, but only coughed.

Akoni made a choking noise. Amelia ran to his side.

"He'll be fine," her dad said.

"Did you save him, somehow?" Amelia asked. "Like you saved me?"

"Don't get ideas, kid," her dad said. "I need him to distribute the Dark that I mine. There was no saving him. I'm just looking after my job."

Her dad coughed. His face went pale and slightly green. He leaned against the rock wall.

Amelia didn't know what to feel. Had he saved Akoni just to keep him working for him? Or did he care about him?

She studied her dad's face. The bloom in his cheeks that appeared when he smiled was completely gone. The stringy hair falling down around his off-color face made him look like a plague victim from another century.

"Are you OK?" Amelia asked.

"No," her dad said. "I mined more Dark. I'm very weak now."

"Why?" Amelia said. "Why did you mine it, when it makes you so sick?"

Her dad bared his teeth at her, and sank to the ground. Propped up against the rock wall, he crouched in the ankle-deep water. His pants were getting wet.

"Because you wouldn't do it. You wouldn't help out an old man," her dad said. "Your old man."

"I can't mine the Dark," Amelia said. "The Dark, it's a bad thing. An evil thing."

"So?" her dad said.

"What do you mean, so?" Amelia asked.

"So what if it's evil? I made money! I lived well. There is evil and good in the world," her dad said. "Make use of what you can."

"I won't do it," Amelia said, a surge of stubborn confidence rushing through her bones. She crossed her arms.

"Who do you think paid those medical bills when you were a baby?" her dad said. "We couldn't have done that without the Dark."

"Mom did fine after you left," Amelia said. "We didn't have any money, but we didn't need it."

Her dad rolled his eyes.

"You got used to being poor," he said. "You could have a much better life, but you don't even realize it."

Amelia stamped her foot, which splashed in the water. "I am never mining the Dark!" she shouted. "I don't like it, at all."

"Wrong," her dad said. "No matter how much that goddess whines in that cave, you are coming with me to mine the Dark."

"Whines?" Amelia asked. Was the goddess in the cave really awake?

"Why don't you say her name and free the goddess?" Amelia asked. "You could do some good, so easily."

"Do some good?" Her dad scoffed at the idea. "I don't know her name. Probably no one does anymore."

Amelia was shocked. Why did she know Alanawaiwai's name, if her dad, who'd been living here for years, didn't?

Maybe Akoni kept it a secret from him, in case her dad had evil plans for the goddess.

"Enough with the stupid questions," her dad said. "Let's go. As soon as I get my strength…" He tried to get up, but fell over. He took a few deep breaths, and lay on his back in the water. Now he was getting really wet, and she was worried he was cold.

Amelia felt the ocean around her. She thanked it, and told it to return to its normal home.

As the water receded, Akoni made another choking noise. He rolled to his side, coughed up sea water, and then opened his eyes.

Akoni looked around briefly, then wasted no time in pulling himself to his feet and shouting at the sorcerer.

"You!" Akoni said angrily. "You turned me into a lizard! I had a…a tail!"

Her dad laughed weakly as he lay on the sand.

"You looked a lot better as a newt," her dad said in a rasping voice. He closed his eyes.

"Oh, no. Dad?" Amelia knelt down to check on him. She worried he had passed out. She smoothed his stringy hair off his face. A smile flitted over his mouth. Or maybe she just imagined it.

"Shows you what you know," Akoni said angrily to her father. "I was a lizard, not a newt."

Her dad made a strangled noise.

"My spells have been off," he whispered. "I'm too weak."

"Akoni, my Dad saved us," Amelia said. She placed

palm leaves under her dad's head like a pillow. He made no movement to stop her.

"He saved us for his own gain," Akoni said. "He probably thinks he can make you mine the Dark."

"It's true," her dad said. His voice came out like a whisper.

"I don't care why he saved us. We need to get him somewhere warm, so he can get some rest," Amelia said.

"It's warm enough here," her dad said. "Leave me be for awhile." His eyes fluttered. As Amelia watched, his head rolled to the side, and he stopped moving.

"He passed out!" Amelia said, alarmed.

"He's just sleeping," Akoni said, still sounding angry.

"Well, you're OK, aren't you?" Amelia said to Akoni. "You were asleep for a long time."

"I feel OK," Akoni said, as he patted his arms and legs. "Nothing broken, not dizzy…no tail."

"I'm glad," Amelia said and squeezed his arm.

"You did some freaky ocean stuff," Akoni said and looked at her with his eyebrows raised.

"I don't know how, really," Amelia said. "I just felt the ocean there and…well, I kind of asked it to come help. Do you think I'm freaky? You know, like my dad?" Her chest was tight with worry. Would he still want to help her if he thought she was using dark magic like her dad?

Akoni looked her in the eyes for a long time. Finally, he smiled.

"Any friend of the ocean is a friend of mine," he said.

Amelia felt the tightness in her heart and stomach relax. Akoni thought it was OK that she could do some magic. It made her feel relieved.

"Now, come with me," Akoni said and he took her arm and looped it through his.

"Where are we going?" Amelia asked. "We can't just leave my dad here. He's sick, or something."

"Shh. Just follow me." Akoni guided her into the palm trees. "Your dad, he's fine."

"Wait!" Amelia said louder, and extracted her arm. "My dad isn't safe there."

"He's safer than us," Akoni said. "He has magic. More than just calling-the-ocean magic, like his daughter. Come on, unless you want to stick around until he's rested?"

Amelia understood what that meant—the cave.

"You know what will happen then. You'll end up back in the cave," Akoni said. "And I'll be scurrying under his feet."

Amelia shuddered. She didn't want to go back there. But maybe there was a good reason to…?

"Akoni, he said the goddess whined," Amelia said. "So, she's really awake, right? Can we free her with her name?"

Akoni looked stunned.

"It's not safe for us to go to the cave when your dad is here on the island," Akoni said. "We should escape. Besides, I don't know what to do to free the goddess. I'm not sure it's just about saying her name."

Amelia felt guilty at the thought of leaving the goddess in that terrible place. But Akoni had a point. They were no match for her magical dad.

"How do we escape?" Amelia asked.

Akoni urged her to walk faster.

"We're going to the house. Your dad looks like he'll be out for a few hours. I've seen him like that before," Akoni said. "We'll get some food and get off the island."

"How long will it take to get back to the house?" Amelia asked.

"One hour," Akoni said. He stepped up his pace, climbing the hillside quickly.

Amelia wasn't sure what to do. She needed food. Her stomach felt like an empty pit. And she had no idea what she could do for her dad, besides hover over him, and maybe give him a drink of water.

But what if the rock dragon came back? If her dad was passed out, would he be eaten by the rock dragon?

Then again, what could she do against the rock dragon? It was her dad who saved her, not the other way around.

She looked at the strong Hawaiian making his way through the lush, green terrain. At least he knew the island. She should stick with him.

Maybe they could escape the island, and then she could find help for her dad. And for the goddess.

She wondered again why her dad didn't know the goddess' name.

Alanawaiwai.

A chill ran up her spine. Maybe no one trusted her dad with her name.

Maybe her dad really was a bad man, and she should stay away from him, ill or not.

Akoni beckoned her to follow, to walk quickly.

For now, she would follow Akoni.

Chapter Twenty-four

Tess, Elizabeth and Susie waited at the busy bus stop on the sidewalk in Honolulu. The sun beat down on them. Tess felt heat rising from the sidewalk, baking her bare legs.

The bus for Nanakuli, a town on the west coast of Oahu, was supposed to come in twenty minutes. It was a long time to wait in the heat. Tess hoped the bus was air-conditioned.

Another text from Susie's mom came in, breaking up the boredom.

I am in a house. Amelia was here. I heard her voice outside. I will escape this house and find her. I feel stronger as her dad weakens. I will call when I can. There is no phone signal. I am using magic to send this. You, Elizabeth and Tess should not go to school while this is happening. Stay safe, stay at home. Love you, Mom.

Susie's face fell as she read the text. She pulled her ponytail nervously.

"My mom's trapped in Amelia's dad's house?" Susie said. "That sounds bad."

Elizabeth tapped her fingers against her dress. "I think it's good news," she said. "She's with Amelia, and she's feeling stronger. I bet she breaks them both out."

"Still, she hasn't escaped yet," Susie said.

Tess squeezed Susie's arm.

"She does say she's getting stronger," Tess said. "I know you're worried, but I think she'll escape like she says. And we know Amelia's OK, if your mom heard her in the house."

"Tess is right," Elizabeth said. "It's mostly good news. And we'll be there soon to meet her. And Amelia. Then we can all go home."

"If this bus ever comes," Elizabeth said jokingly.

"You girls are right," Susie said. "I'm so glad you're here with me."

The three girls held hands for a moment. Tess pulled hers away when it became covered with sweat from the heat. Even her joan shorts felt too heavy for the humid weather.

"It's so hot," Tess said, turning to a lighter subject.

"Yeah, I know," Susie said, even though her jean shorts were designed for hot weather. "I can feel sweat everywhere the jeans are."

"See, what have I been telling you about dresses?" Elizabeth said. She wore her new "Emma" dress, as she called it, from the vintage shop in Berkeley.

"I'm completely comfortable in this Pre-Victorian style,"

Elizabeth said. She did a mock-twirl and tossed her brown ponytail.

"OK, maybe dresses rule in Hawaii," Susie said. "My jean shorts work great in Berkeley!"

"You saying I should move here?" Elizabeth said and smiled.

"Only if you take up surfing," Susie said. "Or beach volleyball."

They all laughed.

"It's too hot for me," Tess said. "Even my freckles are sweating!" She wiped her arms on her T-shirt, and left watermarks.

Elizabeth's phone rang. She pulled it out of her bag to see a video chat request from the Brightcubes.

"Hi, Pete," Elizabeth said to the boy on the screen.

"Hi," Pete said back, and stared from the screen.

Tess and Susie each said hello.

"What's the Amelia search status?" Pete asked.

"Well, she's still missing," Elizabeth said, "but we think we know where she is. And Susie's mom, too. There's an island west of here. We're getting a bus to take us to the coast, and we'll find someone to sail us there."

They watched Pete turn, and heard a bunch of guys' voices in the background.

"Hey," Elizabeth said when he turned back to the screen. "How did the math battle go?"

"Lost it," Pete said. He held up his arm, which had a black armband on it. "But now all effort can be put on the search."

"Wow, thanks, Brightcubes," Susie said and leaned in so her face appeared in the camera.

"Damian wants to know your GPS," Pete said. "And the GPS of the island."

"Um, GPS?" Elizabeth turned to Susie and Tess, who both shrugged.

"We'll find out and get back to you," Elizabeth said.

"Damian also asked what your flight time was," Pete said.

"Flight time?" Elizabeth asked.

"The exact flight time to Hawaii," Pete explained. "We had a bet going."

Tess and Susie shrugged again. No one had noted the time it took to fly.

"Sorry," Elizabeth said.

"Amelia would have known," Pete said. "And we would have won the math battle with her."

"Yeah, we miss her too," Elizabeth said.

Pete turned away, and there was more mumbling between the Brightcubes.

"One last thing," Pete said, when his face returned to the phone screen. "Damian wants to know if you've seen any butterflyfish, yellow tang, or the humuhumunukunukuapua fish?"

178

Elizabeth sighed. "We haven't been to the ocean. We've been in an airport, and a restaurant. You know, searching for Amelia?" Her voice rose to a higher pitch, a sign she was annoyed.

"Take a picture if you see any!" Damian yelled from the background.

Elizabeth rolled her eyes.

"Look, I'll send you our GPS because that sounds helpful," Elizabeth said, "but we need to focus on finding Amelia and Susie's mom. Not on fish!"

Elizabeth had to promise to send a photo if she happened to see any of the tropical fish on the list before the Brightcubes would hang up. She was searching for GPS apps when Mikey came walking up.

"The Brightcubes, now Mikey, and still no bus!" Susie said. She took the tube of sunblock from Elizabeth's bag and smeared it all over her face.

Tess felt a fresh wave of anger when she saw Mikey. But she was more interested in what Mikey's news was, and ignored the anger for now.

"How's Amelia's mom?" Tess asked her brother in a cool voice. She gratefully took the sunblock from Susie.

"She was confused, and didn't know why she was in Hawaii," Mikey said. "I don't think she understands that Amelia is missing. I tried to explain, but she just didn't get it."

"Maybe Amelia's dad cast some sort of spell on her," Elizabeth said. "Did you tell her we're all here?"

Mikey shook his head. "She got dizzy and had to lie down. I didn't want to stress her out more," he said. "We can call her later if you think it's a good idea. I left Didus with her for...you know, protection."

"Let's just let her rest," Elizabeth said. "All our parents know we're out here. I called mine a half hour ago. They're furious and mega-stressed."

"We're all going to get in trouble," Tess said. "Big time."

"I talked to them already," Mikey said and squeezed Tess' shoulder. "They're mad, but they said it was good that I came. They said I should stick with you girls. You know, to make sure you're all OK."

"OK, so you won't get in trouble," Tess said. "But I will." She felt a hot flush appear on her cheeks. Mikey got away with everything.

"Actually, they sounded more worried than mad," Mikey said. "I told them Susie's mom and Amelia's mom were both out here, and they calmed down."

Tess cocked an eyebrow at him. "You lied? The favorite, most perfect son actually told a lie?"

Mikey blushed.

"Tess, don't be mean," Elizabeth said, jumping to his defense.

"Well, it wasn't a lie, exactly," Mikey said. "They are both out here. It's just one of them has a concussion or something, and we lost track of the other one. Anyway, they were also worried about Amelia. I mean, a lot worried."

"Me too," Tess said, her anger replaced by deep concern for her friend.

"Me three," Elizabeth said.

They stood quietly for a moment. Tess hoped Amelia was comfortable and happy wherever she was, and not roasting hot.

"At least I won't get in trouble," Susie said, breaking the silence. "Though I wish my mom were here. I know she could help us with her powers."

The group stood in silence, sweating in the sun. Elizabeth texted the Brightcubes their GPS, and took a screenshot of their map showing the island. Tess broke into a grin of relief when the bus displaying 'Nanakuli' came down the road. Not only because it was shelter from the sun, but also because it was one step closer to finding Amelia.

The bus rolled to a stop. Everyone got on board and looked for empty seats. The ocean was on the left side, so they all sat on that side of the bus. Susie and Elizabeth found two seats together, and Tess and Mikey sat on their own.

The bus rattled down a dry highway, along the ocean. Tess kept her sunglasses on despite the tinted windows, since the sun was still bright. She gazed out at the ocean, searching for islands to the West. So far, she could only see glistening water, with diamonds seeming to dance on it, from the sun.

Tess enjoyed the peace and quiet. She stared out at the ocean for what felt like an hour, but was only fifteen minutes, by her watch. She wondered if Amelia, too, was looking at the ocean wherever she was.

Mikey came over to sit next to Tess, and interrupted her thoughts.

"So…am I forgiven?" Mikey asked.

"Not sure yet," Tess said. She crossed her arms, but she didn't feel angry like before. She was too worried about Amelia at the moment.

"I care about Amelia, you know," Mikey said. "She's my friend too."

The telltale rush of hot anger filled Tess' face when he claimed Amelia as a friend.

"Well, maybe you should have thought about that before you gave her the Valentine," Tess said.

"Look, we need to work together to find her. So, can we do that?" Mikey stuck his hand out. "Truce, for now? Forget the Valentine?"

It was true, Tess realized. They needed to work together. And it would be best if Tess didn't get angry too often. Otherwise they'd have problems not just because of the hot sun, but because of other burning objects.

Tess took his hand with some hesitation.

"Truce," she said. In fact, she felt relieved as soon as they shook hands. Tess was rarely angry at anyone, and she and Mikey usually got along. She didn't like being angry at her own brother.

She touched the amulet around her neck. Though she needed it now to help Amelia, she wasn't sure she liked wearing the Fire amulet. Not for the first time, she wondered why Susie's mom had given her Fire.

Maybe I just can't handle it?

Susie's voice broke through Tess' thoughts. Friendly, sociable Susie was talking to an older man with long, white hair. They were having an intense conversation across the aisle seats.

"We're trying to go to Kahi Kanaka Mai I Hele." Susie said. "Do you know it?"

"That place doesn't exist," the man said. He smiled, showing gleaming teeth in a suntanned and weathered face.

"We have a map," Susie said. She turned around and caught Tess listening.

"Tess, show him the map," Susie said.

Tess felt nervous, considering the response in the pizza place when the staff got so tense about the island. But she pulled out the map and spoke to it.

"Water," she whispered.

The little island to the West turned black.

Amelia was still there.

Tess looked out to the west, but couldn't see anything but ocean. She hoped, wherever Amelia was, she was OK.

Tess held her Fire amulet in her hand.

"Hang on, Water," she said quietly. "We're coming to get you."

Chapter Twenty-five

Amelia and Akoni reached her dad's house, sweaty and panting from running across the island. It looked like an ordinary, wooden house from the outside, but the inside was modern and sleek. Her dad had nice taste.

The entrance hall had a long, vaulted ceiling, and stairs made of a translucent material that spiraled upwards. The inside was at least two stories, though the house appeared to be one story from the outside. Amelia didn't know if that was magic or just clever architecture.

"It looks like a movie star's house in Los Angeles," Amelia said.

"Your dad made a lot of money on the black market," Akoni said. "Just wait until you see all the food. That's my favorite part of the house."

Amelia and Akoni went into the large kitchen, which had big, clean windows and dark, granite counters. They rifled through the cabinets and raided the fridge, stuffing random bits of food into their mouths.

Amelia had never felt so hungry. She ate a banana, which usually filled her up. She couldn't even tell she had eaten it, her stomach was still so empty.

Akoni made a few cheese sandwiches, and Amelia ate two of them with pickles. Akoni ate five. She didn't know how long they spent eating. When the sandwiches were gone, she opened a fancy box of chocolates and snacked on those.

Shuffling sounds seemed to come from upstairs.

"Are you sure we're alone here?" Amelia asked, pointing upstairs.

Akoni shrugged.

"I guess so," he said. "Birds and lizards on the roof make noise sometimes. But let's not stay to find out."

Amelia kept stuffing herself with the delicious chocolates until she felt uncomfortably full. Akoni filled his backpack with crackers and energy bars.

"I can't eat anymore," Amelia said. "Maybe ever." She patted her stomach and groaned. But the chocolates were so good, she wanted to bring them.

"We'll get hungry again," Akoni said. "Come on, let's get to the shuttle."

They left the house in a hurry.

"Is the shuttle nearby?" Amelia asked once they were outside. "I don't think I can walk very far. Too full."

"Yeah, it's parked just outside the house. It will get us to Oahu," Akoni said. "The shuttle is a magic thing that your dad invented."

"Magic?" Amelia asked, feeling sleepy and heavy. "I hope it's not too weird."

"It's just behind these palm trees," Akoni said and led her to the plants. He cleared away the palm leaves and exposed a white sphere with a blue door.

"Um, Akoni? That's not a shuttle," Amelia said, pointing at the strange ride. "That looks more like a carnival ride. It's round…like my full stomach," she said, then hiccuped and started giggling.

"First of all, you've had too much chocolate," Akoni said with a grin. "Second of all, it teleports. It doesn't fly."

"Teleports?" Amelia's insides suddenly felt queasy. "Are you sure we should be using it?" She didn't like the sound of teleportation. What if something went wrong?

"I've done it before," Akoni said. "It's easy. We just light a candle inside the sphere, and the whole thing ends up in Oahu, at Jack's house there."

Akoni opened the door of the sphere. Hot, stale air rushed over them from inside the shuttle.

"My dad has another house? In Oahu?" Amelia said. Her light mood suddenly turned dark.

"My mom works shifts every day, and my dad has two houses? In Hawaii, no less?" Amelia's voice was getting high. She felt angry. She knew about alimony, how other dads gave money to their kids. She also knew they hadn't gotten anything from her dad.

"I think you're tired, girl," Akoni said and studied her. "My sister gets all emotional when she's tired."

"I'm not tired!" Amelia said, although her limbs felt heavy and exhaustion filled her body. Then she shouted at him, "I am not emotional!"

187

Amelia took five deep breaths.

"The Dark," she said. "That's why I'm yelling. I'm not normally like this…so annoyed and angry, I mean."

"I don't feel anything, but…" Akoni studied her. "Well, this shuttle is carrying Dark—a lot of it. It's our…I mean, your dad's next shipment."

"Then I don't want to get in that thing," Amelia said and took a step away from the magic teleport.

"What's the other option? Stay here until your dad wakes up and makes you Darkmine?" Akoni said.

"But if I'm sensitive to the Dark, maybe I shouldn't go in there," Amelia said. "Can we unload it before going?"

"We don't have time. Your dad could wake up any minute," Akoni said.

Amelia wasn't sure she trusted magic enough to use a teleportation shuttle. Especially when Akoni didn't know any magic. What if something went wrong?

The feeling of hate emanating from the shuttle made Amelia take a step back. She didn't like Dark, didn't like it at all.

Akoni grabbed her arm and pulled her to the door.

"We need to go now," Akoni said. "Your dad could come any minute. He doesn't need a shuttle to teleport. He just snaps his fingers, using magic to travel."

Amelia groaned. If her dad gained his powers back after he rested, Amelia was in danger of getting a lot closer to the Dark than she wanted.

"OK, let's get out of here," Amelia said. "But I'm not going to talk when we get in the shuttle. I don't want to start yelling."

"Fine with me," Akoni said and smiled. "Anyway, it only takes a few seconds."

Amelia climbed in the sphere. The seats were comfortable, and it was white and clean inside. A black candle sat on the dashboard.

The feeling in the sphere was negative, and Amelia shuddered with sudden chills, though the air itself was hot.

Amelia held her amulet tightly.

"Water," she said.

Soon she was covered with a light film of water, and she felt loose and flowing. She felt positive and protected.

Akoni climbed in after her, and shut the door. He lit the candle. The walls of the sphere danced in front of her eyes. They shimmered as if they were turning to water. Then everything spun around her. She shut her eyes.

Chapter Twenty-six

The bus lurched toward Nanakuli, and the sun shone bright even through the tinted windows.

Another text from Susie's mom arrived.

Amelia is here! I can't leave the room but I hear her voice downstairs. She sounds OK.

"We need to get there now," Susie said, as soon as she read the text. "Even if Amelia is coming and going, my mom is still trapped in a room!"

Tess had reservations about showing the map to anyone, but Susie took it out of her hands. She gave it to the Hawaiian man she had been talking to.

"See?" Susie said. "We want to go there." She pointed at the little island west of them.

He looked at the map and then gave them a big grin.

"If that island were there," he said and pointed to the map. "You would see it there." He pointed out the window to the ocean.

"Yeah, I thought it was close," Elizabeth said. "I wonder why we can't see anything?"

"There is nothing there," the man said. "This map is wrong."

"Well, where is the island called Kahi Kanaka Mai I Hele then?" Elizabeth asked. "Our friends are there."

The man's big smile turned into a big frown.

"That's a mythical island," he said. "It doesn't exist. Your friends can't be there."

Tess felt her heart tighten as the words sank in. If the island didn't exist, where were Susie's mom and Amelia?

"So, you a surfer?" the man said, turning to Susie and smiling again.

Susie reluctantly began a conversation about volleyball while Elizabeth, Tess and Mikey conferred.

"What if that man is right?" Elizabeth said. "What if the island doesn't exist?"

"What about the map? And the globe that Susie's mom showed us?" Tess said. "That little island west of here was on both of them."

Elizabeth tapped her fingers together as she thought. "I'm texting the Brightcubes," she said and pulled out her phone.

Tess studied her hands with a scowl. Something wasn't adding up. She suddenly realized what it was.

"The waiter at the pizza place!" Tess said. "He said not to go there, remember? But he didn't say anything about it not existing."

"That's a really good point, Tess," Elizabeth said. "They did seem to know about the island. They just didn't want us to go there."

"Let's get off at the next stop," Mikey said. "We'll go back to Honolulu and make a new plan."

"Yeah, let's go back to the pizza place and ask some more questions," Tess said and gave Mikey a weak smile. The thought of walking into that now unfriendly place with the scowling staff gave Tess chills up her spine. But she couldn't think of any other way to find the island.

They got off the bus at a shrimp stall by the highway. There was a thick smell of shrimp in the air. Susie hopped up to the counter and bought pineapple ice cream.

"She's eating again!" Elizabeth held her stomach. "Even I can't think about food right now."

Susie looked at home with her tan skin and volleyball clothes on.

"I think Hawaii agrees with our Susie," Elizabeth said, watching her chat with the Hawaiians at the counter.

"Wish it agreed with me," Tess said as she realized her inner arms and backs of knees were once again sweating. She decided to get an ice cream just to cool off. Mikey had skipped lunch, so he bought the grilled shrimp special.

Elizabeth's phone rang.

"Hello, Brightcubes," Elizabeth said, as she picked up the call. "Who am I speaking with?"

Elizabeth mouthed the word, "Pete."

Tess listened to Elizabeth's side of the conversation as she bought an ice cream at the stand.

"No, we haven't found her," Elizabeth said into the

phone. "And Susie's mom is still missing."

The group searched for a place to sit. All the tables in the shade were busy with Hawaiians and tourists eating shrimp or ice cream. They had to settle with a table outside, in the hot sun.

Tess wished she had a hat, and worried she should reapply sunblock.

"No, we haven't seen any fish!" Elizabeth said and rolled her eyes.

"We're going to the island I told you about, but we're not sure where it is," Elizabeth said into the phone. "The man on the bus said it doesn't exist. We can't see anything to the west, just ocean. But the weird thing is, the island is definitely on the map."

Tess pulled the sunblock out of Elizabeth's bag and reapplied it to her face as she listened.

"OK, thanks," Elizabeth said and hung up.

"Do they have any ideas?" Susie asked.

Elizabeth shrugged. "They're going to look into it."

"What do we have in terms of…magical objects," Tess whispered. She glanced around to make sure no one outside their group was listening, then she pulled the purple candle and little golden key and map out of her backpack.

"We have the magic wallet and the 'veil of mom', too," Elizabeth said. "But I'll keep them in the bag just in case someone notices them." She looked around nervously.

Elizabeth's phone buzzed. She read the text and then relayed the message to the group.

"Hey, the Brightcubes say there is an island where we think there is!" Elizabeth said, excited.

Susie leaned over and read the text.

Water currents clearly show an island three miles by five miles on the map, due west of your current position. The water currents look unexpectedly turbulent there.

"Water currents? How do they know about those?" Susie asked.

"It's the Brightcubes," Elizabeth said. "They know these kinds of things."

"Well," Tess said. "That's sort of good news, I guess. But how do we get to an island we can't see? And I'm not sure we'll be able to get anyone to take us there."

Elizabeth pulled her ponytail as she thought.

"Can we use any of these to help us?" Elizabeth said and indicated the objects on the table.

"What do you think this does?" Tess said, as she turned the purple candle over in her hands. "Is it just a normal candle?"

"It was in the locked cabinet," Elizabeth said. "Right?"

Tess agreed. "If it was just a normal candle, it probably wouldn't have been in the special cabinet. It must do something."

"Light it and see, Fire-o," Susie suggested.

"Flicker," Tess said. The candle lit, and purple smoke curled into the air. Nothing else happened.

"Maybe it's just a purple candle," Susie said and shrugged.

Tess blew it out.

"Hey! Wow! How did you do that?" asked a skinny boy their age. He came right up to the table.

"Was that magic?" the boy asked.

"Just a trick," Tess said and quickly stuffed the candle and key back into Elizabeth's bag.

"I saw you light the candle," the boy said to Tess. "Listen, I know magic. There is a magician who eats here sometimes."

The group gave each other big-eyed, excited looks. They peppered the skinny boy with questions.

"Where does he live?" Mikey asked.

"Is he on Oahu?" Susie asked.

"What magic does he do?" Elizabeth said.

The boy seemed startled when they took a sudden interest in him. He made placating gestures with his hands, and asked them to slow down.

"I can't answer all those questions at the same time," the boy said.

"Where does he live?" Mikey repeated.

"Different places. Are you looking for the magician?" the boy asked.

"We're looking for his daughter," Tess said. "She's our friend."

"Do you know of the island called Kahi Kanaka Mai I Hele?" Elizabeth said.

"Doesn't exist," the boy said and crossed his arms. "I can't help you with that."

Elizabeth rolled her eyes.

"We know it exists," Elizabeth said. "And we know it's there." She pointed west.

The girls were hot, sweaty and desperate to find Amelia and Susie's mom. Elizabeth and Susie stared the boy down. Even Tess gave the boy a stern look

"OK, OK," the boy said. "I give up. There is an island where you pointed. You just can't see it. There is a spell that hides it."

"How do we get there if we can't even see it?" Elizabeth asked.

"Oh, when you're closer to the island you can see it," the boy said.

Tess felt a wave of happiness. "That makes perfect sense! That's why we don't see it–a spell. Do you know where we can rent a boat?"

"You can't get there by boat," the boy said. "The waves are too big at the island," he explained. He raised an eyebrow, and a calculating look came over his face.

"But I can take you to a submarine," the boy said. "For a pineapple ice cream."

A submarine?

Tess exchanged looks with Mikey. Her brother looked skeptical, but shrugged.

Could they trust this boy?

Tess figured they didn't have much choice. It wasn't like anyone else was eager to help them. She would ask more specifics of the boy, to see if he was telling the truth.

"Will you take us to the island in the submarine?" Tess asked. "Can you drive it, I mean?"

The boy shook his head.

"I can't drive it. I wouldn't go to that island anyway," the boy said. "It's too dangerous."

"Because of the currents?" Elizabeth asked, remembering the text from the Brightcubes.

Again, the boy shook his head.

"The currents are bad," the boy said. "But there's worse stuff on the island. Like a really bad rock monster that breathes fire or something. People say that, anyway. And my cousin's uncle got close to there, and he never came back."

Tess shivered. She didn't like the idea of a rock monster, but she guessed it was just a story. She breathed deeply to calm herself.

"We have to go to the island," Tess said. "We don't have a choice. If Amelia and Susie's mom are there, we just have to go."

"Agreed," Elizabeth and Susie said. They hooked pinkies with Tess. Elizabeth offered her pinky to Mikey, who hooked his back, though he blushed red.

"OK, if you have to go," the boy said. "Then get my ice cream and I'll show you the sub."

"Well, how will we get there if we can't drive the sub?" Elizabeth said.

The boy just shrugged.

"I think we should go check it out," Tess said. "Maybe we can figure out how to drive the thing."

Susie ran to the stand and came back with one ice cream for the boy, and one for herself. The boy ate his quickly as he walked down the road, motioning for them to follow.

They walked for a long half hour.

Tess wished they had taken another bus. Sweat poured down her body, especially where her T-shirt and jean shorts covered her.

When the boy finally led them to a beach, all Tess wanted to do was jump into the water to cool off. But there were more important things to do—like finding the sub, and finding Amelia.

The boy pointed out into the ocean. They could just make out a white, torpedo-shaped vessel sitting in the water a short distance away.

"It's there," the boy said. "To get to the sub, we need to take a boat. I'll take you that far, the rest is up to you."

Tess was just thinking how helpful he was for only one ice cream when he held out his hand.

"Since there are four of you, it's twenty dollars each for the boat trip," the boy said. "That's eighty dollars, please." The boy stood very seriously and kept his hand out.

"That's outrageous!" Elizabeth said. "The deal was that you'd bring us to the sub for an ice cream."

"The ice cream got you this far," the boy said and held out his hand, palm up. "Now I need a little more."

"We'll swim to the sub, thank you very much," Susie said.

Tess examined the waves. She was sure Susie could make it all the way out to the sub. Maybe she and Mikey could do it, though it looked a long way. But there was no way Elizabeth could swim that far.

"We can pay you," Tess said.

The boy smiled at her.

"I could tell you were smart," he said. "You need me to get to the sub. You can't swim all the way out there."

Tess asked for the wallet, but Elizabeth glared at her and wouldn't hand it over.

"Let's just pay him, Elizabeth," Tess said. "It's not like we need to save money." They had a magic wallet full of never-ending money after all.

"We'll pay you once we're on the sub," Elizabeth told the boy in a firm voice. "So there are no more surprises."

"Mahalo," the boy said, using the Hawaiian word for thank you. He made a nifty little bow, and they piled into his boat. Mikey, Elizabeth and Susie sat on the port side, the left of the boat, far away from the boy. All the weight made the boat lean toward the left, so someone had to balance it out. Tess sat on the right, the starboard side, next to the boy.

He smiled at her, and shrugged. "I know you're all mad at me," the boy said. "But my family needs the money."

Tess examined his skinny arms and legs. He had holes in his T-shirt. When she thought how the boy and his family probably needed money pretty badly, she didn't mind so much that he asked for a payment to take them to the sub.

Tess smiled at him. "I guess I can understand that," she said.

"You might as well give me all the money you have, anyway," the boy said.

"Why?" Tess asked.

"If you go to that island, you're probably not coming back," the boy said and launched the boat.

Tess wasn't sure if he was joking or not, but she was too frightened to laugh.

Everyone hung on to something as the tiny boat swayed in the waves.

"We'll come back," Tess said, sounding more confident than she felt. "And we'll bring back our friend." She felt her amulet grow warm against her breastbone.

The boy shrugged.

"It's not called Kahi Kanaka Mai I Hele for no reason, you know," the boy said.

Tess' stomach rolled. She held tightly to the side of the boat. She didn't know if the waves were making her feel queasy, or if it was the boy's words.

What if they couldn't find Amelia?

What if there really was a rock monster?

She shook her head of the dark thoughts, refusing to believe them.

They had fire power, they had air power. Surely that counted for something.

They had gotten this far. They couldn't give up now.

Chapter Twenty-seven

When Amelia opened her eyes, Akoni was already out of the shuttle and holding the door open.

Relieved to leave the Dark-infested cabin full of negativity, Amelia climbed out of the sphere-shaped shuttle. She blinked in the bright sun, and was greeted by a lush garden bordered by colorful hibiscus flowers.

The strange pull of the Dark wasn't very strong here. She stopped concentrating on being Water, and let go of the amulet. She turned her face to the sun, enjoying its warmth. Relief flooded more deeply through her.

"Blue sky!" Amelia said.

"I hate that island," Akoni said. "You forget about the sun and sky. That island has only dark clouds and wind."

"It feels like something else lifted too—an evil presence," Amelia said.

"The Dark is strong on that island," Akoni said. "I notice it too, though it affects you more."

"Thank you for getting me off the island, Akoni," Amelia said. "I wouldn't have been able to escape by myself."

"Mahalo for trusting me after, well…you know… helping your dad kidnap you in the first place," Akoni said. He looked down, embarrassed.

"I hope we never have to go back," Amelia said. "I feel so sorry for the ocean goddess trapped in that cave with the Dark."

"She's been there a long time," Akoni said. "One day she'll be free."

Then Akoni smiled and clapped a hand on her shoulder.

"Want to get some pizza?" he said.

"Are you kidding?" Amelia said. "After all that food we ate a few minutes ago?"

But her stomach rumbled. She couldn't believe she was ready for more food. "Actually…yes," she admitted. "I could eat again."

"I know a great place," Akoni said.

"I should probably call my mom," Amelia said. "She must be freaking out. What day is it?" She was extremely worried about her mom, and her best friends. Until now, she had been fully concentrating on surviving the island, and avoiding her dad, and the rock dragon, and Darkmining. Now that she had escaped, her thoughts quickly turned to them.

"Use my cell," Akoni said and handed her the phone. "I'll hide the shuttle." He covered up the spherical craft with a bunch of palm leaves and branches while Amelia made some calls.

Amelia dialed her mom's cell first. Her mom picked up after the first ring.

"Mom!" Amelia said.

"Amelia?" her mom replied. "Is it you?"

"Yeah, I'm OK!" Amelia's voice shook as she poured out the story to her mom. How she was walking across campus when she blacked out, and how her dad kidnapped her.

"Amelia, are you talking about a dream?" her mom asked.

"No, it really happened!" Amelia said. "Dad can do magic. He's a sorcerer!"

"What?" her mom said. "Amelia, did you hit your head? Are you sure you're OK?"

Amelia realized that maybe her mom didn't know about her dad's magic. Maybe he left before her mom could find out he had magic powers.

"Never mind about what I just said," Amelia said. "I meant…magician. He's a magician."

"Your dad is dangerous. Stay away from him! I just hope you're OK," her mom said. "Did you contact the police?"

Amelia climbed onto the back porch looking for shade. She didn't have any sunglasses, and really needed them.

"Um, no. I didn't call the police," Amelia told her mom. "Maybe I should. Dad still has my cell phone, though."

"Where are you exactly?" her mom said.

"In Oahu. I don't know more than that," Amelia said. "Do you know dad has a house here?"

"You're at his house?" her mom said. "Get out of there! Now!"

"I'm outside, Mom," Amelia said. "Don't worry, he won't find me." She hoped that was true.

"Did you say you're in Oahu?" her mom said. "I'm at the airport hotel in Honolulu. Just get a taxi and come here. I just want to see you and give you a big hug."

"OK, mom. Akoni and I are getting pizza," Amelia said, "and then I'll head straight there."

"Akoni?" her Mom asked.

"He's a friend. He helped me escape," Amelia explained. "Oh, can you give me the cell phone numbers of the girls? I don't know their numbers by heart, and I want to tell them that I'm OK. They know I was kidnapped, right?"

There was a long pause on the phone.

"Mom?"

"Did Mikey find you? He was here a few hours ago," her mom said. "He had a dog with him–Didus. The dog is here with me."

"What?" Amelia nearly dropped the phone. She hoped Mikey didn't go anywhere he shouldn't have, like trying to track her down to the terrible island. Hopefully he was still in Oahu.

If Mikey was in Hawaii, did that mean some of her friends were here too?

They might all be in danger if they had come looking for her.

Amelia had too many questions. And what was that part about the dog?

"Here are the numbers…" Her mom recited the phone numbers of Mikey and her friends.

"I'm sorry, Amelia. I'm…I'm very tired, very sleepy," her mom said. "Did you say…did you say you'll come here at once?"

"Yes. Soon, Mom, I promise," Amelia said. "Why are you tired?"

"Hm? Oh, I'm fine," her mom said, though she didn't sound fine at all. "Just exhausted. Bye, now. Come home soon. Bye. Where are you?"

Amelia stared at the phone. "Mom, I told you I'm in Oahu. I'm at one of dad's houses."

"Your dad? What?" Her mom's voice raised in alarm, all over again. "Get away from him! He's dangerous! Amelia, go to the police. Where are you?"

"Mom?" Amelia asked. "Are you OK?"

She heard an immense yawn through the phone.

"Yes. I'm here, just a little…sleepy," her mom said, sounding much more relaxed than usual. "I'll just take a little cat nap. Or a dog nap, with Didus here." Her mom giggled to herself, then yawned loudly into the phone.

"See you soon," her mom said.

The call ended with a click.

Amelia blinked to clear her head. It was strange that her mom suddenly needed to sleep. And also strange that her mom had asked her twice where she was.

Amelia wanted to go to the hotel to make sure her mom was OK. But after everything that happened she had shaky, jittery hands. She would stick with Akoni for now. They could get a quick bite to eat, and then she could find her way to the hotel.

Akoni had finished covering up the shuttle, and they walked out of the garden and down the residential street together.

As they walked, Amelia tried each of her friend's phones, and Mikey's cell, but no one answered.

"That's strange," Amelia mumbled. She told Akoni about the phone silence, and about her mom's confusion.

Akoni only nodded.

"Your dad probably put a spell on your mom," he said. "And your friends' cell phones, too. That way, if you escaped, you couldn't get help."

"Do you think my dad could find us here?" Amelia said. "Are we safe?"

"We're safer here than on that island," Akoni said. "But we should stay on the lookout."

Amelia tensed up with worry. Akoni squeezed her arm.

"Don't worry, your dad hates pizza," he said. "We'll be fine at the pizza place—for awhile, at least."

Amelia smiled, glad Akoni was confident of their safety. But as she and Akoni walked down the bright, hot street bordered by sunny palms, a dark, foreboding feeling crept in. It gripped her, and wouldn't let go.

Chapter Twenty-eight

When the boat carrying Tess, Susie, Elizabeth and Mikey got to the sub, they were met with a nasty surprise. The outer hatch door of the sub was locked. And the boy didn't have a key.

"I didn't lie," the boy said, when Susie said it wasn't nice to lie to people. "I took you to the sub. You never said I had to unlock it."

"Well, how much would it cost to unlock it?" Tess said. She breathed deep, aware of heat building inside her. Though she understood the boy needed money, his tricks were getting to be too much.

"I don't have the key, so I can't unlock it," the boy said and shrugged. "Now, since I'm in a good mood, I'll bring you back to shore in my boat for half price—fifty dollars."

"The key!" Susie said and her eyes lit up.

"What key?" Elizabeth asked her.

"That little gold key from my mom's study!" Susie said. "Let's try it."

"That's true!" Elizabeth said.

Everyone held their breath as Elizabeth pulled the key out of her backpack. It was much smaller than the keyhole in the door. It just had to work. Otherwise, how would they get to the island and rescue Amelia?

When Elizabeth put the tiny key in the keyhole, golden light shone where it entered.

To the group's delight, the wheel on the hatch door now turned. Susie opened the hatch, and soon everyone was climbing into the sub.

"Hey!" the boy said, who was the only one not happy by the open sub door. "That's not fair! That's my great-uncle's sub. You can't take it. I'll get in so much trouble!"

"It's not our fault you didn't think ahead!" Elizabeth said. "You knew we had magic!"

Susie closed the hatch behind them once the whole group was inside and down the narrow ladder. Through one of the many round windows of the sub, Tess watched the boy get back in his boat and head toward shore.

"I sort of feel bad for him," Tess said. "And I sort of don't. He tricked us, after all."

"He tried to trick us," Mikey piped in. "We got in the sub in the end."

"The important thing is Amelia," Elizabeth said. "Remember the mission."

Susie took the pilot seat of the submarine, and Elizabeth took co-pilot. Tess and Mikey sat in seats along the wall, next to the little round windows. A laminated driver's manual hung from the dashboard.

"Pilot, read this manual," Elizabeth said and handed it to Susie.

Susie whipped through it, just glancing at some pages.

"Yeah, yeah, I get the idea." Susie handed the manual back to Elizabeth. "We need to get going."

"Wait, what?" Elizabeth said. "We don't know what we're doing. I'm going to read it, and I can direct you." Elizabeth started at page one, and was immersed in reading immediately.

"Seriously, we need to move," Susie said and pressed a red button that said POWER on it. The lights in the sub flickered on.

"OK, before you do anything," Elizabeth said, as she read from page one, "the manual says here you need to level the—"

"On it! Must be this dial here…" Susie turned a dial and the sub groaned. Tess hoped the metallic, whirring sound was engines starting up.

"And then you have to press depth control…" Elizabeth said, reading from page two.

"Blue button, pressed!" Susie said, her hands flying all over the dashboard. "This looks good. It says 'go deep'." She pressed it, and the sub lurched and shuddered.

"Wait!" Elizabeth said and flipped through the book frantically, checking the index. "Go deep—found it," she muttered.

"Do not press unless one meter deep," Elizabeth said and glared at Susie. "We were on the surface!"

"What could happen?" Susie asked.

They sank very quickly to the ocean floor. Tess felt her

ears pop and she got dizzy. When she opened her eyes and blinked, everyone and everything in the sub looked kind of blue.

Mikey threw up into a paper bag marked 'sick bag' that hung by the passenger seat.

Elizabeth cleared her throat and read from the manual.

"If pressed at insufficient depth, pressure challenges may cause vomiting, dizziness, and death," Elizabeth said.

"Sorry," Susie said. She took her hands off the controls. "Go ahead and read the boring manual and tell me what to do," she said to Elizabeth.

Elizabeth took only fifteen minutes to read it through. Tess watched the fish and sea life passing outside the window of the sub, as it sat on the ocean floor.

"OK," Elizabeth said. "The hard part is actually over. Now you just type in the GPS of the place you want to go, then press that button."

"We don't know the GPS of the island. Do we?" Susie asked.

Elizabeth shook her head no. "The Brightcubes could get it for us," she said. "But we can't contact them from here. I don't have any signal on my cell."

Elizabeth brought the map out and mumbled to herself, thinking very hard.

Susie rolled her eyes and touched the landmass showing on the radar screen.

"Got to be this," she said.

Susie pressed a button and motors whirred into action.

"Wait!" Elizabeth said and skimmed the manual again, frantically looking at the map.

"We're fine!" Susie said.

They started to move, going straight ahead.

Sand and rock covered the ground beneath them. A school of silver fish swam by.

"It's so smooth. I don't feel like we're moving," Tess said.

"We are, though," Mikey said. "And fast." Rock formations passed by the little windows as the submarine whirred along.

"Hope we don't hit anything," Elizabeth said.

"Big things will show up on the radar. Like the island," Susie explained. "That's right there and we're pointed at it."

Elizabeth squinted at the radar.

"See? We're heading due west." Susie showed Elizabeth the compass on the dashboard. "The map shows the island is due west."

"Maybe you're right," Elizabeth said.

"What else would that black thing on the radar be?" Susie asked.

"We can see it on the radar, but not from Oahu with our own eyes," Elizabeth said. "That's weird."

A large green turtle swam by one of the windows. Colorful fish darted along, watching curiously.

"I hope Amelia's OK," Mikey said and sighed. "I really hope she's somewhere safe, and not…you know, in distress.

I mean, her dad better be nice to her."

Tess made a face, and Elizabeth turned to him.

"So you do like her!" Elizabeth's face lit up with joy. "Thinking about her, are we? Damsel in distress?" She batted her big brown eyes playfully.

"No, it's just...well, we're rescuing her, right? We're all thinking about her," Mikey said defensively. "I just hope she's OK."

"Oh, dear, I just hope she's OK," Elizabeth said in a funny voice, mocking him.

Mikey looked humiliated.

"No, seriously!" Elizabeth said. "I think it's so cool you like her. Even though Tess disagrees."

"Is it getting warm in here?" Susie asked. She fanned her face with her hand.

"Oh, sorry," Tess said. "My fault." She felt even angrier when she realized her fire power had gotten out of control, just when she thought she had a handle on it.

"Maybe you should take the pendant off," Mikey said and gave his sister a concerned look. "Just in case you get angry and cause a fire."

"Maybe you should stop talking about my best friend!" Tess's cheeks flushed.

"Whoa!" Elizabeth yelled.

Tess thought she was trying to interrupt her argument with her brother. But the next moment, Susie was also yelling.

"Oh my gosh!" Susie shouted as she tried to turn the wheel.

A big rock column was in front of them, and they were headed straight for it.

The sub veered just a little bit to the left, but they were still on a collision path with the rock column.

"This thing won't turn!" Susie pulled at the wheel.

The rock column towered over them. It was close enough that they could see little fish darting in and out of the cracks.

"Hey!" Elizabeth cried out. "I can feel it!"

"Feel it?" Susie asked. "What do you mean?"

Just before they were about to hit it, the rock column broke apart. Great chunks floated off. A big chunk headed their way, and thunked the window. The whole submarine rattled. Tess held her breath, wondering if the window would crack.

The submarine stopped rattling. Their journey was smooth again, and the water was clear and rock-free in front of them.

Tess let her breath out and sagged in the chair.

"I get it!" Elizabeth said, excited. "I get it now!"

"Get what?" Susie was staring out the window, and tried to straighten their course to get back on target. Her usually tan cheeks were flushed red. It gave Tess a queasy feeling to realize even Susie had been nervous.

"I figured out my power!" Elizabeth said.

"You did that?" Susie asked. "I mean, break apart the rocks? Seriously?"

"Yeah, I think so," Elizabeth said. "It was actually a column of separate rocks. I just encouraged the pieces to be free."

Free, Tess thought. She recognized the feeling.

"I know what you mean," Tess said. "When I say flicker, I feel like I'm releasing something that wants to be free."

The sub manual caught on fire.

"Take a breath, Fire," Susie said and blew out a small flame. "Tess? No more fire words."

Elizabeth was so happy to finally find her magic.

"I didn't think my power would be cool at all," Elizabeth said. "But breaking apart rocks is cool."

"It rocks," Susie said and they all burst out laughing.

"So, we have Air-o, Fire-o, and...Rock-o?" Susie joked. "Rocky? Rock Girl?"

"I wish I had a power," Mikey said.

"Maybe you have the power of love," Elizabeth said and blinked her eyes at him.

Mikey turned red.

"Stop teasing him." Susie swatted Elizabeth.

"Please stop bringing up the love thing," Tess said and rolled her eyes.

"Rock on," Elizabeth said and held up her hand, making a peace symbol.

Chapter Twenty-nine

The pizza place was small and the staff friendly. Soothing ukulele music played in the background. Amelia and Akoni were silent as they focused on eating their slices. The pizza was exceptionally cheesy, and slid down onto their fingers. Amelia had to keep rescuing cheese strands from falling off, piling them back onto the slice.

Once Amelia finished navigating the cheese and was full of the hot, satisfying pizza, she yawned. She felt sleepy and content.

"I know it's wrong," Amelia said to Akoni. "But all I want to do is take a taxi to my mom's hotel and sleep."

"Why is it wrong?" Akoni asked. "I am going to my mom's house to do the same thing. After eating some of my grandma's food, of course." He winked.

"I can't believe you can eat again after this pizza feast. You eat more than Susie!" Amelia said and laughed.

"Who's Susie? Is she one of the friends you tried to call?" Akoni asked.

"Yeah, she's a volleyball star," Amelia said. "She's always practicing, which means she's always hungry."

Akoni sat back in his chair, taking big sips of soda. He looked more relaxed than she'd ever seen him. His black hair was messy and he wore a constant, slight smile.

"She sounds driven. Who are your other friends?" Akoni asked. "You said a few of your friends would be worried, so you would try to call them." He drained his Coke with a slurping noise.

"Well, there's Elizabeth. She loves to read, and is really intelligent in a bookish kind of way," Amelia said. "She isn't smart in the puzzle way, not like me. She loves Jane Austen."

"So she's the one who is most likely to find you with her clever mind?" Akoni asked. "I mean, if you were still lost."

Amelia nodded, though she hoped Elizabeth's skills hadn't led her all the way to Hawaii—or to the terrible island she had just escaped from. It seemed unlikely her friends would actually fly all the way here. Their parents would never let them come.

Amelia touched her amulet necklace. Then again, their friendship was strong. Maybe no one could have stopped them coming.

"I don't know who would be best at finding me," Amelia said. "Susie acts quickly, and Elizabeth reads and thinks things through. Together they would have a good chance of finding me," Amelia said. "And then there's Tess, my other best friend."

"Tell me more about Tess," Akoni said. "It's nice to think about something other than being so angry with your dad. I still sort of feel like I have a tail."

"You don't have a tail!" Amelia said and laughed.

Akoni grinned, but he paled a bit as well.

"Well, Tess and I have always had…I don't know, this ability to understand each other, I guess," Amelia said. "I just look in her eyes and I know what she's feeling. She can do the same for me."

"Wow. Cool to have a friend like that," Akoni said.

Amelia took a sip of her endless glass of refilled water, and felt a twinge of guilt in her heart.

"Yeah, but the last time I saw her, I couldn't really talk to her," Amelia said. "I was hiding something from her, and I think she noticed."

"Was it about your dad?" Akoni said. "Did you know he was stalking you?"

"No, it was…oh, it's embarrassing," Amelia said. She felt the warmth of a deep blush fill her cheeks.

"What was it?" Akoni said. "Now I gotta know!"

"Her brother sort of…asked me out," Amelia said.

"Oh, no. He broke the sister code," Akoni said.

"The sister code?" Amelia asked.

"Yeah. You don't ask out your friends' sisters," Akoni said. "Like me, I think my friend's sister Liana is hot. Well, everyone thinks that. But I would never ask her out without checking with Joe first. And if I asked my friend Joe if I could go out with his sister, I'd end up with a black eye."

"I'm glad you understand," Amelia said. "I thought it was weird when he asked me out. I never thought of him that way. And then I thought Tess would be angry with me when he gave me that Valentine."

"Why would she be angry with you?" Akoni asked.

"Well, I don't know, like maybe it was my fault he asked me? I just felt guilty and weird about it," Amelia said. She gazed out the window at the sunny, blue sky. She hoped Tess had forgiven her for being weird with her, and also for rejecting Tess' invitations to dinner.

What she wouldn't give to have a heart-to-heart with Tess right now.

Akoni was studying her. "I don't think it was your fault. You're pretty," he said. "Guys are simple about stuff like that." He tried to sip his empty Coke.

A waiter brought him a refill, and he drank it gratefully.

Amelia wondered where her friends all were now. They were all at school, she assumed, though she wasn't even sure what day it was.

"What day is it?" she asked Akoni.

"Monday," Akoni said. "Monday afternoon."

Amelia felt surprised. It felt like at least a week had passed. But she'd only been on that terrible island since Friday evening. She suddenly realized what she had missed.

"The math battle," Amelia said and moaned. "I missed it, I can't believe it."

"Sorry," Akoni said.

"Our team practiced so hard," Amelia said. "I hope they got a good alternate."

Akoni looked down at his hands.

"Listen," he said. "If I knew you—if I knew your dad would be so mean to you—I would never have been a part of bringing you to that island. Why don't you hate me?"

Amelia searched herself for angry feelings toward Akoni. But she couldn't find those feelings. In fact, she felt like he was her friend.

Should she feel angry?

Her dad probably tricked him into helping kidnap her. After all, Akoni was turned into a lizard for awhile. That was pretty bad punishment.

"Look, you made up for it," Amelia said. "I'm not angry at you. You helped me escape."

Akoni nodded, though he still looked down.

"I still feel really bad," he said

"Just, don't do anything like that again," Amelia said and patted his arm. "OK?"

He looked up and met her eyes. Then he smiled.

"Deal," he said. "Akoni takes the right path from now on."

They shook on it.

Akoni smiled, his face relaxing. But his eyes still looked guilty.

"I can see why your friend's brother likes you," he said. "Smart, pretty and kind."

"Is that what your girlfriend is like?" Amelia asked.

"Well, from that list...she's pretty, and I'll add...um, she's hot," Akoni said, his tanned face turning red again. "She likes to yell at me, though." He took a long sip of his Coke, his face thoughtful.

"That's because you make me so mad!" said a loud, angry, female voice.

Amelia and Akoni turned to see a young Hawaiian woman with bright red lipstick, hot pink tank top, and stilettos glaring at them through her heavy mascara.

"Honey!" Akoni said and coughed up his Coke. "Amelia, this is my girlfriend Malie. I was just talking about you, how beautiful you are!"

"Don't honey me!" the woman yelled. "I heard you call that girl pretty!"

"No, of course I didn't," Akoni said and stood up. "Well, yes, but it's not that I think she's pretty. It's just theoretical."

"Who is she?" Malie said angrily.

"No one!" Akoni said. "I mean, not no one—she's just a friend. I'm just helping her out. She got mixed up with my boss. That's all, I swear."

Amelia wanted to be anywhere but at the table. She wished she could excuse herself and disappear into the bathroom. But that would mean walking right by Malie.

"My brother called to say his best friend saw you talking with this blondie," Malie said. "When you told me you weren't even in Oahu today!"

"I know, I didn't plan to be here," Akoni said, "it just happened. And then…and then, um…"

"That's it!" Malie said. "You disrespect me. I'm leaving." She walked out, stamping her stiletto heels as she left.

Amelia breathed a sigh of relief.

"Wow, she seemed angry," Amelia said.

Akoni sat down heavily at the table and held his head in his hands for awhile. When he looked up, his eyes were narrow.

"She makes me crazy," he said. "But I can make it up to her. She's all bark, you know. She won't really leave me."

Amelia stayed quiet. She really didn't want to get involved in girlfriend-boyfriend stuff. They seemed so messy and weird.

"It's just that I can't tell her anything," Akoni said. "She doesn't know about magic, or the kidnapping, or the tail." He shivered at the thought.

Amelia realized that Akoni needed some encouraging words from a friend. She suddenly missed Tess with a painful twist of her heart. Tess would know what to say to Akoni to make him feel better. Amelia was terrible at these situations, but Tess always helped.

"It's going to be OK," Amelia said. "If she leaves, you'll find someone better."

"Yeah," Akoni said, sounding tired. "Hey, let's go. I can give you a ride to the airport hotel on my motor bike. Then I'll find Malie and make it all up to her."

As Akoni went to pay the bill, she stepped outside and tried her friends' phones again. Voicemail picked up on all of them. She left a message for each of them, missing them more than ever.

"I'm OK, I'm on Oahu," Amelia recorded on voicemail. "I'm going to go to my mom's hotel near the airport."

When she hung up after the third voicemail, the air sounded eerily quiet. It was strange that not one of her friends picked up. She knew it didn't necessarily mean they were in trouble. But her mood darkened with worry, nonetheless.

Chapter Thirty

Tess gazed out the little, circular window by her seat, feeling relaxed. They had been going for two hours in the sub, and it had actually been a nice ride.

Yellow fish with pointed mouths, green sea turtles, jellyfish, and lots of other sea life swam by. It was a little like being at the movies.

The ocean floor had dropped off pretty deep once they got into their journey. They decided to stay just above the floor so Elizabeth could practice her rock power.

Mikey napped peacefully in the stillness.

Tess took photos with her phone in case Damian from the Brightcubes would be interested in any of them.

While Tess and Mikey were having a relaxing trip, Susie and Elizabeth remained alert the whole time, as pilot and co-pilot. Their eyes were fixed on the scene through the front window.

There hadn't been any more near-disasters, though that was due to Elizabeth sliding rocks out of the way for the whole journey.

"That wasn't anywhere near the sub," Susie said, as a distant rock slid out of view.

"I know, but it's fun to move them," Elizabeth said. "And I think I'm getting better at it."

The radar showed they were getting very close to the island now. The water had been clear for most of their journey, but now it turned dark and murky. Tess could hardly see the bottom of the ocean, much less anything in front of the sub. An octopus appeared from the gloom, floating eerily close to the front window. It seemed to look at them. Elizabeth pressed back in her seat.

"I'm not sure about this place," Elizabeth said. "I'm beginning to see why they call it The Place That People Don't Go."

"Oh, please," Susie said. "It's just dark water. Doesn't mean anything."

"It is awfully dark, though," Elizabeth said.

The big mass of land on the radar got bigger and bigger. A tiny dot on the screen was getting closer and closer to it on the screen.

"We're the little dot," Susie explained to Tess. "We're getting pretty close to the island. Should we stop? I mean, before we hit it."

"Actually, we're supposed to rise to the surface," Elizabeth said. "That's what submarines do, right?"

"Oh, yeah," Susie said. "We get out at the surface."

"The manual says you must first pressurize the cabin," Elizabeth said. "To do that, you follow these steps…"

Elizabeth read the manual out loud, but Susie lept ahead to action.

"This button says lift," Susie said. "Must be it."

She pushed the button.

The submarine lurched as soon as Susie pressed it. Tess' stomach felt like it was bottoming out as the dark water churned around them.

"Ugh," Tess said. "I feel sick."

Mikey woke up from his nap just in time to grab one of the sick bags.

"You were supposed to pressurize the sub before pressing that!" Elizabeth said.

"It worked, right?" Susie said and shrugged.

The front window was now half above water and half under water. Huge waves slammed into the sub.

Everyone was awake and alert now, including Mikey, who was feeling better with an empty stomach.

In between slams of waves, Tess saw the island was close. She remembered that the boy said the spell only hid the island from a distance.

It didn't look like a nice place to visit. Palm trees swayed violently in what looked like a strong wind. A rocky mountain covered with coconut palms loomed close to shore. The sky was dark with storm clouds.

"We'll never be able to swim through those huge waves," Elizabeth said.

"At least we can see the island now," Susie pointed out.

"So, how do we get there?" Mikey asked, rubbing his

sleepy eyes. "Elizabeth is right. Not even a strong swimmer could make it through those dangerous waves."

The group pondered the distance between the sub and the island in silence.

"I can jump it," Susie suggested.

"Forget it!" Elizabeth said.

"Why?" Susie said. "I'll just launch off the sub, and jump as far as I can." She started taking off her sneakers in preparation.

"What if you land in the water?" Elizabeth said.

"That's why I'm taking my shoes off," Susie said. "I might land in the water, but at least I'll clear the big waves."

"OK, but how do we get on the island?" Mikey asked.

Susie shrugged. "Don't know. But at least one of us will be on the island," she said. "Maybe once I'm there, I'll see a way to bring you over."

Elizabeth drummed her fingers on the console, thinking. Then her face lit up.

"I have an idea!" Elizabeth said. "Susie, put those sneakers back on."

"Why?" Susie asked.

"Rocks! They're all around us, scattered on the ocean floor," Elizabeth said. "I can't see them, but I can feel them. I'm going to make us a platform to walk across."

"Is there something I should know?" Mikey asked. "What happened while I was asleep?"

"I got good at moving rocks," Elizabeth said and winked at him.

Mikey looked impressed.

"Let's see…" Elizabeth closed her eyes and concentrated. Deep lines showed on her forehead.

Susie got out of the pilot's chair and paced the sub, in what little room there was to pace.

Tess watched, amazed, as rocks came up to the surface of the ocean.

"Awesome," Mikey said, his eyes wide as he stared out the window.

After a few minutes, Elizabeth opened her eyes and took deep breaths. A bridge of rocks connected the sub to land.

"Are the rocks just floating there?" Tess asked.

"No, they aren't floating," Elizabeth said. "There were enough rocks to build columns that connect it to the ocean floor."

"Wow," Tess and Mikey both said.

Susie clapped Elizabeth on the shoulder, her mouth open in amazement.

"Woo! That's hard work," Elizabeth said, then grabbed herself a well-deserved chocolate bar.

The others joined in. They had a good stash of chocolate bars, so everyone had some. Chocolate seemed like a good way to prepare themselves for whatever they might find on the island.

Mikey climbed up the stairs leading to the door at the top of the sub. He opened the hatch door, looked outside, and motioned to the rest of them to follow.

Susie and Elizabeth climbed carefully up to the top. Tess was the last one up the narrow, metal stairs.

Huge waves crashed into the sub, rocking them side to side, and spraying foam and mist everywhere.

The exterior of the sub was slippery. Susie was OK standing on it, but Tess, Elizabeth and Mikey didn't have her athletic balance, so ended up crawling. They were all soaked within minutes, shoes and all.

"Oh, no. Big one coming!" Susie cried out.

A gigantic wave was coming their way.

Tess and Elizabeth clung to the wheel of the door hatch, and to each other.

Susie jumped up high, using her air power.

When the wave hit, Tess, Mikey and Elizabeth all got slammed with the full force of the blast.

When the wave cleared, Susie landed lightly back on the sub–completely dry.

"You girls OK?" Susie asked.

"Yes," Elizabeth said. "Soaked, but OK."

Tess was still catching her breath. The wave blast had knocked the air out of her, and she gasped. When she looked around for her brother, her stomach turned over with fear when she suddenly realized that he was no longer on the sub.

"Mikey!" Tess shouted. "Where are you?" Her heart raced. Her first thought was the mermaid dream, and how a shark came to bite them. She hoped there were no sharks here.

"I see him!" Elizabeth cried.

Mikey's red hair was plastered to his face as he doggie-paddled toward the sub, bobbing up and down in the waves. He fought to stay near the sub, but he was drifting away.

"Mikey, swim!" Tess shouted.

An orange lifesaver was attached to the outside of the sub. Tess and Susie struggled to get it off.

Finally, the lifesaver came free.

Tess threw it as far as she could. It landed near Mikey. He grabbed it, then all three girls dragged him back to the sub by pulling in the rope.

Tess' arms burned with the effort.

When she and Susie hauled him out of the water, Tess gave him a big hug.

"I was so scared!" Tess said.

"You were scared? I thought that was it for me," Mikey said, terribly out of breath. "The current is really strong."

Tess let him go, and Elizabeth and Susie hugged him in turn. Then Tess threw her arms around him again.

"I thought you were mad at me," Mikey said and tousled Tess' wet curls. He hadn't done that since she was a kid.

"That doesn't matter anymore," Tess said. "I'm just glad you're OK."

"Not for long," Susie said. "Shark!"

They all started screaming as the black fin came straight for the sub.

"We better leave. Now," Susie said. She half jumped, half flew onto the rock bridge. Then she turned and helped the others get from the sub to the rock.

Tess was last. She jumped, and tried not to notice the shark fin in the water, circling between the sub and the rock bridge. Elizabeth caught her, and they ran across the bridge together.

When they came onto the beach, they fell to the sand, tired and crying.

"I thought we'd be eaten!" Tess said.

"I thought I'd drown and then be eaten," Mikey said.

Susie simple lay on her back on the sand, breathing heavily.

"Focus, people!" Elizabeth said. "Look."

She pointed toward the green foliage and rocky mountain wall.

"What is that?" Tess said, breathing heavily, her heart still pounding. "Some kind of rock statue?"

Elizabeth studied it. "Well, it's not normal rock. That much I can tell. That rock formation feels…strange."

Chills of horror raced through Tess when the rock statue she was looking at began to move.

The rocks were alive.

Two blazing, red eyes and a huge jaw opened in what looked like a T-Rex made of stone.

The monster let out a terrible roar. A screech so loud that they had to cover their ears.

"Break it apart, Liz!" Susie said. "Make it go away!"

The rock monster took a giant step toward them, and they felt the beach tremble.

"I can't!" Elizabeth said. "I don't think it's just made of rock. There's something else in there. Something…bad."

Tess felt something coming from the rock monster. It felt to her like a great, burning flame. She saw an orange glow deep in its chest.

"It's also made of fire!" Tess said.

"Do something!" Susie yelled. "It's coming closer!"

Tess shook her head. "I only know how to start fires, not stop them," she said. "I think the only thing we can do is… run!"

The rock monster opened its huge mouth, showing off rows of jagged, pearl-white teeth. It roared again, and took a few more steps toward them.

"Go, run!" Mikey shouted. "There!"

Everyone ran as quickly as they could into the coconut palms.

The rock dragon followed. Heavy, horrible steps chased after them, shaking the ground.

"We've got rock power, fire power, and air power!" Susie yelled as they ran. "What else do we need to defeat that thing?"

Tess' eyes filled with tears as she thought of Amelia, and her amulet.

"Water," Tess said. "We need to douse that fiery monster and put its flame out. We came to rescue Amelia. But she has the Water amulet. Maybe we need her to rescue us!"

Chapter Thirty-one

Amelia climbed onto the motorcycle, feeling a little nervous. She'd never been on a motorcycle before. Normally, she didn't like going fast. She didn't like fast cars or roller coasters. She recited prime numbers under her breath to calm her pattering heart.

The massive helmet Akoni gave her to wear was heavy. When she put it on, it was hot inside and limited what she could see. She took it off and begged Akoni to let her ride without it.

He refused to start the engine until she put the helmet back on.

"Fine," Amelia said. She pulled it back on, and her whole face was already getting sweaty.

She also wasn't prepared for the rumble of the engine—so loud! Her breath came quick when Akoni took off. The vibrations of the motorcycle ran through her as they headed down the road.

As they zoomed south, trees flashed past. She tightened her hold on Akoni's waist.

At first she was embarrassed about holding him for balance, but after getting face-blasted with wind for several miles, she found herself even going so far as to rest her head on his back. He was much taller and broader than she was, and he made a great windshield.

Amelia's whole body rumbled with the roar of the powerful engine, and it was scary to open her eyes. When she did look at the road, it flashed by so quickly and so close that her heart raced along with it.

The motorcycle's engine changed sound. It made a lower noise as they pulled off the road.

Akoni parked on a dirt mound near an overlook to the ocean. He helped Amelia off the bike. Her legs shook, and it took a moment to feel like she was on solid ground again. There was also excitement running through her—a thrill.

"First time on a bike?" Akoni asked.

Amelia nodded, too breathless to talk. She pulled off the helmet and ran her fingers through her now sweaty hair.

"Love it or hate it?" Akoni asked.

She thought about the sting of the wind, the blur of everything rushing past, and the sensation of gliding on the road. It felt like electricity was zipping through her body.

"Love it," she said.

"Yes!" Akoni said. They high-fived.

Standing at the overlook, Amelia gazed out at the ocean. A small island sat straight ahead, across the water. It curved up toward a rise in the center of the island, then smoothly curved back down the other side.

For one panicked moment, she wondered if it could be the island they escaped from—The Place Where People Do Not Go—but it was too close. And there were no low clouds above it. The weather looked clear there, just like in Oahu.

"What's that island?" Amelia asked.

"It's why I took you here. And it's a good place to stop for awhile and rest," Akoni said. "It's Half Moon Island."

"I can see why they named it that," Amelia said, noting the perfect half-moon shape rising up out of the ocean.

"It's named after a legend." Akoni's face suddenly grew serious. His voice became lower.

"My grandmother told me this story many times. She made me repeat it back to her when I was a kid. If I recited it, she would give me dessert," Akoni said. "If not, she would yell. So, I know it well." He smiled at her.

"A long time ago, a beautiful moon goddess, Mahealani, and the ocean goddess Alanawaiwai were friends," Akoni said, reciting the story his grandmother had told him since he was a child.

"Alanawaiwai!" Amelia said. "Is that the goddess in the cave?"

"I think so," he said and nodded. "Mahealani would play on the waves, skipping over them, while Alanawaiwai rode dolphins around her. Alanawaiwai's hair and skin was green. She wove some of her green hair into Mahealani's white hair, as a braid.

"One night, Mahealani came to play in the ocean's darkest water. Alanawaiwai came up from the depths of the ocean to play with her, with cockleshell bracelets on."

Amelia listened, fascinated.

"Kanuike, an ocean god from Antarctic waters, approached them. He wanted Alanawaiwai as his wife, and her father had agreed to the match."

"Did she love him?" Amelia asked.

"No, she didn't. And she said so. 'I don't want to go,' she said in her beautiful voice, which was said to be like the soft sound of calm, ocean waves upon the sandy shore."

"That's beautiful," Amelia said.

Akoni shrugged. "Those are my grandmother's words, not mine," he said. "Anyway…"

Akoni continued the story.

"Alanawaiwai said she didn't like the cold, and didn't want to go to Antarctica. Kanuike wasn't used to being denied. He got angry and slammed a fist into the water. A great waterspout rose up and traveled away. He had a temper.

"'You will come with me,' he said. 'It is decided.'

"'I will not,' Alanawaiwai said and crossed her arms. The dolphins watched along with Mahealani. They were getting nervous.

"'I'll call the sharks,' Kanuike said. The dolphins crowded closer to Alanawaiwai, calling in alarm. But Alanawaiwai was not afraid.

"'The sharks around here know me well,' Alanawaiwai said. 'Many creatures of the ocean in this area are my friends. They won't hurt me.'

"'The sharks will attack your dolphin friends,' Kanuike said. 'If I tell them to.'

"'Why do you want me for a wife, anyway? Alanawaiwai said. 'I hate the cold, so I'll be miserable, which will make you miserable. And I argue. A lot.' She put on her worst face.

"Kanuike stared. His eyes went from angry to thoughtful, and then lit up as he'd just had a great idea.

"'You are right,' Kanuike said. 'I don't want you for a wife.' The two goddesses and the dolphins all felt relieved.

"'I will take the quiet one for my wife,' he said. Before they knew what was happening, Kanuike captured Mahealani in a giant net. If the moon was up, Mahealani would have the power to break the net. But it hadn't risen yet, and she just wasn't strong enough. Mahealani was weaker when the moon was not in the sky.

"'I'll go with you!' Alanawaiwai said. 'Take me instead!' She knew her friend lived in the sky. Her friend would hate the Antarctic waters even more than Alanawaiwai, who was at least an ocean goddess.

"'No, you were right about the arguing thing,' Kanuike said. 'I wouldn't want a wife like that.'

"Oh my gosh," Amelia said and put a hand to her heart. She felt upset about poor Mahealani being taken for a wife, when she just wanted to be free to live her life.

"He started swimming south, carrying the net with struggling Mahealani inside. She looked out at Alanawaiwai through the mesh with big eyes. Alanawaiwai swam as fast as she could, chasing after them. They swam for miles and miles. The water grew colder.

"Finally, it was time for the moon to rise. Just as a curve of white light appeared on the horizon, Alanawaiwai cut the net with the sharp edges of her cockleshell bracelets. Mahealani slipped out and stood on the water.

"Kanuike noticed the net was much lighter, and turned. He was dazzled by Mahealani's beauty. As the moon rose, it sent a glow through her pale skin and white hair, with Alanawaiwai's green hair braided through it. Mahealani glowed brighter than the moon.

"While Kanuike was stunned, Mahealani took Alanawaiwai's arm and danced as fast as she could over the waves back to our Hawaiian waters, back northwards. Alanawaiwai begged her friend to let go, and rise back up into the sky.

"'Go into the sky!' Alanawaiwai said. 'He can't follow you there.'

"But Mahealani refused to leave her friend.

"'He swims faster than you,' Mahealani said. 'He's stronger than you. We need to get you back to your waters, so your friends and family can protect you.'

"Even together, Mahealani and Alanawaiwai were too slow. Kanuike reached them, and created a whirlpool around them. They couldn't swim out of it. They were trapped.

"He called the sharks. Alanawaiwai didn't know the sharks in this part of the ocean.

"She called the dolphins. They were strangers to her, but she quickly explained what was happening, and they agreed to help.

"Kanuike grabbed Mahealani's shining hair. One of the dolphins swam under his arm and knocked it out of the way. A shark lunged at the dolphin.

"Soon a great battle began between the dolphins, the sharks, and Kanuike. Kanuike used two sharks to attack a swordfish who had come to help out the dolphins. Alanawaiwai and Mahealani tried to keep out of the way.

"Mahealani's mother had been looking for her daughter from the moon. Since Mahealani wasn't playing in the usual places she played in the ocean, it took awhile to find her. But Mahealani's mother found her now.

"The moonlit goddess streaked down from the sky and took both Mahealani and Alanawaiwai by the arms. She pulled them into the sky, and dropped Alanawaiwai in safe water outside the whirlpool.

"'Dive!' Mahealani yelled to Alanawaiwai. Her mother streaked into the sky with Mahealani.

"Mahealani was safe, back on the moon. But Alanawaiwai was halfway to the ocean floor when a great roar shook the water. Minutes later, something curled around her ankle and stopped her swimming.

"It was Kanuike.

"'Your friend got away,' Kanuike said and grabbed her. 'She has gone into the sky where I cannot go. But you will be punished. You'll never see the ocean again!'

"He banished her into a cave. A dark cave where she could not see the ocean, or the moon. No one knew where she went, and no one could find her. She could hear the ocean, and smell it, but she could not return to it. She could not escape.

"Kanuike layered all his anger, hate and frustration into the cave to trap her. Over the years, Alanawaiwai became thinner and thinner. She lived in the walls. When she forgot her name, she became truly trapped. Without her name, she could no longer take shape as a mermaid.

"Over the years, Kanuike's anger, hate and frustration became the Dark."

Akoni stopped talking and gazed out at the ocean. Amelia wiped tears from her eyes.

"That's beautiful," Amelia said. "And so sad."

Akoni nodded, his head bowed with sadness.

"My grandma says we keep this story alive because we have hope. Mahealani had hope, too." Akoni pointed at the island. "Half Moon Island is where Mahealani comes every night to look for her friend."

"We have to go back! We have to at least remind Alanawaiwai of her name," Amelia said. "We have to try."

Akoni looked at her. "I don't think I am brave enough," he said. "I can't go through the lizard thing again."

"Why did you take me here, then?" Amelia said and pointed to Half Moon Island. "Why did you tell me the story?"

Akoni shrugged. "I guess I hoped maybe you'd free the goddess one day…somehow."

"Akoni, I can't do it alone," Amelia said. "You have to come with me."

He sighed deeply.

"Let's go talk to my grandmother, Tutu," he said. "She will tell me what to do."

Amelia's heart was heavy. The idea of going back to the island filled her with fear. But the idea of leaving the goddess trapped in that terrible cave was worse.

"Tutu's house isn't far from here," Akoni said. "And at least we'll get some good food there."

Amelia climbed back onto the motorcycle. This time, even the motorcycle ride didn't lift her spirits. All she could think about was the Dark, and how creepy it was. Tears sprang to her eyes when she thought how sad Alanawaiwai must be after all those years trapped in the cave. And how awful it would be to go back to that horrible island.

Chapter Thirty-two

The monster made of rock and fire stood at the edge of the beach. The hostile creature swiveled its massive head toward Tess and Susie, who were by the coconut trees. Tess felt her heart stab with fear as the monster stared at her with its burning eyes.

When the creature roared at them, the horrid sound sent shudders through Tess' bones.

Tess looked frantically at the small cave where Mikey and Elizabeth were hiding. She prayed that Elizabeth would figure out how to use her rock power to stop the monster.

She and Susie both held coconuts, hoping they could be used as weapons.

When the monster took a big step toward Tess, she threw her coconut at it, using her fire power to light it on fire.

"Flicker!" Tess shouted, as the coconut sailed through the air. The burning coconut bounced off the rock monster's arm.

The rock monster didn't even seem to notice.

Susie leapt higher than the trees, using her air power to land on the top of the tallest palm tree. She started to spike coconuts down onto the rock monster's head.

That, the rock monster noticed.

"Spike!" Susie yelled, and sent another coconut down on its head. Tess lit it on fire on the way down, just in case it helped.

The rock monster growled. It raised its massive, clawed hand up to Susie, reaching out to grab her.

Susie doubled up on her coconut attack.

"You're making it angry!" Tess yelled up to her.

"It's already angry!" Susie yelled back. "If I'm going to die in battle, I'm going down playing some V-Ball!"

This fiery coconut hit the rock monster full on the tooth. Tess winced at the sharp sound it made, like rock against rock. One of its rock teeth broke off, and fell onto the ground. Just that piece alone must've weighed ten pounds.

"Score!" Susie said, punching the air with her fist. "Actually, I guess with coconuts, it's called C-Ball!"

"Great, Susie!" Tess said. "Now that thing is really ticked!"

With the rock monster focusing on Susie, Tess managed to sneak farther away from the menace.

"Any time now, Elizabeth!" Tess made sure to shout in the direction of Elizabeth's hiding place.

"I'm trying!" Elizabeth shouted back. "But the rocks in the monster won't move like the ones on the ocean floor did. His rocks seem to like where they are. I don't think I can move them."

Tess couldn't see Elizabeth, but her voice was loud

and clear. She was about to run to the cave to join her and Mikey, but she couldn't leave her friend behind to battle the rock monster alone.

Susie was in real danger.

The rock monster was at the base of Susie's coconut palm. It had two giant front paws on the tree, and was shaking it.

"Whoa!" Susie yelled. She hugged the branches at the top tightly. "I can't hold on! He's too strong!"

The rock monster shook harder. Susie's foot slipped, and then one hand lost its grip on the tree.

Susie was now hanging by only one arm.

"Do something!" she yelled.

The rock monster lifted its open jaw up as high as he could, to catch her in it. Its jaw was only a few feet away from Susie's dangling body. She would be eaten if she fell.

"Jump! Do the Air-o thing!" Elizabeth shouted, as she came running out of the cave.

"There's nothing to jump off of!" Susie said. "I can't launch off anything!"

Elizabeth waved her hands and yelled at the monster. She tried jumping up and down, to distract it, but the monster didn't turn toward Elizabeth. It seemed intent on shaking Susie out of the tree.

Mikey joined Elizabeth, and they both jumped up and down, waving their arms and yelling. But the rock creature remained with its jaw open under Susie.

Tess saw movement in the bushes just behind Elizabeth and Mikey. She squinted to make out the figure.

A girl roughly Tess' height stood among the green foliage. She couldn't see the girl's face, since she was standing in the shadows.

Friend or enemy? Tess wondered.

Another island monster?

Or someone who could help them?

Tess' eyes locked on the girl in the shadows. The girl waved her hands and spoke strange words.

A magic spell.

Water streamed down from the coconut palm and covered the rock monster. The water entered its open mouth, and steam rose into the sky.

The monster made a horrible screeching noise. It ran off into the trees, with smoke rising from its head.

Tess felt her knees turn to jelly as waves of relief and exhaustion ran through her.

The steam made the branch that Susie hung onto slippery. Susie fell to the ground, and shouted with pain.

Elizabeth ran to her, and tried to help her up.

"Liz, I can't put weight on my left foot," Susie said. She moaned in pain, and had to lean heavily on Elizabeth's shoulder.

"A sprained ankle we can deal with," Elizabeth said. "Just be glad that rock monster is gone."

Susie tried to smile but it looked more like a grimace. Tess supported Susie's other side, balancing Elizabeth's efforts.

"Mikey!" Tess called out to her brother, but he didn't answer.

Mikey was still in shock. He stood and stared with his mouth hanging open. But he wasn't staring at any of them.

Tess looked in the direction of her brother's gaze.

The girl who had helped them walked out of the shadows. Though her face was dirty and her blond hair was greasy, it looked like…

"Amelia!" Tess said. Her heart hammered with joy as she ran to her friend.

Elizabeth and Susie both wanted to rush to Amelia. But Susie could hardly stand up, so Elizabeth had to hold onto her.

Tess ran to Amelia. She was about to hug her, but Amelia didn't open her arms. Tess stood in front of her, confused by the cold reaction. Amelia was sending signals that she didn't want to be hugged.

Was she still angry?

"Are you OK?" Tess asked, her voice tight with emotion.

"I'm fine," Amelia said." Everything's groovy."

"Groovy?" Tess asked. The only time she heard Amelia use that word was in the text she sent as code, when she needed help.

Was it code now?

Tess looked into Amelia's watery eyes. Her back immediately tensed up, like something was wrong. And it wasn't just the distance that she felt at the park, before Amelia disappeared. Now there was a worse feeling, and it gave Tess the shivers.

"Amelia!" Elizabeth yelled and waved her over. "Come over here, girl!" She opened her arms.

Amelia went to Elizabeth, but didn't hug her. Susie looked up, blinking tears away.

Tess felt a weight of concern in her heart. Susie almost never cried.

"We found you!" Susie said and sniffed.

"I found you," Amelia said back.

"You're a mess, Amelia." Elizabeth eyed her friend's limp hair, messy clothes, and dirty face.

"Are you OK?" Susie asked. She wiped her tears and dried her nose on her shirtsleeve.

"Fine," Amelia said. "I think."

Mikey was still rooted to the beach in the same spot. Only his head had turned to follow Amelia.

"How did you do that?" Tess asked Amelia. "I mean, drop all that water on the rock monster. That was you, right?"

"Oh, you know, my water power," Amelia said. The girls looked at each other, exchanging glances.

"So, I guess you realized the amulets give us powers?" Elizabeth said.

"Amulets?" Amelia said. She stared at them like she had never heard of their element necklaces.

Tess knew that something wasn't adding up, that something strange was going on with her friend.

Amelia was the one who was best at math and codes. Tess was in unfamiliar territory. If Amelia was speaking in code, Tess wasn't understanding.

Chapter Thirty-three

The clouds gathered over the island Kahi Kanaka Mai I Hele, and a light rain started to fall on the beach. Tess and her friends were unusually quiet. They stared at Amelia, their missing friend, unsure of what to say.

Amelia wore a vacant, surprised look that Tess had never seen on her friend's face before.

Tess was at least glad for the rain. It felt cool on her mosquito bites.

"OK," Susie said. "Back up. Amelia, your water power is from your necklace. The one you always wear?"

"Right. Sorry, I hit my head," Amelia explained. "I mean, my kidnapper hit my head. So maybe I don't seem quite right. Not my, you know…normal self."

"Our element necklaces gave us all magic power," Susie said. "Didus activated them when he dropped the stone into the well, and…" She stopped.

Amelia stared at her.

"Hmm," Susie said. "Well, I guess you don't know about Didus, since you were kidnapped, and weren't there. It's… too much to explain, I think."

Tess thought that Amelia must be getting over the shock of all the recent madness.

"Oh, the power is from the amulet," Amelia said.

"Gotcha. And you all—I mean, we—all have an amulet. So what kind of magic power do you all have?"

"I have air power, so I can jump," Susie said, then looked down at her injured foot. "Right now, I don't know."

Susie's left ankle was red and swollen.

"Let's put your hurt ankle in the water," Elizabeth said and helped Susie up. "The salt water will be good for it."

"I can light things on fire," Tess said, "and we found out that Elizabeth can control rocks with her mind. Though she couldn't break apart that monster...whatever that thing was."

"Rock dragon. It's a menace," Amelia said. "It would take strong magic to destroy it. That creature is extremely old—ancient. And very tough. But it hates getting water in its face."

"You've seen it before?" Tess asked. She felt surprised, though she wondered why. Tess had no idea where Amelia had been the last couple days. For all she knew, the rock dragon had been guarding her in some terrible prison.

Amelia nodded. "Yes, it nearly got me once before," she said.

Tess felt her heart clench. She had no idea what awful things Amelia had been through on this island. No wonder her friend seemed strange.

"My ankle does feel a lot better in the water," Susie said. "Good idea." Though she had to lean heavily on Elizabeth as they stood knee-deep in the waves.

"I think I can put some weight on it – OW!" Susie yelped, in obvious pain.

"Maybe you should just stay off it a little longer," Elizabeth said.

"I'll rest it once we find my mom," Susie said. "Amelia, did you see her?"

Amelia nodded, her face serious.

"Ms. Lang, your mom, came to the island," Amelia said.

"So you did see her?" Susie asked, over the sound of the waves. The water was now up to her waist, and the wind had also picked up.

"Where is my mom? Is she OK?" Susie asked, as she and Elizabeth slowly limped their way to shore.

"I don't know," Amelia said. "She disappeared. I think my dad is more powerful than her."

"Disappeared?" Susie yelled, her voice shrill with fright.

"Maybe we can find her if we look for her," Amelia said. "Here, on the island." She stood up and dusted sand off her jeans.

Tess's gaze flicked over the rock bridge. It looked strong and inviting. They could be in the sub, on their way home.

But they couldn't leave Susie's mom here, if there was a chance she was on this island.

Tess eyed Susie's swollen ankle and Amelia's pale, sickly face. She wondered if Susie and Amelia should rest in the sub while the rest of them searched for Susie's mom.

"Prime numbers," Tess said to Amelia. "Let's check if you have a concussion."

"Oh, yeah! The math thing," Amelia said. "Let's see. One, three, five, seven, nine...um...eleven?" Amelia shrugged. "Is eleven a prime number?"

Susie, Tess, Elizabeth and Mikey stared at each other. Nobody knew what to say.

"You're kidding, right?" Elizabeth said. "You know the primes solid well past one thousand. We've all heard you recite them a million times."

"Oh, my head does feel funny," Amelia said and sat down on the sand. "I'll just sit for a minute."

Tess ran to her in concern. Amelia's hair was dirty, and her T-shirt was soaked with sweat. Her pale face was now a little green in color.

Elizabeth eyed the rock bridge that lead to the sub. It was still standing, visible through the waves.

"Why don't we just go to the sub now, and go to Oahu?" Elizabeth said. "This island gives me the creeps. We can go to the hospital and get Susie's ankle and Amelia's concussion looked at. The police will help us find Susie's mom."

"Will the police help us, though?" Tess said. "With our crazy stories about magic?"

"We don't mention magic to the police," Elizabeth said. "We just say Susie's mom is missing. Deal?"

Tess felt a wave of relief at the plan. Not only would they get help, they'd get off the island immediately. With the frightening rock dragon, big waves, and sharks, this place gave her the shivers.

But Susie shook her head.

"I can't leave my mom here on this island alone," Susie said.

"Yeah, I don't feel good about leaving either," Amelia said. "I think we should look for Susie's mom."

"I agree with Elizabeth," Mikey said. "It's great that you both want to help Susie's mom, after all you've been through. But we're dealing with a powerful, scary man. We should get both of you off the island."

Mikey put a hand on Amelia's shoulder.

Amelia shrugged his hand off and took a step away. Mikey's face fell. Tess felt kind of bad for him, since Amelia was acting so distant.

Amelia even waved her hands around, as if a cloud of mosquitoes had descended, though it looked like she was trying to force Mikey away.

"What are you doing?" Tess asked.

"Huh? Oh, sorry. I just feel so gross that I don't want anyone touching me right now," Amelia said. She turned to Mikey, who looked distressed. "Sorry, man."

"Oh, no!" Elizabeth looked out to sea. "My rock bridge!"

Rocks fell off and were swallowed by the ocean as they watched. The bridge was falling apart.

"Wow," Susie said. "Good thing we weren't on the bridge when it fell."

Elizabeth made a sound of deep disappointment. She looked like she was concentrating hard on the water, then slumped and let out her breath.

"I'm trying to rebuild it, but I can't seem to feel the rocks anymore," Elizabeth said.

"Maybe you're just tired," Mikey said.

"What do we do now?" Susie said.

Tess watched Amelia closely. She swore Amelia was trying to hide a smile.

Something about Amelia was off, Tess could feel it. And it didn't seem to come down to just being exhausted, or possibly having a concussion. Amelia seemed like a different person.

"Let's go," Amelia said. "Before the rock dragon comes back. There's food at the house."

"What house?" Elizabeth said. "Your dad's?"

"You know my dad kidnapped me?" Amelia said. A sharp look came into her eyes, and she sat up straighter.

"We know about his magical abilities, too," Tess said. "Susie's mom is a…well, it sounds weird to say, but she's a sorceress."

"Yes," Amelia said. "Didn't you know that?"

"No," Tess said. "She hid that from us. All of us."

"Oh. Yeah, sorry," Amelia said. "I have trouble remembering what I knew before—my head. Anyway, she fought my dad with magic. But he was too powerful."

"Where is your dad?" Tess asked. "Aren't you afraid he'll come back?"

"No, he's not at the house," Amelia said. "He said he was going away for a few days."

Susie limped toward the group.

"We can't get off the island without the rock bridge," Susie said. "We don't have much choice. Amelia said there is food in the house, so maybe there's some ice for my ankle. Let's go there."

It gave Tess a terrible feeling in the pit of her stomach to stay on the island, and worse, to go to the kidnapper's house. But the others agreed, so Tess would follow.

Elizabeth and Tess hurried to either side of Susie, to help her walk.

"I'll show you the way," Amelia said and started to hike into the island.

The three girls made their slow way behind her. Elizabeth was out of breath quickly.

"This is why wheelchairs, crutches and stretchers were invented," Elizabeth mumbled.

"I don't need any of that!" Susie said.

"Maybe I do," Elizabeth said.

Susie laughed.

Mikey took over for Elizabeth. He and Tess helped Susie along.

"The Gileads to the rescue," Mikey said and nodded to his sister.

Tess tried to smile back. But she had butterflies in her stomach.

Why was Amelia acting so different?

Could they trust this Amelia? She was leading them to the kidnapper's house.

Tess shook those thoughts away. She followed Amelia's long, blond, and slightly greasy hair through the rain-drenched trees.

"Something's wrong," Elizabeth muttered aloud. "I've been getting chills ever since we set foot on this island."

"You and me both, Elizabeth," Tess said, as they followed Amelia.

Even Amelia's walk looked off.

Tess hoped she knew where she was going.

Chapter Thirty-four

After two hours, they were still hiking under the dark clouds. The rain had stopped, but this seemed to give rise to a worse terror—mosquitoes.

Tess and Mikey helped Susie hop along the dirt trail. Despite being free of burdens, Elizabeth and Amelia both panted and sweat heavily as they walked.

Elizabeth was out of shape and always found hikes difficult, so Tess didn't worry about her. But Amelia could usually hike pretty well. Tess wondered again what she had been through. It must have been pretty bad to wear her down like that.

"I'm so hungry," Susie moaned.

"We're almost there," Amelia said, between huge gasping breaths. "Very close."

Tess slapped her wrist, where an insect had just landed. She was covered with mosquito bites, and tried to avoid brushing against the plants and leaves they were trudging through. Every time her wrist or hand brushed a leaf, she came away with more bites. She picked up a stick and tried to push the leaves ahead of her out of the way. That made going ahead even slower, so she gave up the idea.

"I'm getting eaten!" Tess moaned. She showed Elizabeth her arm, which was red and puffy with bites.

"Ooh, that looks bad," Elizabeth said. "I think all the rain must've woken up all the mosquitoes."

"They do get worse in this warm, sticky weather," Amelia said, wheezing in between her words. "Especially after it rains, they're terrible."

They finally came to a little path that led to the house. Amelia gasped for breath and held her sides. She sat on a nearby rock to rest.

"I just need one last rest before the home stretch," Amelia said, completely winded.

Susie leaned on a tree to rest, and propped her foot up on a stone. Tess and Mikey stretched out their arms and shoulders. Tess felt lighter without Susie leaning on her, and stretched out her sore legs.

"I'm glad you're thin," Mikey said to Susie, who gave him a dirty look. She stuck her tongue out at him.

"Maybe you're just strong, Mikey," Elizabeth said. "She actually weighs a ton."

Susie picked up something that looked like a nut and threw it at her. It missed Elizabeth, who giggled.

"Let's go!" Amelia stood up. "I think I can make it now."

The last trudge was only fifteen minutes.

When they saw the little house, Tess wanted to cry with relief. Anything was better than the mosquito-filled hike. She could put ice on her bites.

"No more walking!" Elizabeth said happily. She actually kissed the door as soon as they arrived.

The door was unlocked.

"Hello!" Susie called, but no one answered.

They waited by the front door while Mikey checked out all the rooms, just in case. He came back a few minutes later and gave them a thumbs-up.

"All clear," Mikey told them.

Tess was hit with a sudden hesitancy to enter the sorcerer's house. Even though she wanted to rest in a mosquito-free place, her stomach turned with nerves.

"Wait," she said, as the group started to enter the house. "I don't feel good about this."

Amelia ignored her and walked tiredly into the house. Her body was slumped. She looked exhausted.

Susie followed her, hopping on one foot.

"We won't stay long," Mikey said. "We'll just eat something quick, then go look for Susie's mom."

Tess reluctantly followed the group inside. It was true, they didn't have much choice. They all needed to rest.

Susie and Amelia lay down on two sofas in the living room.

"Food," Susie moaned. "I need food! And ice."

"My gosh, look at all this food!" Elizabeth said from the kitchen. Elizabeth quickly got to work, preparing plates of food for everyone.

Tess found ice in the freezer and made an ice pack for Susie's ankle. She rubbed an ice cube over her mosquito bites, which cooled their fire.

Mikey said he'd walk around outside, to alert them if anyone was coming. Elizabeth made a sandwich for him, which he ate as he walked.

Elizabeth carried heaping plates of food to the living room. Hunks of cheese, bread, stir-fry over noodles, green soup and sliced pineapple. Everyone dug in gratefully.

Susie finished her first plate, burped loudly, then filled her plate again. The rest of the group ate almost as fast.

"I'm sorry about the rock bridge," Elizabeth said, as she chewed some pineapple, the only thing left on her plate. "I thought it was strong enough to hold up for the way back to the sub."

"What are you sorry about? It was amazing!" Susie said. "It was so cool how you thought of making a bridge with ocean rocks. We wouldn't have made it to the island without your rock-ability."

"Well, we wouldn't have gotten far without you pelting the rock dragon with your aerodynamic spikes," Elizabeth said. "That was awesome!"

"I'm bummed about my ankle, though," Susie said. "I wonder when I can play again?"

"Is it still swollen?" Tess moved the ice pack from Susie's ankle and winced at the sight. It was red and swollen. A purple bruise was forming.

"Ouch," Elizabeth said, noticing the bruised ankle.

"Amelia, how are you feeling?" Tess asked.

"OK. Headache," Amelia said. Her face was pale.

"Do you want some Advil or something?" Tess said. "I don't know what there is in the house, but I can look."

"No, nothing," Amelia said. "I'll be fine. Just need rest."

Everyone quieted down, allowing Amelia to rest and recover. She had been through more than any of them. None of them had ever seen her so tired, so weak.

"Wait!" Elizabeth said. "She can't sleep if she has a concussion. They say not to go to sleep."

"My cell phone won't work," Susie said. "Annoying."

"No signal on this island," Amelia said. Her voice was almost a whisper.

"Elizabeth is right," Tess said. "Amelia, you've got to sit up. You can't go to sleep with a concussion."

Anger flashed through Amelia's eyes.

Tess took a step back. She could feel a fiery heat building inside of her, a reaction to Amelia's hard look.

Amelia had never looked like that before.

What was wrong with her?

Amelia's face softened, and the anger in her eyes disappeared. She smiled at Tess.

"If I'm not allowed to sleep, can I take a shower? That'll make me feel better," Amelia said. The girls agreed, and Tess helped her to a sitting position.

"But I need a minute, before I stand," Amelia said and turned paler.

"I knew we should have gotten to the sub—somehow, some way," Elizabeth said, her normally calm voice sounding panicked. "Amelia needs a hospital."

"I told you, I'm fine," Amelia said. "Just let me rest for a moment. I'm sort of hot, all this hair."

Tess tied up Amelia's hair as she'd done a thousand times before, using a ponytail holder around her wrist. Then she noticed something funny. The string that usually lay around Amelia's neck was missing.

Had Amelia taken off her amulet?

But she never took it off.

"You're the best nurse we have, Tess," Susie said and Elizabeth nodded in agreement.

"Hey, Fire?" Susie said. "We never thanked you for setting fire to those coconut spikes."

"I'm not sure how much that helped," Tess said. "I mean, the rock dragon was made of fire!"

"It annoyed him, for sure," Susie said.

"Yeah, good going, Tess!" Elizabeth said. "I only wish my rock bridge could have been stronger. Maybe if I had fit the rocks together differently, or picked different rocks."

Amelia shook her head and mumbled something.

"What did you say, Amelia?" Tess prompted.

"The more basic the spell, the easier it is to undo it," Amelia said. "It wasn't a problem with the rocks. It was the spell."

All three girls stared at her.

"What do you mean?" Tess said. "How do you know?"

"Whatever can be done…can be undone. The power in the doing…matches the undoing." Amelia stared at them. "Don't you know those sayings?"

When everyone else looked at her with blank stares, Amelia put a hand to her head.

"Oh, I don't feel well. Sorry, maybe I'm talking crazy," Amelia said.

"Where did you hear all that about magic spells?" Tess asked. She stared closely at Amelia.

Something was definitely wrong.

Amelia didn't know the primes, yet she knew about spells. And she wasn't wearing her amulet.

"Oh, I read some books in the house," Amelia said. "And I know because of my water power."

Susie and Elizabeth looked confused. But Tess was starting to feel like she knew what was going on. Cold chills ran through her, and she hoped she was wrong about Amelia. She would ask some questions to find out.

"Your water power," Tess said. "Right, that's how you helped us defeat the rock dragon, right?"

"Helped? I am the one who defeated him," Amelia said, then looked up. "Oh, wait—what am I saying? I meant that I only helped, with my water power."

"There's only one thing wrong with that statement," Tess said.

"What?" Amelia said.

"You're not wearing your amulet," Tess said.

Chapter Thirty-five

Amelia sat on the sofa while Tess stood over her, looking down, arms crossed. She felt angry, and her cheeks flamed with heat.

"Wait, what?" Elizabeth said. "If Amelia didn't have her amulet on, how did she use water power to defeat the rock dragon?"

"My point exactly," Tess said. "This can't be Amelia speaking."

"So?" Amelia said. "What's so wrong with me not wearing my necklace? I took it off. It was...constricting."

"We have powers from the amulets," Tess said. "So, if you don't get your power from the amulet, and your dad is a powerful magician, I'm guessing..."

Amelia blinked at them.

"What are you saying, Tess?" Elizabeth asked. "Are you saying she's under her dad's spell?"

"She doesn't know the primes," Tess said. "Concussion or not, I don't think Amelia is her normal self today."

"What? How could you say that?" Amelia looked up at Tess. "Don't you trust me?"

"See!" Tess said, her face growing flushed. "That's not how Amelia would react!"

"Well, if that's not Amelia talking," Elizabeth said. "How do we break the spell?"

Amelia hung her head and sniffed, acting like she was crying and upset, giving weak little sobs.

"You girls don't trust me," she said. "My best friends don't trust me!"

"Hey, girls! Let's not be too hard on her. I don't know the primes either," Susie said. "Maybe she needs a doctor, you know? Maybe she really did hit her head, or she's under some weird memory spell. If her dad really is a powerful sorcerer, there's no telling what he did to her."

Mikey walked in at that point.

"All clear," he said.

Tess had a sudden idea. But Mikey would have to play along, and there was no way of knowing if he would. She decided to take a risk.

"Mikey. You're Amelia's boyfriend," Tess said.

"Huh?" Mikey said. His cheeks grew pink.

"What are you talking—" Susie said, but was cut off when Elizabeth clamped a hand over her mouth.

Tess felt thankful Elizabeth guessed her plan.

"Yeah," Elizabeth said. "To prove it's Amelia, you've got to kiss her. You'll know if it's really her by her sweet, passionate, slobbery kiss."

Mikey tried to speak, but nothing came out of his mouth but air.

"Um," Amelia swallowed. "I don't feel too well. I'm not sure about this. Though, of course, I…I love you," she said to Mikey. "Honey."

Mikey turned a deeper shade of pink.

Tess felt more and more certain the girl sitting next to her was not really Amelia.

"Well?" Tess prodded Mikey forward. "Don't you want to show her your love?"

Everyone watched in silence as Mikey approached the blond-haired girl on the sofa. Amelia got greener in color, then tensed up when Mikey sat next to her and leaned in.

"OK!" Amelia moved quickly to the other side of the couch. "Stop right there! Don't you dare kiss me."

"Clever girls," the blond girl said in a lower, more masculine voice. She waved her hands around, and a gray tornado formed around her. When the tornado disappeared, Amelia's lanky-haired dad sat looking at them.

"OMG," Elizabeth said. "Shape-shifting."

"Ugh!" Mikey groaned, and wiped his mouth, even though he hadn't kissed anyone.

"I knew it!" Tess said and got far away from the sofa. She stood on the other side of the room.

Susie made a muffled sound, and Elizabeth took her hand off her mouth so she could talk.

"Eww! Gross!" Susie said.

"What do you mean...eww, gross?" Amelia's dad said, mocking her. "You're in my house, eating my food. Not to mention that you're all alive only because of my spell, which saved you all from the rock dragon."

"We wouldn't be here if you hadn't kidnapped Amelia," Elizabeth said. "So technically it's your fault we were in danger. Um, sir. Mr. Hilton."

Amelia's dad scoffed. "Ungrateful, all of you."

Tess hardly heard a word of it. All she was aware of was the anger she felt. It burned like...fire.

Amelia's dad's hair started to smoke. The water glasses on the table were boiling over.

"Tess, is that you?" Elizabeth said. "Don't light any fires!"

"Sorry," Tess said. She quickly tried to calm her anger. "He just made me so angry."

"Oh, please," Amelia's dad said, waving her off. "I'm not afraid of your cheap amulet tricks. A simple counterspell to your child's magic is all I need."

"If it's so childish, why is your hair still smoking?" Tess said. Her face flushed with deep anger.

Mikey stared at her. "Sis, calm down," he said.

"I don't want to be calm!" Tess screamed. Steam rose up from a half-eaten soup on the table.

"Everyone!" Elizabeth said. "We need to focus! The real Amelia could be here, trapped in the house. Is she?" Elizabeth said to Amelia's dad.

"Well, that's the thing," Amelia's dad said. "She escaped. But now that you're all here, I feel certain she'll come back." His voice was weak, and his hair still smoked. He waved his hands feebly, about to cast a spell. Then the life seemed to drain out of him, and he passed out.

Mikey took Tess' amulet off her neck.

The soup and water glasses stopped boiling.

Mikey grabbed a cold glass of water from the kitchen, then poured it on the sorcerer's hair, to stop it from smoking.

"Seriously, Tess," Mikey said with his teeth clenched. "I can't believe you made me almost kiss that gross man."

Everyone watched the sorcerer breathing deeply on the sofa. His face was pale and his eyes were shut.

"Amelia escaped," Susie whispered. "I think we should too!"

Elizabeth nodded. "Let's get out of here. Now."

Tess felt a twinge of guilt as she looked at the old man, exhausted on the sofa. All the anger she had felt with the amulet on, was now gone.

"Do we just leave him there?" Tess said. "He doesn't look well."

"A minute ago you were burning his hair!" Elizabeth pointed out.

"I know," Tess said and looked embarrassed. "But I don't feel so angry now that the amulet is off."

"He's breathing, so that's good enough for me. Let's go," Susie said, ready to leave the sorcerer's house.

"Wait! This is the time to tell you some good news," Mikey said. "I found an airplane outside."

"Airplane?" Tess said. "None of us know how to fly an airplane."

"I don't see why that should stop us," Susie said. "We need to leave this place."

"Let's get out of here," Elizabeth said.

"If Amelia escaped," Tess said, "then we need to get off this island before she comes back to rescue us."

A sinking feeling stole through Tess. It would be just like Amelia to come save them, if she found out they were on the island.

Mikey and Tess helped Susie up, and they crept out of the living room. Amelia's dad made a grunting noise, and shifted on the sofa.

They froze.

Footsteps sounded from the floor above them. Heavy footfalls made their way down the stairs.

"Someone's coming down the stairs!" Elizabeth whispered. She sounded panicked. "Mikey, I thought you said all the rooms were clear?"

"I checked all the rooms! I didn't see anyone," Mikey whispered back. "I don't know how someone would've gotten inside the house without us noticing. Unless they used magic."

"Let's leave, now!" Susie said and made a move to go out the front door.

"Wait a second!" Elizabeth stopped her from leaving. "Susie's mom texted that she was trapped in a house, right?"

"Right," Tess said.

"So if that passed-out sorcerer over there was lying to us, pretending to be Amelia all along," Elizabeth went on, "then maybe what he said about Susie's mom escaping wasn't true, either."

"You're right, Liz," Susie said, agreeing with Elizabeth. "Maybe that was another lie, about Mom escaping."

"You think she's still trapped in this house?" Tess asked.

All three girls turned toward the noise of footsteps, hopeful that it wasn't another evil sorcerer.

Tess felt her stomach flutter with nerves as she waited to see who would come into the entrance hall where they stood, so near the front door.

Elizabeth put her hand on the doorknob, ready to open it in case they had to run from whoever it was walking toward them.

"Mom?" Susie said.

Tess felt great relief when a very sleepy Elaine Lang walked from the lounge into the entrance hall. Her hair was a mess, and she looked terrible, but her dark eyes were bright and kind, like always.

"Mom!" Susie yelled, and launched herself into her mom's arms.

Ms. Lang staggered, but kept her balance.

"Shhh!" Elizabeth warned. "He could wake up!" She pointed dramatically to the sofa, where Amelia's dad now snored.

"Let's go," Tess whispered, and helped the exhausted Ms. Lang out of the house. Susie followed, hopping along behind them.

Once they were outside in the humid air, Ms. Lang took turns hugging everyone.

"What happened to you?" Tess asked her. "Are you OK?"

Ms. Lang tried to smooth down her hair, which looked like a messy spider web around her head.

"Amelia's dad cast a spell on me, which is making me sleepy," Ms. Lang said. "But I'm fine."

Ms. Lang's face went from happy, to confused, then back to happy once again.

"Why are you all here?" Ms. Lang asked.

"We had to find Amelia," Susie said. "And you!"

"Is Amelia with you?" Ms. Lang asked, searching the group. She looked Susie up and down, and her eyes and face turned to alarm when she noticed her daughter's bruised, swollen ankle.

"Susie, what happened to your ankle?" she asked. "Did Amelia's dad do that to you?"

"I sprained it fighting a rock dragon," Susie said.

Ms. Lang hugged her daughter tightly. "Oh, I never meant any of you girls to face monsters like that. I'm so sorry you got involved in all this."

"It's OK," Susie said, clinging to her mom. "We're fine. I'm just glad you're safe."

"We still need to find Amelia before we escape this island," Elizabeth said. She pulled the magic map out of her backpack.

"Good idea," Tess said. "Elizabeth, you check and see if Amelia is even on this island."

"While you're doing that," Mikey said, "let's get to that plane I found. If Amelia is still here, we can fly around looking for her."

This seemed a solid plan, and they all agreed.

Susie and her mom linked arms with Mikey, and he helped them through the green plants around the house. Tess and Elizabeth followed.

Elizabeth had a smile on her face. Surprised, Tess asked her why she looked happy.

"We're in danger, and you look happy!" Tess said, as they walked along. "We could have been attacked by sharks, or eaten by the rock monster, or kidnapped by an evil sorcerer. Not to mention that we're still trapped on this horrible island. And you're smiling!"

"I know," Elizabeth said. "But now we have Susie's mom back. And soon we'll find Amelia, I just know it. It's only…I was just thinking that I haven't wanted to read my book the whole time we've been on this island. Actually, not since we landed in Honolulu."

"Well, we haven't exactly had time to read a book," Tess said. "We've been a little busy rescuing people. And getting into trouble. And getting out of trouble."

"That's my point," Elizabeth said. "It's not just that I haven't read one. I mean, I actually haven't wanted to read one. Normally, I find life a little…I don't know…awkward and boring, I guess. That's why I prefer a fictional world, like Emma's world, or any world created by Jane Austen."

"Yeah, I know," Tess said.

"But life has been so exciting since we landed in Honolulu," Elizabeth said. "Discovering magic, and searching for Amelia, and the whole submarine thing…"

Tess shoved a palm leaf aside so they could walk.

"This world we're in now," Elizabeth said, "it's even more exciting than one of my books. I actually want to be in it!"

Sweat dripped down Elizabeth's face, but she smiled, almost glowing.

Tess let out a long, slow breath, trying to understand. She slapped a mosquito on her arm.

"Well, I'm happy for you, girl," Tess said. "But I think I'd prefer to be curled up in my own bed with a novel. And bug spray."

Chapter Thirty-six

The real Amelia was completely sweaty when they arrived at Akoni's grandmother's house. Her hair was wet at her neck, and her jeans felt far too heavy for the weather. But she'd rather feel like this, hot and sweaty, than covered with chilly goose bumps.

Akoni's grandmother's place was a low, white house made of wood. Akoni explained that he lived with his parents and sister in the house just next door, and his aunt and uncle had a house down the street.

Amelia imagined how nice it would be if she and her mom lived on the same street as all the people she loved most, like her best friends.

Colorful wind chimes hung just outside the white house. It looked inviting, with a hibiscus plant next to the door. And the door itself was decorated with bright orange flowers.

Akoni knocked.

The door opened almost immediately.

An old woman in a flowery, shapeless dress stood before them. Her hair was a gray cloud around her face, but her dark eyes were bright and alive. She examined them both closely, and then grinned with a big smile, showing a few missing teeth.

275

"Aloha," the old woman greeted them.

"Aloha, Tutu!" Akoni said. "I'm back."

Tutu hugged both Akoni and Amelia, even before Akoni introduced her. They were hurried into the kitchen where Akoni's grandmother laid plates and glasses on the table for them before they could stop her.

"I have been wondering when I would see you, grandson," Tutu said. "You looked so tense last time I saw you. Now, you look better. Who is this lovely girl?"

She gently took Amelia's arm and sat her at the table, then organized lau lau (pork wrapped in leaves) and a pitcher of POG (pineapple, orange and guava juice) in front of them.

"Mahalo, Tutu," Akoni said. Amelia also said "Mahalo" and Tutu smiled.

"So, Akoni?" Tutu said. "Tell me all."

"Well, Grandma…" Akoni shifted in his chair. "I maybe got involved with the wrong job, that's clear. Amelia's dad…my boss…well, he kidnapped her."

Akoni told the story of how Amelia's dad kidnapped her, and tried to force her to mine dark magic.

His grandmother's face quickly went from happy to very angry as Akoni talked.

"You were involved in kidnapping this sweet, young girl?" Tutu said with a scowl.

"I didn't know!" Akoni said quickly. "It all happened so fast, but…yeah, I guess I could have stopped it. I didn't really know what was happening. But I will never work for him again...not ever." His face grew twitchy and his eyes shifted around with nervousness.

"I knew that man was bad news," Tutu said. "I told you not to work for him, but you didn't listen! And now look at you—a kidnapper!"

"Akoni helped me escape," Amelia said. She didn't want him to get in trouble, especially after having gone through the lizard experience. He had been through enough.

"Eat, eat," his grandmother said to Amelia, the smile returning to her face. "Drink some POG. It sounds like you have been through some tough days." She felt Amelia's arm. "You are too thin!"

"It's delicious," Amelia said truthfully.

She bit into another of the tender and juicy lau lau and drank down a glass of POG. Tutu refilled her glass from the pitcher, and then fixed her eyes on Akoni.

"Grandson," she said to Akoni. "I can see there is more to the story."

"Well, yes," Akoni said. "I think we found the cave where Alanawaiwai is trapped. I think Amelia woke her up."

Tutu stared at them for a long time, her dark eyes deep and serious.

"Is this true?" she asked Amelia.

"Maybe," Amelia said. "I was in the cave all night. My dad trapped me there with magic. So I started to sing, and a voice joined in. A woman's voice. Akoni thinks it's the ocean goddess."

"If it's true," Tutu said to him, "then you must go back. You must try to free her, in case it is Alanawaiwai. She must be reminded of her name."

"That sorcerer, though," Akoni said. "He has a lot of power. He turned me into a—oh, never mind. The point is, we wouldn't be safe going back to the island."

"You must go back," Tutu said. "Have I told you Alanawaiwai's story a million times for nothing?" She fixed a stare at Akoni.

Akoni cowered, slumping in his chair.

"Why did you not try to free Alanawaiwai and then leave the island?" his grandmother said in a loud voice. "The poor goddess has been trapped in that cave for hundreds of years!"

"Tutu, it was dangerous to stay on the island," Akoni said in a meek voice. "It was dangerous for Amelia to be there, too."

Amelia felt sorry for Akoni. Though Tutu was very nice to her, the fire in her eyes toward him was fierce.

"You eat this island's coconuts, you eat the poi I make from this land's taro, and you disrespect the goddess because you are…afraid?" Tutu said.

"I'm sorry! We'll go," Akoni said. "We'll go right now."

Amelia nodded.

"I'm not afraid to go back to the cave," Amelia said. "Especially after this delicious food. Thank you."

The old woman's face softened again. She smiled at Amelia, then came and squeezed Amelia's shoulders.

"You should marry this one," his grandmother said.

"Tutu, please!" Akoni said and pushed a fist against his head. "I can't believe you said that. You know I have a girlfriend."

"That silly Malie?" Tutu said, sounding angry again. "She's lazy!"

"We've been dating three years now!" Akoni said. "We're serious!"

"Three years is nothing. You are young, so your foolish head is turned by a nice pair of—"

"Um, I'm going outside for a minute," Amelia said, interrupting the argument. "I'd like to call my mom, see if she's OK."

"She calls her mom. See? She speaks with Aloha. She's a nice girl," said Tutu.

"Thank you…I mean, mahalo," Amelia said. "Though I don't know what speaking with Aloha means."

"Aloha is a word full of love," Tutu said, beaming at Amelia. "It means love, compassion, all beings connected as one—wonderful things."

Then Tutu turned to Akoni and scowled.

"That Malie does not speak with love!" she yelled. "You should marry a girl like Amelia!"

Amelia felt herself blush with embarrassment. She excused herself from the table and hurried out of the house. She walked out into the garden to get away from the tense kitchen scene.

Amelia dialed her mom's number while trying to block out the voices of Akoni and his grandmother, who was getting very loud. Akoni was really getting an earful.

Her mom picked up the call immediately. She sounded worried.

"Where are you?" her mom said. "In Berkeley?"

Amelia felt her eyebrows pinch in concern. Didn't her mother remember their last conversation?

"No, Mom, I'm in Oahu," Amelia said. "Like you."

"Oahu?" her mom said. "I'm in Oahu! Just come to my hotel. Take a taxi. I'll be here. At the hotel."

Amelia stared at the phone a moment. "Mom? Are you sure you're OK? You sound, I don't know…really confused. You already know I'm in Oahu."

"Do I?" her mom said. "Oh, I feel dizzy. I need to get off the phone. Come to my hotel. In Oahu."

Amelia felt like crying, but kept it together. She told her mom that she would do whatever she could to get to the hotel in a few days.

"Listen, Mom, if you feel weird or anything, call my friend's grandmother," Amelia said and gave her Tutu's address and phone number. She made her mom write it down and repeat it back.

If her mom was affected by magic, under some kind of memory spell, then maybe Tutu would know what to do. When Akoni and Tutu came out of the house, Amelia shared her worries.

"It sounds like that bad man gave your mom some bad magic," Tutu said, her face wrinkling with tension. "You leave it to me. I will get your mom out of that hotel and bring her here."

"Mahalo," Amelia said, thanking her.

Tutu smiled at her and hugged her grandson, but pinched him as well.

"Find your courage, boy," Tutu said to him.

Once Tutu went back into the house, Akoni's shoulders slumped. He looked defeated, not big at all.

"Man! She's so mean sometimes," Akoni said.

"Hey, it was your idea to ask her what we should do," Amelia said. "We could have been to the island by now."

Akoni shrugged. "I'm still glad we came," he said. "Partly for the lau lau, and partly because of this."

He showed her a necklace made of turquoise stones.

"She says this is protective," Akoni explained. "So if your dad tries any more of his tricks on me, they won't work." He pulled the necklace over his head.

"Did you tell her about the lizard thing?" Amelia asked.

Akoni shook his head. "I was too embarrassed," he admitted. "Don't you tell anyone, either. Understood?"

"Yes, I promise," Amelia said. "Again, I promise."

"Let's go. I'm not so worried about your dad now," Akoni said. "I don't think he can hurt us."

"Really? Why?" Amelia asked, surprised. "Because of the necklace?"

"Well, that and…" Akoni showed her the tattoo around his wrist. It was almost invisible now.

"What happened to your tattoo? Does it wash off or something?" Amelia asked.

Akoni shook his head. "This tattoo was made by a spell," he said. "It has been dark for a year, since I started working for your dad. But now, it's almost gone! Remember what I told you about sorcerers, when they get weak or die?"

"Their spells break," Amelia said.

"Yeah. So maybe he is too weak to bother us anymore," Akoni said.

She felt the weight of sadness in her heart. She didn't want her dad to be sick, or worse.

"We go to the island, quickly free the goddess, come home, and then sleep for days. Deal?" Akoni said and stuck out his hand.

"Deal," Amelia said and shook his hand. She smiled at him, but it was a forced smile. She was nervous about going to the island, and felt sick at the idea that her dad was ill.

As she put on her helmet and climbed behind him on the motorcycle, a sinking feeling filled her heart. Her throat grew tight, as if she'd swallowed a stone.

She wished she could just go to her mom's hotel and forget about Alanawaiwai, and the cave, and her dad. A long sleep, then some time curled up reading a math book would be just the thing.

But she had to go to the island.

Alanawaiwai had woken up, that seemed clear. So they had to try to free her. The goddess would suffer more if she was awake and trapped in the cave, rather than asleep and trapped.

Her dad was more complicated. He was likely to be ill or dying. And even though he was mean, he was still her dad. She had just found him, and she wasn't sure she was ready to lose him again.

Amelia touched the heart pin that was still in her jeans pocket. She brought it out and pinned it onto her T-shirt.

Amelia felt unsure of everything.

Thinking of the dark gray stormy sky of the Place Where People Do Not Go, she shivered, despite the hot sun, and the hot motorcycle seat.

Chapter Thirty-seven

As Tess followed the group through the thick plants, she looked back at the sorcerer's house, which loomed close behind them. The sky above was stormy. Dark clouds gathered so low they seemed to sit on the roof.

She prayed that Amelia's dad wouldn't wake up anytime soon. And she hoped that Amelia was somewhere safe, away from sorcerers and rock dragons.

Mikey handed her the Fire amulet and Tess put it on. She might need it if Amelia's dad woke up.

Tess wished they were moving faster, as the group followed Mikey's lead. She felt irritated—by everything—and wondered if it was the Fire amulet that was giving her a short fuse.

Tess got at least five new mosquito bites on the short walk through the rain forest. Though she slapped bugs constantly, she just couldn't keep up. Some of the creatures slipped through.

The itchy feeling made her feel even worse. Furious. She wished she could burn up all the mosquitoes.

Her brother stopped in front of a big, oddly-shaped bush. When Mikey cleared away some of the leaves, a blue and white airplane stood before them.

"Ta-da!" Mikey said, grinning. They gathered around the plane and looked through the little windows. It had six seats.

"Perfect!" Susie said. "I'm pilot!"

"With that foot?" Elizabeth said.

"Sure! I'll just use the right one." Susie said and hopped to the door.

"Where will we land?" Elizabeth said. "Honolulu airport?"

Susie waved her off. "We'll figure it out when we get closer. Maybe there's a nice field or something we can see once we're in the air." She yanked open the door of the plane, then froze.

"What is it?" Elizabeth asked. "Susie, what's wrong? Please tell me it's not a snake. I hate snakes."

"We should never have let you watch that Snakes on a Plane movie, Liz," Susie said and rolled her eyes. "It's not a snake, but something…weirder. See for yourself."

They all peered into the plane. Instead of a dashboard with switches and buttons, there was just a single, black candle.

"Magic plane," Ms. Lang said sleepily. She yawned, then said, "Amelia's dad really is clever. This airplane is powered by Dark magic."

"So, it'll be easy then," Susie said. "Tess can light the candle and we're off."

Tess peered at the candle on the dashboard. It looked a little menacing–unusually dark. She felt like the candle, or something else in the plane, was giving off a weird vibe. Negative energy.

"Black candle?" Elizabeth said. "That doesn't seem too inviting. Is it OK, Ms. Lang, do you think? It's giving me chills just looking at it."

Ms. Lang's head was slumped on Mikey's shoulder. She was literally asleep on her feet, snoring softly in his ear. Poor Mikey looked uncomfortable, but he was being a gentleman about it. Tess almost laughed, but she was too nervous about Amelia's dad waking up.

"Let's just get off this island," Mikey said. "Black candle or not, I think we're safer anywhere but here."

"Do we still have the purple candle?" Susie asked. "Let's switch the black one for the purple candle and light it. If it's my mom's magic candle, it must be OK."

"Not a bad idea," Elizabeth said. "Tess, Mikey, what do you think?"

Tess opened her mouth to answer, when she felt a sharp pain on the back of her knee. It felt like a needle was going in. She yelled really loud, then slapped the area, hoping to get the mosquito.

Suddenly, the plane was gone.

"Tess!" Elizabeth said.

"What? What did I do?" Tess said.

"You lit the candle! The black candle lit up all on its own," Elizabeth said. "Then the plane disappeared."

"I'm sorry! I didn't mean to light it," Tess said and touched the amulet at her neck.

Her fire amulet was hot.

"I guess I got angry at that mosquito," Tess said. Shame filled her face with heat. She knew she was probably as red as her hair.

"Watch it!" Susie said, then started smacking Elizabeth's bag with her hand. A thin stream of smoke trickled out from the dirt-covered backpack.

"Don't tell me," Tess said, staring at backpack.

"Yep, you must have lit the purple candle too," Susie said.

Tess realized that her fire power had gotten away from her—again. It was out of her control. All because of one mosquito. Tears filled her eyes, and her face grew warm.

"I can't believe I sent the plane away," Tess said in a voice that was husky with emotion. "And now we can't get off the island. And we haven't found Amelia!"

She started to sob. Tears streamed down her face.

Susie launched herself at Tess, to give her a big hug. Elizabeth and Mikey tried to make her feel better too.

"We can hike back to the sub," Elizabeth said. "I'll make another rock bridge."

"We'll find Amelia," Mikey said. "I know we will."

"I don't deserve this," Tess said. She unhooked the Fire amulet and gave it to Elizabeth. "I keep screwing up."

"You need that for protection!" Elizabeth said. She tried to put it back around her friend's neck, but Tess wouldn't allow her.

"With all these mosquitoes," Tess said, "I just get too angry."

"Mosquitoes, huh?" Elizabeth said. A smile tugged at her mouth, and she laughed into her hand.

The girls and Mikey exchanged glances.

Tess wiped the tears from her face, and got her breathing under control.

"The evil sorcerer doesn't make you angry, sharks in the water don't make you angry, but mosquitoes, of all things, make you incredibly angry," Elizabeth said. "So… mosquitoes basically turn you into…a rock dragon! A Tess Dragon? Mosquito Monster?"

Susie and Mikey grinned, seeing the humor in it too.

Elizabeth laughed louder, but Tess was still upset. She didn't think it was funny at all.

Mikey squeezed Tess' arm, so she wouldn't feel bad.

"They're your kryptonite, Tess!" Susie said.

Mikey let out a loud bark of a laugh.

Tess finally grinned.

"Yeah, I'm not up to more mosquitoes today," Tess said. "Bring back the rock dragon. I'll face him instead."

"Don't even say it!" Susie said. "Don't mention him!"

Susie laughed so hard she had to sit on the ground.

"Don't mention what?" said a new voice. It came from the direction of the trees.

A girl's voice.

The group stopped laughing at once.

They all froze, immediately serious.

Susie pulled herself up to her feet, using Tess as support. Tess searched the trees for the girl who spoke.

The girl stepped out of the trees, and rushed toward them with her arms outstretched.

Tess' heart skipped beats.

It looked like Amelia, though it could be a trap.

The girl wore one of her favorite peach-colored T-shirts, which was stained and smeared with dirt. The pin Amelia got from her Aunt Ada was in place. Her hair was in a ponytail, and looked wet with grease. Most importantly, Tess could see the Water amulet around her neck.

Although the girl looked greasy and dirty, her face was clean, smiling and happy.

"Elizabeth! Susie! Tess! Mikey!" the girl said. Then she noticed Ms. Lang, who was sleeping against a palm tree.

"What's wrong with Susie's mom?" the girl asked. "Is she OK?"

The girl opened her arms wide, as if to hug them all.

"Stop right there!" Susie held up her hand.

"We've seen that trick before, whoever you are," Elizabeth said.

The girl stopped. Her peach-colored cheeks blushed deep pink and she looked confused.

"Why? What's wrong?" the girl asked.

"What are our names?" Elizabeth asked. "Our real names."

"You mean, like...you're Earth, Susie's Air, and Tess is Fire?" the girl said.

Tess stared at the girl. Her heart told her it really was Amelia. But she had been tricked before.

"Primes! Recite them," Elizabeth asked. "Your dad could have guessed our element names. We told him about the amulets."

"You met my dad?" the girl said, her eyes wide open with alarm.

"If you really are Amelia," Tess said, "start reciting the primes so we can be sure it's really you."

"Um...OK," the girl said. "Two, three, five, seven, eleven, thirteen, seventeen, nineteen, twenty-three..."

"So far so good," Elizabeth mumbled.

Any doubt in Tess' heart lifted as the girl smoothly recited the numbers, higher and higher, without hesitation or a single mistake.

"Forty-one, forty-three, forty-seven," the girl said. "Fifty-three, fifty-nine, sixty-one, sixty-seven, seventy-one..."

"Keep going," Susie said, smiling with excitement.

"Seventy-three, seventy-nine, eighty-three, eighty-nine, ninety-seven, hundred and one, hundred and three, hundred and seven, hundred and nine…"

The girl went on and on, reciting faster. Her tears stopped, and her face looked peaceful.

"Hundred thirteen, hundred twenty-seven…"

"OK, you can stop," Tess said. "It's definitely her."

Tess had seen that look of peace on Amelia's face before, when she was doing math.

Her dad wouldn't know that. And even if he did, Tess doubted he could fake her expression.

"I think so, too," Susie said.

"How do we know for sure, though?" Elizabeth studied the girl in front of them. "I want to believe it, but her dad could have learned a math spell, or some kind of prime number enchantment, you know."

"Amelia gets blissed out reciting the primes," Tess said. "I doubt her dad knows that. And I don't know anyone else crazy enough to find peace in primes!"

"You're right, Tess. It's me!" Amelia said. "And you would know out of anyone." She ran to Tess and threw her arms around her.

Tess hugged her back, her heart warm. It felt like her friend, the real Amelia.

"I missed you!" Tess said.

"I missed you!" Amelia said at the same time.

Tess wanted to cry with relief.

There were hugs all around, even one for Mikey.

"Now that we're all together," Mikey said, smiling big, "we just need to find a way off the island. Then we can go home."

Tess let go of Amelia long enough to smile at her brother. But something caught her eye in the bushes.

A strong-looking Hawaiian man walked toward the group. Tess' back tensed up.

Susie and Elizabeth also saw him.

"Aloha," he greeted them with a smile.

"Stay back!" Susie yelled. She got ready to jump off her good foot, and Elizabeth floated a very large, very heavy stone above his head.

"Stop! He's OK! That's Akoni," Amelia said. "He's a friend." She linked arms with Akoni.

"A friend?" Mikey said. He stared Akoni in the eye.

"Really, I am," Akoni said. "But I can't recite the primes."

Tess laughed.

"A friend of Amelia's is a friend of ours," Tess said.

Elizabeth and Susie relaxed, and the stone lowered gently back to the ground.

"Liz, I didn't know you could do that," Susie said. "Rip huge rocks out of the earth, and make them fly. That is so cool!"

"It just sort of…happened," Elizabeth said. "I wished it to come up, then bam! The stone was above his head."

"You can do magic?" Amelia said to Elizabeth.

"We all can," Susie explained. "The amulets give us powers. After we found the envelope with the instructions, and the green stone, Didus took it and dropped in the well, and that's when–" She broke off as soon as she noticed Amelia's confused look.

"Green stone? Envelope?" Amelia said.

"Sorry," Susie said. "There's a lot to explain."

"Yeah, we'll tell you about Didus and everything later," Elizabeth said.

"I have water magic," Amelia told them. "I didn't even think that it could be from the necklace. That explains a lot."

"I've seen her water power," Akoni said, jumping into the conversation. "When I first saw Amelia call the ocean, I thought she was magic like her dad. But I'm feeling happier that it's her necklace. Her dad's an evil man."

"We know," Susie said. "

"We have to get off this island," Akoni said, "before Amelia's dad wakes up and turns us all into…"

"Turns us into what?" Susie asked him.

Akoni shivered. "Oh, never mind. Let's just go."

A sinking feeling stole over the group. Tess' stomach tightened with nerves.

They weren't nearly far enough away from the sorcerer's house, and the plane was gone. With Susie's bad ankle, it would take a long time to hike back to the beach, where they parked the submarine.

Was there another way to escape?

Chapter Thirty-eight

"When did you meet my dad?" Amelia asked, looking concerned. "Are you all OK?"

"Yeah, we're fine," Tess said. "Your dad shape-shifted into you and tricked us. We just escaped the house maybe ten minutes ago, when he passed out. He had Susie's mom trapped there."

"That's why we asked you to say the primes," Susie said. "We had to be sure it was you."

"How did you all escape?" Amelia asked.

"We had to get Mikey to pretend to kiss him," Tess explained. "Your dad freaked before Mikey could, and revealed himself. That's how we found out your dad was only pretending to be you."

Amelia was so shocked that she laughed out loud, picturing the whole thing in her mind. But then she turned sad eyes to Mikey.

"Oh, that must have been awful," Amelia said to him.

Mikey looked terribly embarrassed. Maybe not as embarrassed as Akoni when he was turned into a lizard, but close.

"Well I…thought it was you at first…so it wasn't awful… at first…" Mikey said, then stopped, turning a darker shade of red.

"Mikey was heroic," Elizabeth said. "George Knightley in a past life."

"Um, isn't George Knightley a fictional character, Liz?" Susie said.

"I'm sure he was based on someone real," Elizabeth said. "Anyway, Mikey was awesome."

"He was," Tess said and smiled at her brother. She was honestly happy and totally over the Valentine thing.

Or maybe the joy of finding Amelia was bigger than any irritation she felt.

"Ow!" Tess scratched her arm, which was full of bites. But she was only a little annoyed.

She wasn't really mad at all.

Why was that?

Tess wasn't wearing the fire amulet, so maybe that was why she wasn't nearly as annoyed at the mosquitoes. She gave her amulet to Elizabeth after she accidentally made the plane disappear. The Fire amulet made her angrier in general. She was definitely more chilled without it.

The thought made Tess a little freaked at the amulet. Maybe she should never put it on again.

Susie was showing Amelia her swollen ankle under her sock. Susie was trying to act like it was nothing, no big deal, but it was a bad sprain with a deep purple and black bruise.

"Did my dad do that to your foot?" Amelia asked.

Susie shook her head no. "I fell from the top of a coconut tree. We were fighting the rock dragon," she said and grimaced. "I was bashing coconuts on the rock dragon's head, while Tess lit them on fire."

"Oh, no! The rock dragon!" Amelia said, alarmed. "It almost ate Akoni and me."

"How did you get away?" Elizabeth asked.

"My dad saved me," Amelia said. "He saved Akoni too."

Akoni rolled his eyes.

"Your friend is too trusting," Akoni told the group. "Her dad just wanted her to mine the Dark. And I'm sure he didn't save me on purpose. I'm not a Darkminer."

Amelia shrugged. "He did save me, though," she said. "So I guess I really do owe him something, even though he tried to make me mine the Dark."

"Mine the dark?" Elizabeth asked, confused. "What does that mean?"

"It's a lot to explain," Amelia said and shivered. "It's like this evil energy or something, stored inside of rock. I don't like it. I don't want to touch it."

"Rocks?" Elizabeth said. "That sounds like my territory. Is the rock the evil part? Or is it just evil inside the rock?"

Amelia was about to answer, but Mikey jumped in. He scanned the trees nervously.

"Let's get to safety first," Mikey said. "We have to get away from this house. He'll be after Amelia if he wants her to mine…evil Dark rock, or whatever it is. We should go."

"Let's move," Akoni said. "Though he won't be following us anytime soon, I don't think."

Akoni held out his arm.

The tattoo around his wrist had faded to nearly blend in with his skin. Tess had to squint to see it.

Amelia paled as Akoni explained that it meant her dad was very weak.

"He looked really awful after that Amelia shape-shifter spell," Elizabeth said. "He passed out, and that's how we escaped from his house. I think that's why Susie's mom could escape, too. His magic was getting weak."

"We have to help him," Amelia said. "We can't leave him unconscious."

"We can leave him," Akoni said. "He'll recover. He always comes back from his unconscious time. And one of us should help the goddess first."

"Goddess?" Elizabeth asked. She and Susie exchanged wide-eyed looks of surprise.

"Yeah, we're sort of on a goddess mission," Amelia said. "That's why we came back to the island."

"You came back?" Tess said. "Does that you mean you escaped already? Your dad said you did, but I wasn't sure if he was telling the truth."

"Yes," Amelia said and linked arms with Akoni. "Akoni helped me."

Mikey tensed and blushed a deep red. Tess felt bad for her brother, and went to link arms with him. He seemed to need the support.

"I know it sounds crazy, but we had to come back," Amelia said. "There's so much to explain."

A moaning sound from Susie's mom stopped the conversation. Susie went over to her, where she was slumped against a tree, and smiled with relief as her mom woke up.

"Oh, goodness!" Ms. Lang said, slightly embarrassed as she noticed everyone around her. "I'm sorry, I must've fallen asleep. Although…I do feel much better."

Susie helped her to her feet.

"Amelia!" Ms. Lang said and threw her arms around Amelia. "You're here! Is it really you?"

Ms. Lang held her at arm's distance and scanned her up and down, checking her over.

"It's really her," Tess said.

"You look exhausted," Ms. Lang said. "Are you OK?"

Amelia nodded. "I could use some sleep," she said. "But really, I'm fine."

"We were just asking her why she and her friend Akoni came back to the island," Tess explained. "After they had escaped the first time."

"You came back?" Ms. Lang asked. "But this is such a dangerous place to be."

"We came back to free the goddess," Amelia said. "She's been trapped for hundreds of years."

Everyone stared at Amelia.

What goddess?

Tess didn't believe in ancient legends like that, and she didn't think any of her friends would, either. Then again, magic turned out to be real…so why not?

"A goddess?" Ms. Lang said. "I didn't think they still existed."

"The goddess Alanawaiwai is trapped in a cave here on the island," Amelia explained. "We can free her by saying her name…well, maybe. We're not sure about it. But we have to try."

"There are lots of gods and goddesses around," Akoni said. "We Hawaiians know about them. Her name is—"

"—Alanawaiwai."

Everyone jumped when a man's hoarse voice came from the green plants. Then the dark figure slowly stepped out of the shadows.

Amelia's dad.

A chill stole through Tess as the sorcerer came into view. He propped himself up on a tree.

"I may be weak," the sorcerer said. "I may not have had the strength to hold that woman in my house any longer…"

Susie squeezed her mom's hand.

"…but for many long years I have searched for the name of the goddess. And now that I have it…"

The sorcerer laughed hoarsely, then had a terrible coughing fit. Everyone huddled close together, with Ms. Lang urging the group to get behind her.

"I am sure I will be feeling better very soon." Amelia's dad took a shaking breath in and out.

Tess' heart turned.

Why did he want the name of a goddess?

Amelia's dad waved his arms around, but nothing happened. He cursed under his breath.

"I'm so weak!" he said. "I can't even transport."

He took out a stone in his pocket and rubbed it, then began to chant.

The group stared at him, stunned. It was Tess who found her voice first.

"Stop him!" Tess yelled.

Ms. Lang waved her hands around weakly, but Elizabeth was faster. The stone the sorcerer was holding lifted out of his hand and flew through the air to Elizabeth.

"I'll take that," Elizabeth said and grinned smugly.

The sorcerer narrowed his eyes, a frown on his face.

"That was very good, Elizabeth," said Ms. Lang.

"Stone's my thing," Elizabeth said and shrugged.

A wind blew through the clearing, making them all cough. When it stopped, it took awhile for Tess to rub the dirt out of her eyes. She counted the group members as soon as she could see, but Amelia got there first.

"Uh-oh," Amelia said, looking at the trees.

"What?" Tess asked.

"My dad's gone," she said.

Chapter Thirty-nine

The place where the sorcerer stood a moment ago was empty. Mikey searched through the surrounding plants, but couldn't find him.

"What if he found a way to transport to the cave?" Amelia asked. "We have to get there as soon as we can to help Alanawaiwai." She pulled at Akoni's arm.

"What?" Tess said. "You can't possibly want to follow your dad! What if he traps you again? Or worse, traps all of us?"

"We need to save the goddess, we have to try. I don't have time to explain," Amelia said as she grabbed Tess' hand. "But if you knew Alanawaiwai's story, you would want to help her, too."

"Well, I know the story," Akoni said and touched the turquoise medallion around his neck, as if it gave him comfort. "And I don't want to go into that cave while your dad is there."

"How can you not want to go?" Amelia said, her tear-shaped blue eyes flashing with emotion. "Alanawaiwai needs us!"

"I'll go with you," Mikey said, stepping close to Amelia. She gave him a bright smile and his cheeks grew red.

Tess sighed. If Amelia and Mikey were going to risk their lives and go to the cave, she had to stand by them.

"OK, I'll go," Tess said and squeezed Amelia's hand. "For you…I would walk through fire."

Susie and Elizabeth said they were in, too, and held hands with Tess and Amelia.

All four girls stood in a circle, together again.

"OK, Element Girls," Akoni said. "I guess if you are all going, I have to go too. If I don't even try, and something happens to the goddess, my grandmother will kill me."

"Thanks, Akoni," Amelia said and took his hand.

"Between your dad and my grandmother…" Akoni, as big as he was, looked fearful. "I'd rather take my chances with your dad's spells than face her anger."

Ms. Lang watched them closely. Her face looked tired, her hair was a tangled cloud, and her eyes were pinched with worry.

It made Tess nervous to see Susie's mom not looking like her normal, got-it-together, confident self.

"I can tell you girls won't be talked out of going to that cave," Ms. Lang said. "If you girls are certain, then I'm in too. I think that sleep spell is finally wearing off."

At least Susie's mom sounded like she was back to normal, even if she didn't look it.

Clouds gathered low in the sky, and big drops of rain started to fall. It looked like it was almost night in the sudden darkness.

At least the rain felt cool on her mosquito bites.

"Amelia?" Tess said. "If we're doing this, we better go now. Before we drown!"

"Good idea," Elizabeth said. "I've been thinking, maybe your dad isn't even there. He said he was too weak to even teleport. If he went back to the house to rest or something, let's go now before he gets his strength back."

Ms. Lang smoothed her hair down in the rain. It somehow helped Tess' spirits to see it looking more tame. A bit of the sharpness was returning to her eyes, so she didn't look so tired and confused.

"I'm sorry to say it, but Amelia's dad is surrounded by a source of darkness and power. I can feel that," Ms. Lang said. "Which must be the cave, the exact kind of darkness that could trap a goddess."

"You can feel all that?" Susie asked. She wasn't the only one staring at her mom. Tess was stunned, too.

"The cave has a lot of Dark in it," Amelia said to Ms. Lang. "Do you know about Dark?"

"Unfortunately, I do," Ms. Lang said. "A terrible thing. Dark is powerful magic."

"Please, let's go right now," Amelia said, "before my dad does something even worse to the goddess. Especially now that he has her name…which is totally my fault."

"I can take us all there in half a second," Ms. Lang said. "Though I will be the only one going into the cave. Understood? It's far too dangerous for the rest of you."

"Sounds good to me!" Akoni said.

"You mean…" Susie looked at her mom. "You can just magic us all to the cave?" she asked.

Ms. Lang nodded.

"So cool," Elizabeth said. "Are you as powerful as Amelia's dad?"

"I haven't done magic like this in over a decade," Ms. Lang said, "so there's no telling how rusty I am, or how powerful Amelia's dad has gotten." She swirled her arms and twirled in place like a ballerina.

"Teleporto Air, Earth, Fire, Water, Akoni and Mikey!" Ms. Lang said.

Tess felt a shift under her feet. It was as if the Earth itself was sliding. Trees raced past her like she was in a speeding car. But there wasn't a strong wind like she would expect if she were moving fast.

The air was still and everything was quiet.

Tess didn't even hear the rain falling. She felt a yank, and suddenly found herself on top of a hill.

The sound of the rain came back, and heavy drops pelted her again.

Tess was standing on a hill. They were so high up that she could see the ocean from here.

Her friends stood next to her.

A cave in the shape of a hunched ghoul stood nearby. Tess shuddered, and chills ran up her back.

Amelia shivered too.

"The Dark is here," Amelia said. "I can feel it. It's so strong, so…gross."

"Is that what it's called? Dark?" Tess asked. "I can feel it too." She realized it was the same negative energy feeling she sensed from the black candle in the airplane.

A man's raspy voice came from the cave.

Amelia's dad was chanting, casting a spell.

"Alanawaiwai mi reviva!" the sorcerer said.

"Oh, no!" Amelia yelled. "We can't be too late! We can't be!" She ran into the cave and disappeared into the darkness.

"Amelia!" Ms. Lang called out. "Don't go in there!"

Tess' heart squeezed tight. She couldn't bear to lose Amelia again.

Frightened, she followed Amelia into the dark mouth of the cave.

Akoni followed, mumbling to himself. "If those girls are both braver than me, I won't be able to show my face to my grandmother ever again."

Tess crashed into Amelia in the darkness.

A moment later, she felt the solid weight of Akoni as he crashed against her back, nearly knocking them over.

The cave was pitch black.

They couldn't see anything at all. Not the walls of the cave, and not each other. Tess, Amelia and Akoni found each other's hands, and held tight.

"I can't see!" Amelia whispered.

"I don't have my flashlight," Akoni said quietly.

"Flicker!" Tess said, hoping to light something. But then she remembered she wasn't wearing her Fire amulet.

She hoped Susie's mom would come soon.

Where was she?

A dry laugh filled the cave.

"Little girls in the dark," said Amelia's dad, his voice sounding stronger. "How can you possibly stop me?"

"I'm not a girl," Akoni said.

"No, you're a lizard!" the sorcerer said.

"Alanawaiwai!" Amelia yelled. "Be free!"

"It will take more than that," her dad said, laughing. "And when I'm done, she will never be free!"

A woman's voice came through the cave. It was beautiful, melodic, and smooth as honey.

"Amelia, Water, my friend!" the woman's voice said. "Is that my name, Alanawaiwai? It feels…familiar. This man is taking my power, my life."

"My mortal life is spent, it's over," the sorcerer said. "But soon I will be renewed with the life force of the goddess!"

"Alanawaiwai, hang on!" Amelia said into the darkness. "We need someone with more powerful magic. We need Susie's mom."

"I'll go," Tess whispered. "I'll get her."

Tess ran outside to get help. She squinted at the bright light of day. When her eyes adjusted to the daylight, she couldn't believe what she saw.

The rock monster was back.

Steam rose off its body as the rain came down. But the fiery creature didn't seem to mind the rain.

Tess' heart tightened with fear when she saw that it had Mikey cornered. Her brother crouched by the cliff's edge, behind a tree.

Ms. Lang leapt in front of Mikey to protect him. She spread her hands out and a soft, blue light formed a shield in front of her and Mikey.

The rock dragon tried to move toward them, but bumped into the shield.

A coconut flew from the sky onto its head.

The rock dragon opened its great, fanged jaws and let out a terrible roar. It turned its head to look at something in a coconut palm.

Susie was in the tree.

Once again, she was a coconut warrior. From her perch high in a tree, she spiked coconuts down onto the rock dragon. She was only hanging on with one hand and leg, with her injured ankle dangling out into thin air.

All the hair stood up on Tess' scalp. She could see no way to help them without her fire power.

"Ms. Lang!" Tess yelled. "Elaine! We need you!"

Ms. Lang didn't hear her. She had her hands full, concentrating fully on the rock dragon, trying to protect Mikey and Susie.

Tess watched as the rock dragon shook its head madly after another coconut was spiked onto its nose.

Tess felt so helpless. She couldn't help Alanawaiwai in the cave, and she couldn't help Susie, or her brother.

Suddenly she felt something laid around her neck and shoulders. A rush of heat flowed through her.

The amulet necklace was back where it belonged. Turning around, she found Elizabeth.

"You've got this, Fire," Elizabeth said.

"I don't know," Tess said. "What if I make everything even worse?"

"You won't screw up," Elizabeth said. "And we need you, Fire-o. We need you badly. Let's go help the goddess."

Tess was worried she'd burn the wrong thing, or hurt someone, or ruin everything…but she had to try.

Tess grabbed a nearby stick. "Flicker," she said and suddenly held a torch in her hand. She and Elizabeth ran into the cave.

Chapter Forty

The fire was enough to brighten the tunnel. Tess could see Akoni and Amelia holding hands in front of them.

All four of them ran down the tunnel and into a chamber, where they discovered Amelia's dad, who was right in the middle of casting a spell.

The stringy-haired sorcerer had both of his hands on a shining, white part of the stone wall.

His whole body glowed.

"Dad, stop!" Amelia yelled.

"Stone, repel him!" Elizabeth shouted. Nothing happened.

"Names are important in magic, my dad said so," Amelia said. "Try saying his name! Jack…no, wait. It's…David!"

Amelia remembered her dad's real name.

"Stone, repel David!" Elizabeth shouted.

Amelia's dad flew away from the stone. He howled in fury as he was hurled through the air, then landed rough. He sat up, holding his head in his hands.

"That hurt," the sorcerer said. "Your magic is getting stronger, girl."

"Um, thanks," Elizabeth said. "Go near that weird glowing wall, and I'll I do it again."

"No. You won't," the sorcerer said, though he didn't explain. He was shaken up. He stayed sitting on the floor of the cave, holding his bleeding head.

Amelia ran to the white stone. She put her hands on the cave wall and called out to the goddess.

"Alanawaiwai!" Amelia said. "Is that you? Can you hear me?"

"Water, is that you?" said a woman's voice. It came out of the stone, sounding weak, hardly a whisper.

"How can I free you?" Amelia said.

"Say my name again," the woman said. "I feel a little stronger…each time…you say it."

"Alanawaiwai," Amelia said. "Alanawaiwai!"

"No, I'm too weak," the woman's voice said. "It's too late, he took too much power from me."

Amelia lay her forehead on the stone.

The sorcerer stood up, dusted himself off, and turned to Elizabeth. He had a furious expression on his face.

"Oh, you're in trouble now, girl," the sorcerer said, glaring at her. "Which one are you? Tell me your name. Now!"

Elizabeth backed up, away from the sorcerer.

Tess had to do something. Amelia's dad had the meanest look in his eye, glaring furiously at Elizabeth.

The sorcerer waved his hands around.

At the same moment, Tess yelled, "Flicker!" She concentrated on his clothes.

His jacket burst into flame.

"Now what's going on?" the sorcerer said. He sounded annoyed, but not scared in the least. When he snapped his fingers, the flame died out. He examined the black holes that now covered his jacket.

"Nice one, Tess!" Elizabeth called to Tess.

"Child's trick," the sorcerer said. "But you've ruined my favorite jacket. And that makes me angry, Tess."

Amelia's dad snapped his fingers again. This time, blue light surrounded Tess. She could no longer move.

Tess tried to light his jacket on fire again. She couldn't speak. She couldn't even move.

The sorcerer faced Elizabeth.

"Incantus, incantus Susie newt!" he said, waving his arms around.

Nothing happened.

"Maybe you're not Susie," the sorcerer said, coming closer. "What is your name, girl?"

No one answered him.

"I said, tell me your name!" the sorcerer yelled.

Elizabeth just shook her head, biting her lip. Tess prayed he wouldn't guess her name, or her element.

Amelia was talking to the white stone, trying to coax Alanawaiwai out of it.

"You are strong enough!" Amelia said. "Come out, be free! Maybe water can help you. You're an ocean goddess!"

Water flowed from Amelia's hands onto the stone.

"Ah, the water!" Alanawaiwai said. Her melodious voice sounded stronger. "It feels so good!"

Amelia's dad turned his attention to Amelia.

"Amelia, stop!" her dad yelled. His face filled with fury, more angry than she'd ever seen him.

Amelia turned around.

Her tear-shaped blue eyes met his eyes. They were the same, a pair in Amelia's young, beautiful face, the other in the sorcerer's gaunt, worn-down, skeletal one.

"Incantus…" her dad began to say, but then he dropped his arms.

"You're wearing the pin I gave you for your birthday," he said in a softer voice. "Don't you hate me? After all I've done to you?"

Amelia shook her head.

"I don't like what you've done," she said, "but I can't hate you. You're my dad. I care about you too much. I could never hate you."

"Please," he said to Amelia in a much softer voice. "If you care, get out of the way. I need Alanawaiwai's power to live."

"I don't want you to die," Amelia said, a tear running down her cheek. "But it's not fair to take Alanawaiwai's life."

"Life isn't fair," her dad said, though his voice was gentle. Then he straightened up his back and squared his shoulders.

"Now, move, Water." He waved his hands, and Amelia slid away from the rock. The slide was gentle, and she wasn't hurt.

"Leave her alone!" Tess yelled, surprised to find that she could speak again. "Don't you dare touch her!"

When the sorcerer used his power to shove Amelia out of his way, it seemed to unlock the holding spell.

Tess guessed that Amelia's dad must still be pretty weak if he couldn't keep two spells going at the same time.

The flaming stick she held burned her fingers, so she had to drop it. The light went out and the cave was pitch black again.

Tess heard shuffling noises, followed by a crash.

Someone yelled, "Ouch!"

A hand grabbed hers in the dark, then something cool and narrow was pressed into Tess' hand.

"The candle," Elizabeth whispered into her ear.

"Flicker," Tess said. The candle immediately lit up the cave, providing just enough light to see.

Tess examined the scene in front of them.

The sorcerer was face down on the cave floor.

Akoni lay on top of him.

The strong Hawaiian had the sorcerer pinned to the ground, restraining him. He must have tackled him.

"This is for turning me into a lizard!" Akoni yelled, and yanked the sorcerer's arms behind his back.

"Incantus, incantus Akoni newt!" the sorcerer shouted angrily, over and over.

The spell didn't work.

"Thanks, Grandma!" Akoni said and kissed the turquoise necklace hanging around his neck.

Amelia ran back to the white part of the stone, the glowing part, and put her hands back on it.

"Tess! Elizabeth!" Amelia called. "Help me!"

Tess and Elizabeth ran to the white stone. All three girls put their hands on it. Water flowed from Amelia's hands.

Amelia started to sing True Colors.

Tess wasn't sure why they were singing. But she trusted Amelia, so it must be for a good reason.

Humming came from the inside the stone wall.

It was the same tune.

"Hey!" Elizabeth said. "I can feel something in here. Some of that Dark stone is in here, blocking the white stone. Maybe I can convince it to move."

Elizabeth closed her eyes and concentrated hard.

"Sing louder!" Elizabeth said. "The Dark stone doesn't like the song. I can tell."

Tess and Amelia sang louder.

Amelia's dad yelled in frustration. He was still face down, with strong Akoni sitting on top of him.

"It's not working! I'm trying to silence their awful song!" the sorcerer yelled. "Why won't even my simple spells work?"

"It's my grandmother's necklace!" Akoni said. "You've newted your last newt!"

"That necklace only protects you, fool," the sorcerer said. "Why can't I even move the girls away from the rock?"

Alanawaiwai was growing stronger.

The goddess' voice matched perfectly with Amelia and Tess. Alanawaiwai's voice grew louder and louder, until it filled the cave with a beautiful melody.

A green mist poured out from the rock.

It swirled around until it formed the shape of a woman. The green mist woman studied her hands and mermaid tail, amazed.

Tess' heart beat fast with amazement.

The goddess was beautiful.

"I'm free!" Alanawaiwai said.

"Amelia, Water, you and your friends saved me," Alanawaiwai said. "I have spent hundreds of years trapped inside the rock. It feels so good to be free again."

"Noooo!" the sorcerer cried with frustration and anger. "This can't be happening!"

"Go!" Amelia said to Alanawaiwai. "Go to the ocean! He's powerful. You need to get away!"

"Mahalo, Amelia, water-girl," said Alanawaiwai, then turned back into a green mist. "I will not forget you."

The green mist swirled around Amelia, and then raced out of the cave.

"Look at your hair!" Elizabeth said, pointing to Amelia. "There is a green braid in it!"

"A gift from Alanawaiwai," Akoni said and smiled.

"I can't believe she's free!" Amelia said. "We did it together. It took all of us."

Tess, Amelia and Elizabeth hugged each other.

The three girls sang True Colors together, linking arms. Tess felt giddy with relief and happiness.

"Um, Amelia?" Akoni said. "I hate to ruin the good mood…but your dad just passed out."

Akoni carefully climbed off the sorcerer. Amelia's dad lay flat with his eyes closed. Amelia ran to him.

"I'm not sure he's just passed out," Akoni said. "I think this time it's worse."

Akoni held out his wrist. The tattoo was gone.

Chapter Forty-one

Amelia's dad lay facedown on the cave floor. Amelia ran to him, and put a hand on his limp arm. She was silent for a long time, then began to cry for him.

Tess felt tears well up in her own eyes as she watched Amelia sobbing next to her unmoving father.

Tess was conflicted. She didn't want Amelia to be sad, but she also thought they would be better off without the evil sorcerer. Maybe it was better if he was gone? No danger to anyone, not anymore.

But that meant Amelia would lose her dad.

Tess wasn't sure what to say. Elizabeth stood beside her, shuffling her feet. No one seemed to know what to say, or what to do right now.

The sound of quick footsteps approached.

Ms. Lang ran into the cave. She stared at the scene in front of her.

"He's not OK," Amelia said to Susie's mom in a high-pitched, thin voice, full of pain. "Maybe he's dead."

Ms. Lang took one look, then shook her head.

"He's still breathing, just a little," Ms. Lang said. And then she noticed the candle that Tess was holding.

"Tess? Where did you get that candle?" Ms. Lang asked.

The purple candle in Tess' hand was still lit.

"Oh. Um, sorry," Tess said. "We kind of took it from your office. Sorry."

"Is that how you defeated him?" Ms. Lang said.

Tess felt confused. "No, I don't think so," she said. "Akoni was the one who jumped on top of him."

"Akoni would not have been able to do that if Amelia's dad had his powers," Ms. Lang said. "That's an anti-Dark magic candle. Whenever it's lit, Dark magic won't work."

Tess was shocked into silence. She had no idea the candle was so powerful.

"Anti-Dark magic, of course!" Elizabeth said. "I bet the candle weakened the Dark in the rock. It must have! Tess, your fire power freed Alanawaiwai!"

Tess shook her head. "No way. I mean, you were the one who moved the Dark rock away from Alanawaiwai," she said. "It was you that really freed her."

"Amelia's water also helped," Elizabeth said thoughtfully. "And the song! That helped too, so..."

The experienced sorceress stepped up.

"You all saved her," Ms. Lang said. "You all did such an amazing job. It took all three of you to free the goddess. You too, Akoni."

The Element Girls all looked very proud. Even Akoni smiled sheepishly.

Ms. Lang turned toward Tess, who worried she was in trouble for going into the secret cabinet.

But Ms. Lang squeezed her shoulder and smiled.

"Now, Tess? You keep that candle lit," Ms. Lang said, "in case Amelia's dad wakes up."

Tess nodded, suddenly conscious of her responsibility of keeping the candle lit.

"Good thing you took back your amulet, Tess," Elizabeth said.

Tess squeezed her hand.

"Good thing you believed I could do it," Tess said.

All was silent, which struck Tess as strange. She suddenly realized why she couldn't hear any more of the rock monster's screeching cries.

Susie's mom must have gotten away from it.

But how?

"Ms. Lang? What happened to the rock dragon?" Tess asked. "Are Mikey and Susie OK?"

"Everyone's fine," Ms. Lang said. "Something very powerful came shooting out of the cave—some kind of green mist. It flew around the rock dragon, and must've done something to it. Next thing we knew, that awful rock dragon went running down the mountain as fast as it could go."

"That was Alanawaiwai," Amelia said, looking up from her dad. Her hair shimmered in the light of the candle. The green braid looked beautiful against her blond hair, even though it was all greasy.

"So you all freed the goddess, who saved us in return," Ms. Lang said.

Tess felt a gentle hand on her shoulder.

"You've all been through so much," Ms. Lang said, giving Tess a soft squeeze.

"Um, excuse me?" Akoni interrupted. "Can we leave now? I never liked this cave."

The Element Girls laughed, so did Ms. Lang.

Tess felt the closeness of the cave around them. She had a sudden desire to see the sun and blue sky.

"Yeah, good call, Akoni," Elizabeth said. "I can feel a darkness in all this rock. The Dark stone is really foul. And really sort of…disgusting."

"My dad wanted me to mine the Dark," Amelia said. "But I didn't want to. That's how this all started."

Tess and Elizabeth threw their arms around Amelia, hugging her.

"You're safe now," Tess said, warmth in her heart glowing like a happy ember.

"Let's go home," Ms. Lang said.

"Can we take my dad too?" Amelia asked her. "If he's sick, I don't want him to be all alone in this cave."

Ms. Lang squatted down by the sorcerer.

"He used to be my friend," Ms. Lang said, "back when we were little. We had fun together."

"You knew my dad?" Amelia asked. "When?"

Ms. Lang sighed.

"We went to school together," Ms. Lang said. "Not a regular school, but a school for children with magic."

Everyone was shocked into silence.

"But once David…your dad," Ms. Lang said, looking at Amelia, "started to use magic for evil…"

"What?" Tess asked.

"Well, none of the teachers wanted to teach us anymore," Ms. Lang said. "So the school doesn't exist anymore. So now, kids with magic abilities don't even know about their powers."

"That's too bad," Susie said. "A school for magic would be way cool."

"It's complex," Ms. Lang said. "Maybe it was for the best that the school shut down."

"Do you think I might have powers?" Amelia said. "I mean, without the Water amulet?"

Ms. Lang studied her. "I don't know, Amelia. Magic is hereditary, so there's a very good chance that you do. Susie might, she might not. It's hard to know."

"OK, I'm all for talking, but we need to go!" Akoni said.

Ms. Lang agreed, it was time to leave.

"Tess, keep that candle lit," Ms. Lang reminded her, though Tess wasn't planning on putting it out.

Ms. Lang waved her arms as she twirled around in a circle, while chanting her transport spell.

Tess saw the dark cave slide by, and suddenly they were all outside. The sun was out, and she could see blue sky.

Mikey and Susie were standing among the coconut palms just outside the cave. They both stared, and Tess realized how weird it must be to see people magically appear. Susie's mom swirled her arms around again to transport everyone to the sub.

More scenery rushed past their eyes.

Green plants and coconut trees slid by, and she swore she saw the rock dragon stamping its feet in the waves. She felt a yank, and a second later they were all in the submarine.

Chapter Forty-two

Tess blinked her eyes, looking all around. Even though the purple candle was the only light, which made it very dim inside, it felt much nicer here. It had a clean smell, much better than the musty smell of the cave. And there was no Dark here.

They were back inside the submarine.

"Thanks, Mom!" Susie said.

"Yeah, thanks, Ms. Lang," Elizabeth said. "That was way easier than walking."

"And no mosquitoes," Tess said. The girls laughed.

Susie hopped into the pilot seat. She pushed a few buttons, flipped a few switches, and the sub came alive.

The engine was running and the lights were on, bathing them all in a warm, yellow glow. The sub had windows to look out, and comfortable chairs. It seemed so clean and peaceful, in contrast to the cave.

Elizabeth sat in the co-pilot seat. Instead of reaching for the sub manual, she found something better.

"Ooh, look here," Elizabeth said.

Their chocolate stash lay on one of the low tables in the sub. They shared pieces all around.

Tess sank gratefully into one of the passenger chairs, delicious chocolate melting in her mouth.

The candle was still lit.

Tess looked around for somewhere to put the candle, but there wasn't a good place.

Elizabeth grabbed the manual and instructed Susie in how to sink one meter before diving.

This time Susie listened.

The submarine slowly sank below the surface of the water, then dropped when Susie pressed the button marked 'go deep'.

The sub sank through the dark water, all the way to the ocean floor, roughly five meters below the surface.

No one was sick this time. The descent felt much smoother.

From its resting position at the bottom of the cove, Susie pulled the sub up a few meters. That was easy, but it took ages for the sub to turn around before they could head east, back to Oahu.

Soon enough, they were chugging away from the island.

Amelia curled up on one of the passenger chairs and immediately fell asleep. Tess watched her breathing deeply, and felt a warm glow in her heart to see her friend safe.

But was she safe?

Tess glanced nervously at Amelia's dad, where he lay on the floor. He was still unconscious, but at least he was breathing. Tess worried he'd wake up, feeling strong, and find a way to overpower them all.

Akoni was studying his own arm. His tattoo still hadn't come back. He kept rubbing his wrist, and that's when he caught Tess' eye.

"Never again," Akoni said to her. "I'll never work for a sorcerer again."

Tess held the purple candle, still lit, close to Amelia's dad. She wasn't sure how far the candle's magic reached, and wanted to stay near him, just in case he woke up in a severely bad mood. She recalled what Akoni had said back in the cave—something about being turned into a lizard.

"It's OK, Tess," Ms. Lang said. "The candle works even from several yards away."

Tess eased her arm back in, and rubbed it.

Ms. Lang frowned with concentration for a second, then took some paper from a magazine she found lying in the sub. She formed an origami candle holder, then said some words over it. When she handed it to Tess, Tess was surprised to find it felt solid-heavier than paper.

"It's so strange to think of you as having magic," Tess said, as she fit the candle into the magic candle holder. She placed it by her chair, then smiled at Susie's mom.

"Thanks for everything, Ms. Lang," Tess said. "It's amazing what you can do with magic."

Elizabeth turned in her seat, her brown eyes wide.

"Yeah, we all thought you were a pretty cool mom before all this magic stuff," Elizabeth said. "But now…you're like the coolest mom ever."

Ms. Lang smiled.

"It's a relief not to hide it," she said. "But I am not a big fan of using magic in the everyday world. It feels dangerous, like having too much power. And if anyone found out…" She scoffed and said, "I'd probably be arrested! Or worse, taken away to be studied."

As the sub moved through the ocean depths, Susie and Elizabeth were focused on getting back safely. Elizabeth slid a stone out of the way and turned in her chair.

"Is magic why your garden grows so quickly?" Elizabeth asked. "We can never get anything to grow in ours, but your lemon tree, the mint, the cucumbers—" Elizabeth ticked off the plants on her fingers. "They all grow so well."

Ms. Lang looked embarrassed. "OK," she said, "I admit it. I do use a little magic on the garden. But for most things, I promise that I don't use any spells."

"I knew it!" Elizabeth said. "I knew there was something funny about your garden. Can I tell my parents? They love all that gardening stuff."

"Goodness, no! Please don't tell them," Ms. Lang. "They don't need to know about magic. Though I can come tend your vegetables when we're back, and you'll find they grow better." She gave Elizabeth a knowing smile.

Elizabeth turned back to the front window, an echoing smile on her face. The ocean was lighter now, which meant they must be out of the bad weather of the island.

Yellow fish swam by.

"Tess?" Ms. Lang said. "I feel really in the dark about everything that's happened. All I know is, we came to find Amelia, and we landed in Honolulu. That's when I passed out. When I woke up, I was in that house. I don't even know where Maggie is, or what happened to her."

"Amelia's mom is at the Honolulu airport hotel," Tess said. "She's OK, but confused."

Ms. Lang didn't look happy.

"Well, it's a relief that you know where she is," Ms. Lang said. "And I hope the confusion is a temporary spell from David. I will go see her as soon as I can."

She studied Akoni, who was still rubbing his wrist.

"Hello, Akoni. I'm Elaine," Ms. Lang said, extending her hand. "I'm not sure we got a chance to introduce ourselves back on that island."

"Aloha," Akoni said. Then he seemed to realize something. His eyes lit up and he turned to the others.

"Aloha, all of you," Akoni said. "Tess, and Elizabeth, and Susie. And you too, Mikey. Amelia told me about all of you."

"Nice to meet you, Akoni," Tess said, giggling. It was true, they hadn't really met formally. They just sort of fell into a wild adventure together.

"Hey, Akoni?" Elizabeth asked. "Are you and Amelia… you know, like…a couple?"

Tess held her breath as she waited for the answer. Mikey leaned out of his passenger chair, studying Akoni's face. Tess knew he'd be disappointed if they were going out.

Akoni smiled deeply as he looked at the sleeping Amelia.

"You honor me," Akoni said. "She's an amazing girl. But I have a girlfriend, Malie. No, Amelia and I are just…close friends. We've been through a lot together."

"How did you meet her?" Tess asked. "Were you also a prisoner on the island?"

To her surprise, Akoni lost his smile.

"Actually," Akoni said, "I will let Amelia tell you that story when she wakes up." He brought his knees into the seat, and looked moodily out the window.

Tess wondered what Akoni's story was, especially since it seemed to be a dramatic one.

"I'm surprised you all didn't know each other," Ms. Lang said. "It's just that you all seemed so close, when I met you in that clearing."

"Actually, we only met Akoni pretty much when you did," Tess explained to Susie's mom. "I guess because Amelia trusted him, we did too."

"So, Tess?" Ms. Lang handed her a piece of dark chocolate. "Tell me…what happened to you?"

Chapter Forty-three

Tess started to tell the story of what happened to them all. She started at the beginning, with the text about the green envelope back at Amelia's house.

"Just when your text came, Didus was there at the kitchen window," Tess said.

"Ah, yes," Ms. Lang said fondly. "He's always reliable. Didus was looking out for a sign from me. I let him know he might be needed before I went to Oahu."

"You talked to him?" Tess said. "Can you talk to dogs?"

Susie gave her mom a weird look from the pilot seat.

"Not really," Ms. Lang said. "Didus is special."

Susie's shoulders relaxed.

"Just so you know, Mom," Susie said. "I'm OK with magic…but it would definitely weird me out if you talked to animals."

Her mom smiled.

"Noted," Ms. Lang said. "And I'm very glad you're OK with magic."

Tess continued to fill Ms. Lang in on their search, how they took some magic objects from her office, and how they discovered each of their element powers.

"I kept accidentally lighting fires," Tess said and laughed dryly. "Susie jumped up to the ceiling in a volleyball game.

And Elizabeth, she found her rock power in this very sub, on the way to the island."

By the time Tess explained all the things that happened to them before they met Amelia in the clearing, an hour had passed. She was thirsty from all the talking and explaining.

"So cool how you all have amulets," Mikey said. "I felt really useless this whole time. I could barely help."

"You weren't useless," Elizabeth said. "You helped a lot! You kept us harmonious, you were dependable, and very brave." She winked at him.

Mikey shrugged, and looked down.

"Yeah, maybe," Mikey said. But he smiled.

"Well, at least you didn't make a whole airplane disappear," Tess said to Mikey. "And you didn't keep setting maps and hair on fire by accident."

Mikey grinned at his sister.

"You were the hero in the end," he said, "with that purple candle."

Ms. Lang was shaking her head.

"I would never have given you those amulets if I knew you would try to take on Amelia's dad," she said.

"The amulets helped us. Probably saved us, too," Tess said. "We would have gone after Amelia with or without magic."

Ms. Lang's eyes watered. "You girls are inspiring," she said. "And so much has happened to all of you."

Tess realized they had only been gone a few days. But so much had changed. They had rescued their friend, freed a goddess, fought an evil sorcerer, and discovered their element powers.

And she felt protective of Mikey. That was a new feeling. All her life, he had protected her.

Tess didn't feel like the nervous, insecure Tess pre-adventure. She somehow felt stronger. Older. Even though she had made mistakes…like the disappearing airplane, and accidentally setting things on fire…she still felt a lot different.

Tess had an important question for Susie's mom.

"Ms. Lang? Why did you give me the Fire amulet?" Tess asked. "I mean, thank you, and everything–but I never thought of myself as fire. Is it because I flicker?"

"Well, no," Ms. Lang said. She looked at the purple candle burning in the origami candle holder. Then she pointed to the unconscious sorcerer lying on the floor.

"He was good, once," Ms. Lang said. "But he never examined his actions. He saw the power Dark magic would give him, and he didn't hesitate."

"He loved Amelia and her mom," Ms. Lang went on. "I'm sure he thought he was helping them, making more money. But he never really thought about his choices, whether they were good or bad. And Tess, you always examine your actions. I knew you'd try to do good despite fire's desire to burn everything it can."

Tess felt her cheeks warm. She had thought the fire element to be the weakest one, and she always thought she was the most unsure and hesitant of her friends. But now Susie's mom was saying it was given to her because of her strengths.

"Thanks," Tess said and wished she could think of something bigger to say. "Thanks so much. I mean, for seeing that. I do try. And I want to use the fire power for good. But it sometimes has its own ideas."

Ms. Lang reached out and squeezed Tess' hand.

"It sometimes used my anger, I think," Tess said. "I felt angrier with the amulet on. And that's when I lost control of the fire power."

Ms. Lang nodded.

"The fire element has the most destructive power of all the four elements," Ms. Lang said. "I thought you were the most responsible one, and the one most likely to be able to handle its power. That is why I chose you for Fire."

Tess' heart warmed. She hoped she could learn to control it even more, and never misuse it. She couldn't imagine turning into someone evil, like Amelia's dad.

The submarine passed into brighter waters.

They were over halfway there.

Tess gazed out the window and counted small, pink jellyfish. She pulled out her phone and took some photos for the Brightcubes.

"Well now, Tess," Ms. Lang said, breaking into her momentary quiet. "You've told me how you, Susie, Elizabeth and Mikey got to the island. But how did you learn about the goddess…Alanawaiwai, right? Stories about gods and goddesses are extremely old, and you don't come across them every day."

"Oh, yeah! I want to know that too," Tess said. "I have no idea who she was, but she was very beautiful—a green, misty, mermaid goddess."

Akoni had been listening. He opened his mouth to answer, but someone else got there first—someone else who knew the story.

Amelia sat up in her chair, with her tear-shaped blue eyes focused on Tess.

"She's an ocean goddess," Amelia said, waking up. "She was trapped in that cave for hundreds of years by this really mean ocean god who wanted to marry her. Akoni can tell you the whole story. It's so sad."

"My grandmother taught me the story," Akoni said. "She made me repeat it word for word, so many times."

Akoni rolled his eyes.

"Yeah, but it paid off," Amelia said. "We found her, didn't we?"

"Grandma was right, as usual," Akoni said and smiled thinking about Tutu.

Amelia turned back to Tess and Susie's Mom, to fill in more of the story.

"Mahealani, her best friend, never stopped looking for Alanawaiwai," Amelia said. "Just like you all never stopped looking for me."

"Wow," Tess said. "Where do you think Alanawaiwai is now?"

"I think she probably went to find her family," Amelia said. "And her best friend, Mahealani, the moon goddess."

"I hope Alanawaiwai and Mahealani find each other again," Tess said.

Amelia touched the green braid in her hair.

"I'm sure they will," Amelia said. "Friends like that always find each other."

Amelia beamed at Tess, and Tess' heart glowed.

"I'm so glad you're here with us, safe," Tess said.

Amelia's face darkened, and her eyes misted up, as if remembering something difficult.

"It was scary sometimes," Amelia said. "When I was in the car, when my dad first took me. I didn't know where we were going, or what was happening. And then I was trapped in that cave all night. My dad did some ankle-shackling spell."

Tess' eyes teared up. "I was scared too. I dreamt you were captured, in a big net," she said. "You cried out 'Daddy'. Now I know what it meant."

Amelia's eyes brightened.

334

"A big net?" Amelia said. "That's how Mahealani was first taken. Then Alanawaiwai freed her, and was captured herself."

Tess wondered what the parallel meant. Maybe two sets of best friends faced the same kind of problems, only hundreds of years apart.

"I knew you would find me," Amelia said. "I didn't give up hope. When I was trapped in the cave, in the dark, hungry and all alone...I thought of you three. It kept me going, made me feel better."

"I worried we wouldn't find you," Tess said. "I wish I had your hope."

Amelia held out her pinky. "I have enough hope for both of us," she said. "For all of us!"

"Let's make a pact to always have faith in our friendship," Amelia said.

Tess agreed.

The bond between her and Amelia felt stronger than ever. They called out to Elizabeth and Susie, too.

"I'll pinky to that!" Susie said. From the pilot's seat, she reached one arm back to join them.

The four girls hooked their fingers together.

"Friendship pledge?" Tess asked.

"For you, I would walk on water," Amelia said, smiling at Tess.

"For you, I would walk on air!" Susie said. "Even with one good ankle!"

"For you, I would walk the Earth," Elizabeth said.

"And for you, for all of you, I would walk through fire," Tess said.

There was a blip on the radar screen.

"Hey, check it out!" Susie said, turning to the monitor. "The ocean bottom is sloping up. I think we're close to Oahu."

Chapter Forty-four

The submarine slowed to a stop, and rose slowly to the surface. Tess couldn't believe they were finally back in Oahu, safe and together.

"We're rising slow this time!" Susie announced. "Maybe we can figure out where to go by the time we surface."

"Pizza?" Elizabeth said.

"I think I have a plan," Ms. Lang said. "I've been thinking about it all through the trip. But first…"

Susie's mom went over to her daughter and placed her hands on her injured ankle.

Rainbow light came from her hands.

"Wow!" Susie rotated her ankle. "It's all good now! Why didn't you do that before?"

"Well, for one thing, I wasn't sure it was the right thing to do," her mom said.

Susie's face darkened. "What do you mean?"

"It's hard to explain…" her mom said.

"Wait a second," Susie said. "Remember in third grade, when I pulled my calf muscle running? Why didn't you heal it? I couldn't race with the team! Or when I fell off my bike in sixth grade and split my lip. Or my first volleyball tournament, when I took a spike to the face and got that huge black eye. Why didn't you fix all those?"

337

"Because you had to learn," her mom said. "Magic doesn't solve everything. We need to learn to be careful, and we need to learn that our bodies can be injured, and should heal naturally."

"So why did you just fix her ankle now?" Elizabeth asked.

"Well, she injured it fighting a magical creature—the rock dragon. So this time I made an exception," Ms. Lang said. "Broken by magic, healed by magic."

Susie still didn't look happy, but she nodded.

"I guess it makes sense," Susie said. "Thanks for fixing my foot, Mom." She got out of her chair and did some practice jumps.

"Yeah, that's much better," Susie said and smiled as she kept jumping.

"Are you going to heal my dad, too?" Amelia asked.

Ms. Lang's face became serious. "I'm afraid he is too sick to be returned to health," she said. "And I'm not so good at healing spells. Not ones that powerful."

Amelia lowered her head in sadness.

"So he's going to die?" Amelia said, sniffing. "I only just met him."

"I can try to heal him," Ms. Lang said, "but just in case it works...I should probably erase his memory at the same time."

"So he'll forget about kidnapping me?" Amelia asked. "And mining Dark?"

"Can you make him forget about magic completely?" Elizabeth asked.

"You've always been so clever, Elizabeth," Ms. Lang said, smiling at her. "Yes, I think I better erase any memory of magic. Though, it is possible he could rediscover his powers."

"OK, so we won't do any magic in front of him," Elizabeth said. "Right?"

Tess, Amelia and Susie agreed.

"And we can't tell anyone what happened on the island," Elizabeth said. "It has to be our secret."

"That's safest," Tess said. "No one would believe us anyway."

"My grandmother," Akoni said. "I have to tell her what happened. She would never forgive me if I didn't prove I tried to help free Alanawaiwai. I have to redeem myself."

"Redeem yourself from what?" Tess asked.

Akoni and Amelia shared a look. Tess felt like she was missing part of the story.

"OK, fine," Ms. Lang said. "Akoni, you can tell your grandmother what happened. No one else. Now, this may take some time."

Susie's mom crouched by Amelia's dad. Rainbow light poured from her hands onto Amelia's dad's body.

The submarine surfaced.

Though they were back in sunny Oahu, no one moved to get out of their chairs. Everyone was quiet.

Tess watched blue waves lap at the little circular window of the sub. She enjoyed the peace, and let her mind drift like waves.

"Hey, I got a phone signal!" Elizabeth's excited voice interrupted Tess' thoughts.

Elizabeth called the Brightcubes to tell them Amelia was safe. Tess smiled as she listened to their conversation.

"She seems OK," Elizabeth said into her phone. "She can recite the primes."

"Practice tomorrow?" Elizabeth said, after a pause. "I don't think she'll make it to math practice tomorrow. Next week, maybe."

After another pause, she turned to Tess.

"Did you see any of the species on Damian's list?" Elizabeth asked.

"I don't know what species I saw," Tess said. "I took lots of pictures, though."

Elizabeth told the Brightcubes that she would send the fish photos as soon as she could. Then she rolled her eyes and hung up.

"They wanted to let us know it's 80.5 degrees in Oahu today," Elizabeth said. "I mean, is that relevant?"

"Maybe it's their way of bonding, Liz," Susie said. "I love those guys."

Akoni called his grandmother. He poured out the story of how they freed Alanawaiwai, and how he helped. At the end of the conversation he smiled.

"For once, Tutu is proud of me," Akoni said. He sat up straighter in his chair.

Ms. Lang stepped away from the sorcerer.

"That's it. That's all I can do," she said and stretched out her sore hand. "All we can do now is wait to see if he wakes up."

Tess' stomach rumbled. She was extremely thirsty now, and so was everyone else.

"Man, I'm hungry. And thirsty," Susie said, echoing Tess' thoughts.

Akoni announced that he had some excellent news.

"Amelia, your mom is at my grandma's house," Akoni told the group. "Tutu invites us all there. There will be a lot of food. And it will be good!"

Ms. Lang sighed and said, "OK, one last magic trick, then we go back to normal." She waved her hands around, and recited the teleportation spell.

Tess watched the ocean speed by her, then a sandy beach whooshed past. She felt a familiar jolt, and the next thing she knew, she and everyone else were standing outside a low, white house in the sun.

Akoni's grandmother waved from the porch. She hugged them all in turn, saving Akoni for last. She gave her grandson an extra long hug, her crinkled face smiling with pride.

A woman came out of the house into the sunshine.

"Mom!" Amelia shouted.

Amelia's mom launched out of the house, laughing. She grabbed Amelia and held her tight. They heard a bark from the house, and saw a beautiful brown and tan Collie at the door.

Didus ran to them, panting and greeting each of them with joyful brown eyes.

"Maggie, are you OK?" Ms. Lang asked her. "The girls told me you felt confused, and something about a possible concussion."

"I'm fine now," Ms. Hilton said. "Suddenly, everything became clear again. I still don't know exactly what happened. Amelia, are you OK?"

"I'm OK, Mom," Amelia said and gave her another big hug.

"What happened?" her mom asked. "You look terrible. You're covered in dirt, and your eyes are all red. Have you slept?"

"I...don't remember," Amelia said. "But I'm OK, I promise. Just need some sleep. And a shower."

"And the rest of you! Are you OK? What happened?" Ms. Hilton asked, looking around with worried eyes.

"We don't know either," Susie said.

"We think some kind of drug was used," Ms. Lang said. "It made us all forget what happened."

"A drug?" Ms. Hilton looked at the unconscious man Akoni was tending to. "Amelia, why is your dad here?"

"I do remember him capturing me," Amelia said. "I was in a car with him. That's all I know. Right now, he's really sick."

"He kidnapped you?" Ms. Hilton said. "We need to call the police."

Ms. Lang put a soothing hand on her arm.

"Maggie, I promise that he is not going to hurt anyone in the state he's in," she said. "I'm not even sure he's going to wake up."

Amelia's mom's face crumpled into sadness.

"I don't want him hurt or…dead," she said. "I just don't want him anywhere near my daughter."

Since he was the strongest, Akoni picked up and carried the sleeping sorcerer into the house. He laid him down on a bed upstairs. Tess followed with the purple candle, just in case.

Akoni dusted himself off. "I hope I never have to see that guy again," he said to Tess. "I can't forget what he did to me."

"What did he do?" Tess asked. She wondered if it had something to do with the lizard comment Akoni made in the cave. Had he turned Akoni into a lizard?

Akoni looked horrified. "I…I can't say it. Never mind." Then he hurried back down the stairs.

Tess imagined being turned into a lizard was not something easy to get over. She wondered what the sorcerer did to Amelia's mom, to make her so forgetful.

Ms. Hilton knocked gently on the door.

She and Tess stood over the sleeping sorcerer. He didn't look like he was going to wake up anytime soon.

"I just want to keep a close watch on him, in case he goes after Amelia again," Ms. Hilton explained. "I haven't seen him in twelve years. I thought I hated him, but he looks so…pitiful. And old."

"What did he do to you to make you hate him?" Tess asked.

"Oh, he got mixed up with the wrong crowd when we were young," Ms. Hilton said. "We were robbed—twice—by some of his so-called friends. He refused to admit it, and refused to stop hanging out with them. I found drugs in his pockets more than once. He went down a bad road, and I didn't want Amelia to get mixed up in all that."

Tess looked sadly at the unconscious sorcerer. The part of him that looked a little bit like Amelia made her heart warm to him.

Tess put the burning purple candle by his bedside, though Amelia's mom didn't understand why.

"If it's important to you, Tess, I'll keep it lit," Ms. Hilton said. "Though I'm not sure it will help. Oh, I feel so lost about a lot of things."

"Don't worry," Tess said. "There are things I don't understand either. But maybe with time they'll become more clear."

Ms. Hilton looked at her with big eyes.

"When did you get so grown up?" she asked Tess.

Tess only smiled. Even if she could explain the whole story, and if she hadn't promised to keep it quiet, she really couldn't explain the effect everything had on her. She just felt so different.

And hungry.

Tess' stomach growled in response to all the delicious smells coming up the stairs. She told Amelia's mom she'd bring her a plate of food, and hurried downstairs to join the feast.

Chapter Forty-five

Tutu's cooking was truly amazing. She had made lots of traditional Hawaiian food including tender and smoky kalua pig, lau lau, lomi salmon and the starchy yet tasty poi. Everyone's spirits lifted as they ate in the comfortable living room on sofas and armchairs.

Didus had an armchair to himself.

After finishing a plate heaped with food, Tess felt full and content. Deep waves of sleepiness were hitting her.

Tutu gave Akoni a second helping of kalua pig, and Amelia smiled at him.

"Looks like your grandmother is happy with you," Amelia said to Akoni.

"I'll enjoy it while it lasts! Probably only twenty-four hours," Akoni said and they both had a good laugh.

Tess smiled, watching them. Akoni and Amelia seemed like old friends. She realized they must have been through a lot together, and she hoped Amelia would tell her more about it one day.

Mikey leaned close to Amelia. "I'm so glad you're safe," he said.

"Thanks, Mikey," Amelia said. "And thanks for coming to the island to rescue me. And Susie's mom."

"And, um…if you want to go out with Akoni, I'm fine with that," Mikey said. "I mean, disappointed, but OK."

"Mikey!" Amelia said. "I don't want to go out with Akoni. But I don't want to go out with you, either."

Mikey looked crestfallen—even the tips of his ears turned red. He nodded soberly.

"I guess you just want to do math battles," he said.

Amelia thought about it. "Yeah, I guess I like math because it's so clean and logical. So predictable, in a way," she said. "Real life isn't like that. I learned that in these last few days. I think I'll start doing something else, too. Something watery. Like swimming."

Mikey smiled. "And listen, I didn't mean to freak you out like that—you know, by asking you out. I'm sorry. Can we just go back to being friends?"

"Of course! We are already friends," Amelia said. Then she politely excused herself to go into the kitchen.

Elizabeth had been listening to their conversation, watching Mikey closely. When Amelia got up for some more POG to drink, Elizabeth came over to him.

"I decided…I'm sure of your power now," Elizabeth said.

"What power?" Mikey said. "I don't have any magic."

"Sure you do," Elizabeth said. "I've told you before. You have the power of love."

Mikey blushed deep red.

"That's not a power!" he said.

"Of course it is! Look, you patched things up with Tess, and now Amelia," Elizabeth said. "You kept our group harmonious. I wasn't kidding about that."

Tess nodded. "I completely agree," she said. "You kept trying to be my friend, even when I was mad at you. And I'm not mad at you anymore. I feel closer to you than ever. I think a lot of that was your special power."

Mikey shrugged, but he liked the idea.

"I just care about all of you," Mikey said. "That's all."

"Well, that's a lot," Elizabeth said. She handed him what looked like a small bowl of fruit. "This is so good. Here, try some. There's ice cream at the bottom, and it's all creamy and good."

Mikey took it, and smiled as he ate it. "It is amazing!" he said. "I think this is my new favorite dessert."

Elizabeth reached for a second treat. "As of tomorrow morning, I'm going on a diet," she said. "But not tonight."

Susie joined them on the sofa.

Elizabeth turned to her. "So, Susie, I guess you can't wait to play volleyball! It's been what, like, days?"

"Yeah, I guess," Susie shrugged. "I mean, I want to play, of course. But not as much as I usually want to play. I don't think anything is going to beat spiking coconuts at that rock dragon."

Tess stared at Susie in amazement. Susie never expressed less than one hundred percent enthusiasm for volleyball. Tess realized she wasn't the only one who felt different after their wild weekend.

"I think I'm ready to do something else too," Susie said. "Maybe I won't play volleyball every day. Maybe just six days a week instead. One day a week, I'll go swimming with Amelia."

"Yes!" Amelia said. "I'd love it if we could swim together."

"Me too!" Elizabeth said. "I want to swim!"

"You hate exercise!" Susie said.

"That's true," Elizabeth said. "But I want to be able to hike up the next mountain, if one of us is ever in danger again. I mean, without panting."

"You did great," Susie said. "You kept up just fine."

"I was panting and sweating more than you and Tess combined!" Elizabeth said. "Anyway, with you girls, swimming will be fun. I do have a summer dress I can wear over my swimsuit–it'll be perfect."

"You're going to swim in a dress?" Susie asked.

"Of course!" Elizabeth said. "You can do anything in a dress."

"What about you, Tess?" Amelia asked. "Are you up for swimming with us?"

Tess didn't know what to think. She was so full, and so sleepy. She was just happy to be here, in this group, with her best friends around her.

"I don't know," Tess said, thinking out loud. "The thing is, before the island, I realize I always felt like I was doing something wrong. I was sure I did something to make Amelia mad at me before all this started."

Amelia reached over the sofa and squeezed Tess' hand. "I'm so sorry I didn't tell you about the Valentine. I shouldn't have shut you out."

"It's OK," Tess said and squeezed her hand back. "I understand it was weird for you. It wasn't just that. I mean, when Mrs. Riley asked me to do the summer camp, I thought I would just mess up. And when I lit the black candle and the airplane disappeared, I just felt like a total failure. Like, great, of course, it had to be me that screwed up so bad."

"Hey, if we had lit the purple candle in the plane like we planned," Elizabeth said, "we wouldn't have had it in the cave. Then Amelia's dad might have won!"

"Yeah, I guess so," Tess said. "Thanks, Earth. But I think I need to find my confidence. I need to find my own thing. I don't want to feel like I'm screwing up all the time."

"Believe in your fire!" Susie said.

"Something like that," Tess said and smiled. "I need to think about it some more. Maybe I'll start with being a camp counselor this summer."

"You totally should!" Susie said and gave Tess a hug. "And you can still come swimming with us! It'll be, you know, in preparation."

"They have pools in camp, you know," Elizabeth said. "Best to be prepared!"

Tess laughed and nodded. "Yeah, I guess you're right," she said. "OK, I'm in on the swimming."

A squeak on the staircase made them all jump.

Amelia's dad was awake.

Ms. Hilton was helping him down the stairs because he was too weak to do it on his own.

Tess wondered what he remembered.

Did he still have his powers?

And where was the purple candle?

Chapter Forty-six

As the sorcerer walked down the stairs, assisted by Amelia's mom, Tess felt her heart tighten with fear. She made a move to get up. She wanted to rush upstairs to get the purple candle, to stop him if he dared to try and go after Amelia again.

As if to restrain her, Susie's mom grabbed Tess' arm. She leaned toward her, as if she knew what Tess was thinking.

"It's OK," Ms. Lang whispered. "It will work from up there."

Tess sagged back into the couch with relief. She still thought about checking it was still lit, though.

Amelia's dad didn't look like a threat anymore. He looked…fragile.

"That's it…" Ms. Hilton said. "Good. Next step."

The sorcerer looked like he'd aged twenty years. Gray hair hung down over his wrinkled face. He limped as he walked, and his tear-shaped blue eyes were cloudy, almost as gray as his hair.

When he spoke, his voice was tired and thin.

"Oh, hello," Amelia's dad said, looking confused. "I'm sorry, but do I know you? Any of you?" He looked around the room. "I've just met Maggie, here…she's helping me." He patted the arm of Amelia's mom.

Then his eyes met Amelia's, and grew clearer.

"Now, you I remember, young lady," he said. "What's your name again?"

Amelia came up to him.

"I'm Amelia," she said. "You're my dad. But I don't know you very well. I didn't grow up with you."

She hugged her dad gently.

"Why didn't you grow up with me?" her dad asked. "Was I away somewhere?"

The group exchanged confused looks.

What could they tell him about his past? They certainly couldn't mention magic.

Susie's mom jumped to the rescue.

"You were lost," Ms. Lang told the ex-sorcerer. "We don't know where you went. But you're back now, and that's all that matters."

Amelia led her dad to the sofa. He sat there quietly, looking around at everyone, looking very confused.

Tess ran upstairs to get the purple candle, just in case. She felt better when it burned right next to the sofa where he was sitting.

"See," Ms. Lang said quietly, when Tess returned with the candle. "Responsible. You."

Tess felt her cheeks burn with a pleased kind of embarrassment.

"Everyone," Akoni's grandmother said as she came shuffling in. "Have some haupia, made with fresh coconut."

"Seriously? Ice-creamy fruity stuff, and now yummy coconut sweets?" Elizabeth said. "Well, if we're going to start swimming when we get back, I'm going to have one."

"That fruity ice-cream dessert is called halo-halo," Tutu said. "And of course you will eat some haupia. You cannot leave Hawaii without trying it. It is time for sweets and celebration. A goddess isn't freed every day, you know."

"SHHH!"

A chorus of hushing sounds made Tutu jump. Tess caught her eye, and gave a pointed look at Amelia's dad.

She quietly explained to Tutu not to mention anything about magic in front of Amelia's dad—even if he seemed pretty harmless at the moment.

"I mean, on my TV show," Akoni's grandmother said. "I'm excited because on the show, a goddess was trapped in a cave, and freed just today."

Tess took a square of haupia from Tutu, and they exchanged smiles.

Tess bit into the dessert. It was creamy and delicious. Even Amelia's dad smiled a little as he tasted one.

Didus wasn't allowed to have one, but Tutu gave him something else as a treat.

Didus leapt up next to Susie, and she rubbed behind his ears.

"Mom?" Susie said. "I always wondered, why is Didus still so healthy? I've always known him as an adult dog, you know. But don't they only live around ten years or something?"

Her mom winked.

"Don't worry, Susie," she said. "Didus will be with us a long time yet. Or should I say…Professor Didus."

Susie stared at the dog, eyes wide.

Tess suddenly imagined Didus with glasses on, lecturing in a classroom. She found the image kind of suited him.

"Was he a professor in the magic school?" Susie asked, whispering.

Ms. Lang nodded.

"Don't worry," Ms. Lang said. "Didus has his own ways of keeping young."

Didus stared at Susie and Tess with big, brown eyes. Tess swore he looked kind of proud of himself.

"Mom, I don't get why you hid magic," Susie said quietly. "I mean, it's so cool. And you're so amazing at it!"

Ms. Lang looked nervously at Amelia's dad. He was licking his fingers after eating the square of haupia, and the color of his face looked better—less pale. And he was paying absolutely zero attention to their hushed conversation.

"We'll talk about it later," her mom whispered back. "Let's just say that sometimes, I wish there was no…M-word. It can be too much power. Just look at what happened with Amelia's dad."

Susie shrugged.

"Personally, I think it's a good thing," Susie said. "Just look at my ankle!" She got up and jumped all around, higher than she probably should have. "I think that if I had the M-word, I'd be loving it."

"I didn't always hide it," her mom said. "In the old days, I was much more open with it. But your dad…that's why he left."

"He left because of magic?" Susie said loudly.

She got shushed by everyone in the house, and quickly lowered her voice.

"You told me he left before I was born," Susie said quietly. "But you never said why. I figured you guys just had issues."

"We did," her mom said. "The issue was the M-word. And after he left, I decided it would be safer to hide my abilities. To give you a normal life."

Susie nodded, pulling her ponytail.

"I think I get it," Susie said. "Maybe. I'm not sure."

Her mom gave her a hug.

"Take your time," her mom said. "I'll tell you more if you want. Just ask me."

Ms. Lang gave a careful look to Amelia's dad, who was closing his eyes sleepily, and about to fall right into his second helping of halo-halo.

"I think we should talk about it later, once we're out of his earshot," her mom said.

"OK, Mom," Susie said. "Anyway, I'm too tired for anything but more dessert. But first…"

Susie got up to use the bathroom.

Tess touched her Fire amulet.

"I hope you don't mind, I was listening," Tess said to Susie's mom. "I'm not sure about the M-word, either." She held up her Fire amulet. "I get angrier with it on."

Ms. Lang understood perfectly well.

"It affects us, it changes us," Ms. Lang said. "At the school, I saw a lot of people change as they became more powerful. No one went quite as a bad as him."

Didus whined.

Ms. Lang turned to pet him.

Amelia's dad had fallen asleep on the sofa, his mouth partway open. He didn't look like someone who did terrible things.

Amelia and her mom were studying him too.

"I don't think he looks evil," Amelia said to her mom. "Not now, anyway."

"No, he was never evil," her mom said. "Just mixed up with the wrong people."

"What do we do about him now?" Amelia said. "Will we leave him here?"

Her mom took a deep breath. "I can't do that," she said. "He doesn't remember anything. He's all alone."

"Mom?" Amelia whispered. "I know dad has a house on that island–well, two houses, actually. But maybe he shouldn't go back there? I mean, if he was mixed up with the wrong people, maybe it's better if he doesn't remember them. We could sell both his houses and get him a place in Berkeley. Near us."

She could tell her mom was thinking about it.

"Let's see if he wants us to do that," she said. "When he wakes up. OK?"

"OK, Mom," Amelia said.

After such a tremendous meal, everyone was soon sinking into the cushions of the couch and plush chairs.

Tess felt ready to explode from all the food she ate.

Akoni was on the phone in the kitchen. Tess could hear him talking to someone, apologizing.

"Of course you're the only one for me!" Akoni was saying. "You're the hottest of the hot!"

Amelia came to sit by Tess, and elbowed her.

"He's talking to his girlfriend," Amelia explained, pointing to the kitchen.

Tess giggled. "Akoni's girlfriend sounds like a handful."

"Oh, yeah," Amelia said. "Believe me, I know."

Akoni's grandmother came over. She put a gentle hand on Amelia's shoulder.

"I still think he should marry someone like you," the old woman said. "But maybe, one day…" Then she winked at Amelia before making an announcement.

Akoni's grandmother told everyone that she had made beds for all of them. The four girls would sleep upstairs in

358

bunk beds, and Mikey would sleep downstairs on the sofa. Akoni had his own room.

After the weekend they all had, everyone agreed without a fuss that a good night's rest was in order.

Tess went upstairs with the other girls. She tucked herself into the lower bunk bed, exhausted.

Susie and Elizabeth climbed the ladders to the top bunks, and got comfortable.

Soon it was quiet, except for the deep breathing sounds of the girls.

Tess closed her eyes for a minute. When she opened them again, Amelia was watching her from the neighboring bed. She was pretty sure that Susie and Elizabeth were already asleep.

"Are you OK?" Tess whispered.

Amelia smiled deeply, her dimples showing in the dim light of the moonlit room.

"So much has happened," Amelia said quietly, "but I feel better than OK. I can't believe you all came to find me."

"Of course we came to find you," Tess said. "What are friends for?"

"It's still a lot," Amelia said. "What about you, Tess? Are you OK?"

Tess considered how tired she was, and how her mosquito bites itched. But she also felt very happy, full of food, and curled up in a warm, safe bed.

"Yes, I'm OK," she answered truthfully. "I feel better than OK. I feel closer to you and the others than ever. And I can't believe we found you. And how we freed the goddess. It all makes me realize something."

"What?" Amelia asked.

"All the things I was worried about, like the summer camp counselor thing, and starting high school in the fall..." Tess sighed, but it sounded relaxed. "I'm not so worried about those things anymore."

"You'll do fine," Amelia said. "Better than fine. You'll do great. I know you will."

"Thanks...it's not just that," Tess said. "It's that now I know I won't have to do it alone. With all of us, and Mikey, and Susie's mom, I know I've got help when I need it."

Amelia beamed. She hooked pinkies with Tess.

"You're right, Tess," Amelia said. "None of us have to face anything alone."

"That's right. Hey, we're the Element Girls now," Tess said and grinned.

"Element Girls," Amelia repeated. "I like it. That's what Akoni called us, right?"

Tess nodded.

"For you, I would walk through fire," she said, reciting her part of the friendship pledge.

"For you, I would walk on water," Amelia said with a smile.

Their arms, with hooked pinkies, swung back and forth between the beds for awhile. Then Amelia couldn't hold back a huge yawn.

"Sleep," Tess said, as they let go. "You must be exhausted."

Amelia nodded, and closed her eyes. She breathed deeply, and was asleep in an instant.

Tess felt tired too, but she wasn't ready to go to sleep just yet. Her mind spun with all that had happened. She thought about all the other people who had helped them on their journey. Even the tricky boy at the shrimp stall had helped them, by leading them to the sub. That was crucial in getting to the island.

Tess thanked him silently, and wished him a pineapple ice cream.

She whispered to Alanawaiwai, wishing her love. She hoped the goddess was safe, and had found her family and best friend.

"And thank you, Cyndi Lauper," she whispered as she fell asleep. "For the song."

As soon as she fell asleep, Tess dreamed of mermaids, and dolphins swimming all around them.

All four Element Girls were swimming in the ocean, singing a song together.

A green mermaid sang with them.

It was Alanawaiwai.

The moon rose, and a streak of white light played on the waves. A beautiful woman made of light came down on a moonbeam, and laughed with joy when she saw them. She hugged Alanawaiwai, and danced on the water. She had a green braid in her hair.

It was Mahealani.

A shark swam near, but Tess wasn't scared. She knew what to do.

Tess had a strong, beautiful red tail, and she beat it at the shark. She smacked its nose with her tail, and it swam a little ways off.

When the shark came back, she was ready.

Amelia, Susie and Elizabeth linked arms with Tess, and they faced the shark together. The shark looked frightened, then quickly swam away. Far, far away.

Together, they had found their powers. Together, they were the Element Girls.

Susie — Air

Amelia — Water

Elizabeth — Earth

Tess — Fire

About the author

Giulietta M. Spudich enjoys writing everything from children's stories to grown-up fiction, and poems in between. She lives in Cambridge, England where she moved from California in 2002. She is inspired by cats, especially her late black cat, Smokey.

Find Giulietta on Twitter @spudichpen.

Discover more at:
www.handersenpublishing.com

A special thank you to our readers in Hawaii for their helpful comments on the pre-published version of this book.
Lisa-Anne Tsuruda & Sean, Brandon and Emma.

Also by Giulietta M. Spudich
Discover the stories of
The Amber Giant &
The Ice Giant
Now available at wwww.handersenpublishing.com

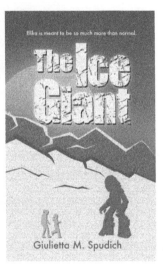

Thank you for purchasing and reading *Element Girls*.

Handersen Publishing is an independent publishing house that specializes in creating quality young adult, middle grade, and picture books.

We hope you enjoyed this book and will consider leaving a review on Goodreads or Amazon. A small review can make a big difference.

Thank you.